"I think I need the services you're offering," Malachy said

"*You* can't get a date?"

"It's not that." He gazed at her thoughtfully. "If I tell you something now, is it confidential?"

This was the last thing she'd expected. "I really can't counsel you," Scout told him. "I mean, you're someone I know. It's too close. It's not ethical or professionally correct."

"I don't care about the ethics," he said. "I think you might be able to help me."

"*I* care about eth—"

"I've found the woman I want to marry. And I need help closing the deal."

Dear Reader,

We are influenced by our childhoods and by the landscapes of our lives. I lived for only three months in the place where I was born, yet I've always found a deep connection with place.

Both Scout Berensen and Malachy MacCullagh, the main characters of *Where We Were Born,* were born and raised in Alaska. Malachy's childhood was shadowed by his parents' choices, while Scout grew up in the Alaskan bush, an environment with which she felt at odds. Like Scout, I always felt out of sync with the place where I grew up.

Scout dislikes rusticity, dislikes harsh environments and wants the comforts of the world outside Alaska. Malachy is at peace with the place where he was born—and, to a lesser degree, with the unusual circumstances of his birth. As Malachy sets out to help Scout learn to like Alaska, he shows her something that was absent in her childhood—an adaptability, an acceptance of change. Most of all, he teaches her that home is where we find the people we love.

I hope you enjoy this story. Thank you so much for reading!

Wishing you all good things,

Margot Early

WHERE WE WERE BORN

Margot Early

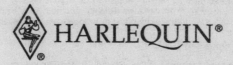

TORONTO • NEW YORK • LONDON
AMSTERDAM • PARIS • SYDNEY • HAMBURG
STOCKHOLM • ATHENS • TOKYO • MILAN • MADRID
PRAGUE • WARSAW • BUDAPEST • AUCKLAND

ISBN-13: 978-0-373-71376-9
ISBN-10:   0-373-71376-2

WHERE WE WERE BORN

ABOUT THE AUTHOR

Margot Early is the award-winning author of thirteen novels and three novellas. She lives high in the San Juan Mountains of Colorado with two German shepherds and twenty tarantulas. When she's not writing, she's outdoors in all seasons, often training her dogs in obedience.

Books by Margot Early

HARLEQUIN SUPERROMANCE

HARLEQUIN SINGLE TITLE

With love for Lisa

ACKNOWLEDGMENTS

Thank you to Warren Breslau for answering questions for this book and Lisa Knight for checking for mushing mistakes. All technical errors in this fictional work are mine.

CHAPTER ONE

McGrath, Alaska
June

SCOUT BERENSEN HAD never been beautiful, except to those who think good health, fitness and unique features equal beauty. She was a big, strong woman with broad shoulders, big hands and feet. Her figure remained good in part because of genes, in part because she'd been forced to be physically active in childhood and finally because she realized that her hot—if Amazon-scale—body was her best feature and did her best to exploit it. Her hair was an unexciting brown, and her eyebrows, if left ungroomed, nearly joined in the center. Her aesthetician in California had always shrugged. *One eyebrow's common enough. Here's what we'll do....*

Outside—in the Lower 48—Scout always gave her appearance intensive, focused and sometimes expensive care. And Outside was where she'd lived her entire adult life, through college until now. In fact, it was where she'd planned and *hoped* to live till she died. Outside, she could devote unreasonable quantities of time and money to making the absolute most of her looks and no one would raise an eyebrow—professionally shaped or otherwise.

Alaska had different standards, as she well knew.

Growing up in the bush, she'd rarely considered her looks; there were other, more important areas where she hadn't measured up. When she'd finally gone to high school in town for the winter and boarded with a family there, she'd been too glad to live in town to spend much time envying petite girls with cheerleader looks, and she could at least pretend that in the bush she'd learned a host of skills that even most of her Alaskan contemporaries didn't possess. She could drive a dog sled (allowing for skunks and epic wrecks), start a fire in the rain (possibly before death from hypothermia), dress out a caribou with her father standing over her screaming imprecations (well, she'd done it once, sort of, before developing hunting-related post-traumatic stress disorder), and fly an airplane badly enough to be the only member of her family without a pilot's license. She could spin dog hair into yarn that resembled knotted twine, preserve almost any edible plant without breeding botulism, and sleep for a total of maybe twenty minutes in a night with only tree boughs between her sleeping bag and the snow. She'd been raised right—at least, her father said, he and her mother had *tried*—she had a keen sense of who she was (someone who stood a better chance of reaching old age Outside) and she'd learned to survive things very difficult to survive. Looks were extra.

All of that was fine until she'd fallen in love for the first time, and then she'd keenly wished she was good-looking, because her first love, which in some ways remained, fifteen years later, her keenest, had been with a male of profound good looks, and the sort of mysterious past that made him irresistible to her, if not to all women. And though he had valued her as his friend—and was willing to share a more-than-friends one-night stand—he'd gone for love to a fellow genetic celebrity, a competitive surfer born and raised in Laguna Beach.

Now, climbing out of the bush plane that had taken her to the village of McGrath, famous for being the site of Alaska's first airmail delivery and a checkpoint on the Iditarod Trail, Scout reflected that she'd come to the one place where she'd be treated as though she was just as desirable as Halle Berry or Keira Knightley. High school in Alaska wasn't that different from high school Outside. But cheerleader types grew up and left Alaska for gentler environments. So now, being adult, female, and human in Alaska, Scout was also high status. She didn't even have to be competent; showing up was adequate.

But today, no one would guess she'd grown up in the bush north of the Yukon River, only about two hundred miles from McGrath.

She was a city girl now—or looked like one. For a five-year partner in a successful business, she was rich—rich by the standards according to which she'd been raised. Wire-rimmed glasses had been traded for designer tortoiseshell rims, and then for laser surgery, no glasses. Her business partners, who were also her two best friends, said that her eyes were the color of a wolf's. Scout always replied that she'd been raised by wolves. (Bitten by many sled dogs was more accurate, although some of these had been more than a small part wolf.)

The hair she'd worn long, in two practical braids, was now bobbed at chin-length.

The pilot moved to get her pack, but Scout took it from him easily, and he lifted his eyebrows at this sign of her physical strength. "Thanks." Scout shouldered it and fastened the hip belt over the smooth stretch-khaki fabric of her bell-bottom hip-huggers. With those, she wore backpacking boots, a silk T-shirt and a flannel shirt to help keep off mosquitoes—as if *that* would happen. Mosquitoes were at the top of the list of things she disliked about Alaska, closely followed by sled dogs of savage disposition.

Her partner, Dana, picking her up to drive her to the airport, had exclaimed in mock horror, "You're already letting yourself go, and you haven't even got up there yet!"

Scout had assured her that she didn't intend to start chewing tobacco before the Fourth of July, at the earliest.

Of course, the reality was that it had taken her very little time after moving *away* from Alaska to get used to hot baths, pedicures, an occasional eyebrow wax or chemical peel, a personal trainer, and other things that her family of origin found, rather than extravagant, simply incomprehensible.

But Scout was not wedded to these things, and she already felt a familiar relaxation seeping through her at the thought that within a few weeks she wouldn't be bothering to paint her nails or wear mascara or…

That's not why you came up here.

She'd come to McGrath to do a job. To establish a business office, then to branch out. In short, to continue to make piles of money. She had not come back to Alaska to stay. Her time here was *temporary,* and she had agreed to come because she and her partners had decided she was the best person for the job.

Her first glance at the area near the airstrip was what she'd expected. A few—very few—rather spindly conifers, two Quonset huts with sled dogs staked outside, barking at her, barking at the plane. Town reached out to her as she left the airstrip. More dogs, four-wheeler training devices, dogs in nearly every yard, sleds leaning against cabins and old Victorian-type houses and 1950s-style summer dwellings that had been beefed up for year-round occupation. A few small western-looking storefronts, rustic and charming. A modern post office, out of place beside a wood-sided general store. A total absence of city planning of any kind.

She found the real estate office easily and wondered, when she reached it and peered at the property listings, if there was *anywhere* that wasn't doing a booming business in property sales. She saw a house for sale for $150,000, and while she considered "Victorian" a loose description for the building in question, she was surprised that property in McGrath, Alaska, could hope to earn so much.

The Realtor's name was Graham Pork. He did not resemble a pig, which Scout thought must've been the saving grace to such a name. He wore his dirt-colored, silver-salted hair long, with a long, thick, elaborate mustache. Tinted wire-rimmed glasses hid his eyes. His secretary, who was, Scout had learned, also his wife, kept her short yellow hair fluffed out in a way that must have been achieved with a curling iron or hot rollers. She did have more of a porcine look than her husband, but she'd kept her maiden name, Angela Frye.

"You must be Scout," she exclaimed in the Texas drawl Scout remembered from their many phone conversations, during which Angela had expressed fascination with the Harmony Agency and the services it offered. *Well, dear,* she'd finally opined, *you might have more luck with an escort service. There's no shortage of money, and men up here would certainly pay for companionship, but as for teaching them how to behave—well, they'll sign up, all right, but I doubt you'll make much headway. You know what they say about Alaskan men, don't you, dear?*

Yes, Scout knew. She suspected she knew *all* the things said about Alaskan men and about the women too.

"Your boxes arrived," Angela said, "and Graham hung up your shingle like you asked, and we set up your answering machine the way you said. You know, you don't look at all like I expected."

Scout figured it was better not to ask her to clarify this.

"You look like you're from the city, and here you told me you grew up in the bush, so I was expecting something completely different."

"Illusion," Scout replied. "I've eschewed handkerchiefs and silverware my whole life."

Angela hooted.

Graham brought Scout the keys to the downtown building she'd rented. "I'll take you over there," he said. "I hope you'll like it, but you're from Alaska, so you know how things are."

Trying to give an encouraging smile—and hide her doubts about "how things are"—Scout followed him out the door, carrying her heavy pack, striding easily down the sidewalk of two-by-fours until it ended. Then they walked on the dirt road.

Yes, McGrath was like a hundred other bush villages. A general store with a post office, a bar, a laundry and a one-story structure beginning six feet above street level, that called itself a hotel.

Her building was nestled against another high wooden sidewalk, rammed up beside a diner called The Tug. A mushing reference, to the tugline. Scout gritted her teeth. This was a mushing town, which she suspected might be the downfall of the Harmony Agency's ambitions for McGrath, but they'd chosen the town, in part, because racing kennels meant money. Still, Scout guessed that if it came down to a team of sled dogs or a relationship with a member of the opposite sex, the dogs would win.

When she'd announced to Dana and Victoria, her partners, that she might make the same choice—*and I don't even like the vicious mutts*—Victoria had advised, *You might want to keep that sentiment to yourself.*

Of course, neither of her business partners had actually accused her of not having worked through her own issues with men. But sometimes Scout thought that was just because they didn't dare.

Scout had issues with men from which there truly was no healing.

As Graham fitted the key in the front door, a wooden affair with a rather picturesque four-pane window that looked like an invitation to a very cold winter, Scout gazed up at her shingle. It hung from the awning that extended over the sidewalk above both her building front and that of The Tug. The diner seemed busy. A bearlike giant grunted, "Graham," to the Realtor as he ducked in the door. It smelled like fried food, all-day breakfast, hamburgers, the kind of food that made Scout suddenly acutely hungry.

Her sign read:

> **THE HARMONY AGENCY**
> **BRINGING HAPPINESS TO INDIVIDUALS**
> **THROUGH THE WORLD OF FULFILLING**
> **RELATIONSHIPS**
> Scout Berensen, PhD, MFT, Life Coach
> Individual, Couples and Family Counseling
> Mail Order and Dating Service
> Life Skills

And her new local phone number.

You'll see your family, Dana had said hopefully.

Do you have any idea how big Alaska is?

Victoria had said, *Maybe you'll go visit them.*

Scout suspected that she was doing a poor job of hiding her cynicism about love. To be and asset to the business she must at least *seem* like a person more wedded to hope than indifference.

Victoria and Dana just kept urging her to spend time with her family of origin.

Well, that was part of her plan. To see Holden, anyway, her brother, her twin. Because they did keep in touch—through e-mail—which Holden checked whenever he was somewhere with Internet access. Anywhere but the home where they'd been raised, in other words, and where he still lived. Also, she sent text messages from her cell phone to his e-mail and she'd discovered heretofore unknown literary powers in his text messages back to her. In fact, it was Holden who'd thrown out

McGrath as a possible location when Scout had told him the Harmony Agency might open an Alaska office. Surprisingly, her brother's idea had turned out to have merit.

But Scout saw certain problems with facing even Holden again.

One problem was that part of the point of leaving Alaska had been to leave the people she knew best, who didn't understand her at all. To some degree, that included the brother who'd shared the experience of her upbringing—and also of having a literary name, bestowed by a mother who'd chosen a life that left her with no time to read. Scout believed that *Catcher in the Rye* and *To Kill a Mockingbird* represented more than her mother's favorite books. They represented the free time Dora had relinquished when she'd joined her life to Frank Berensen's.

Scout and her twin *liked* each other, yes. But Holden didn't really understand her. In their family, he'd fitted in, which was easier for him, and more difficult for her than fitting in with the rest of the world.

The big problem with seeing her family was that none of them, not her mother or her father or her brother, knew about Danny. Of course, they'd known she had married Danny. Her parents and brother had even come to California for the wedding, to celebrate an event they'd clearly doubted would ever occur—Scout marrying.

And they knew that she was no longer married to Danny. It had been five years, and of course they knew.

But there were a few details that Scout had failed to mention. She hadn't even been able to say the words, *There was someone else.* Because that wasn't *precisely* true either, not the whole truth and nothing but the truth. *There were two other women* was closer to gospel but still didn't cover it.

Scout didn't want them to know all the facts. It was mortifying, and they would say, *I told you so,* as though the appalling thing Danny had done would never have happened if she'd stayed in Alaska.

Scout didn't believe that.

But she didn't want to hear her parents and brother say it, either.

Not that she herself needed any of the services Harmony offered. In fact, when she and Dana and Victoria had started the business, part of the basis of its appeal, to Scout, anyway, was that she wholly believed in its unstated mission—*bringing hope to the hopeless.*

Harmony made its money by opening offices in areas with more men than women, men actively seeking partners, and helping to polish up the diamonds in the rough who came through their doors. Or so Scout had heard Victoria explain to their accountant.

What had been so astonishing about the end of Scout's relationship with Danny was that when she was free of it, she found she had qualities the men around her seemed to find irresistible.

One: She didn't want to marry.

Two: She didn't want a relationship.

Three: She didn't want a date.

That combination was an aphrodisiac whose power she could never have imagined when she was a student and *longing* for all of the above.

"The stove's here. The chimney's been cleaned,"

Graham said. "Double-paned windows. Sorry about the floor. I told you what to expect."

"It's fine." Hardwood, in need of refinishing. In the meantime, she'd give it another good mopping and throw down the rugs she'd sent ahead. The curtains in the windows facing the street were yellowed. She'd order blinds that would keep the warmth inside in winter. The wallpaper had been redone badly; it was a sort of dark-blue faux Victorian print that was supposed to be hung vertically

In the front room, the Realtors had installed the furniture she'd ordered and had delivered, but they hadn't removed the plastic from the chairs and couch. She followed Graham back to the downstairs kitchen, where bullet holes riddled the entire wooden wall on both sides of a stainless steel sink, then upstairs. Unlike the downstairs, which had been divided into separate rooms, the apartment upstairs stretched across the whole floor, with a kitchen, surprisingly clean, at one end. Behind dingy curtains at the other, French doors opened onto a balcony. "Is it safe out here?" she asked. "It won't collapse?"

"Not under your weight. The owner reinforced the railing."

The landlord, Scout guessed, lived out of town. In any event, Graham Pork managed the property.

"He said the balcony seemed strong enough. Not that I'd recommend getting a crowd out there."

"I understand."

"The building has an interesting history. It used to be a brothel."

"That is interesting," Scout agreed. Up here, the wallpaper was an unappealing post-brothel duck pattern.

Yet the building still had a pressed-tin ceiling with most of the panels in place, and the baseboards were of some dark hardwood. She'd done nothing about bedroom furniture, preferring to wait until she saw the place where she'd be living. For now, she'd use her sleeping bag and an air mattress.

Graham showed her the renovated bathroom in the upstairs apartment and the other bathroom downstairs, which definitely had a rustic feel. He told her that the building's *recent* history included being a bar, then a gift shop, then a preschool and day-care center. All of these businesses had failed.

When the Realtor had gone, Scout returned to the downstairs front room, where the Porks had plugged in her phone. She'd brought another phone, having been assured that there was also an extension upstairs.

She saw that she already had messages.

"Hi. This is, um, Everett Nairn…. I was curious about your sign. About mail order…women. My number is…"

The next two messages were also from men inquiring about the Harmony Agency, the last apparently under the impression that it was an escort service. The following message was from Dana.

"Scout, it's me. Your folks called and they didn't know you were going up there, and I suppose I blew it because I assumed they knew because your brother knew…I thought. I didn't give them your number, but I told them I'd ask you to call. I'm sorry," she said.

Holden had known she was returning to Alaska but not when, and Scout had asked him not to mention it to her parents. Clearly he hadn't.

A fist banged on the front door.

Scout rose from the plastic-covered chair she'd been sitting on and went to the door. She opened it, reminding herself that her pack was upstairs, wondering which of the boxes stacked against the wall of *this* room might contain pen and paper, wishing her appointment book was at hand.

The person on the wooden sidewalk outside wore a uniform that identified him as an Alaska state trooper. At first she registered only that the officer was tall, tall enough that his name tag, at eye-level, demanded her attention.

MALACHY MacCULLAGH.

She almost shut the door again—a sort of reflex action. Shut door, make go away.

Instead, she lifted her eyes to the face.

Back when they were in college, she'd been impressed with a number of things about him. The first—that he was from Alaska. Like her, he was from Somewhere and Nowhere. Another interesting quality—his looks. Very dark hair that he used to wear long, skin that was always the color of unblemished wood evenly stained. She had written bad poems to that skin, calling it shades from whisky to earth. He was half-Aleut and had looked Amerindian.

He was still gorgeous. Now the long hair was short enough for a marine corps recruiting poster. He'd filled out, but the excellent facial bones remained. Strong cheekbones, straight nose, the look of a man put on earth to break hearts.

He must be thirty-four now, she calculated, to her thirty-two.

No doubt he could still break hearts. But not hers.

"Hi," she said rather indifferently. She hadn't known he was in Alaska and didn't like that he was in Alaska, whether he'd originally come from Alaska or not. She especially didn't like that he was in McGrath, where she happened to be.

Immediately, she wondered if he was still in touch with her twin, with Holden.

No, he couldn't be, or her family would know the real story about Danny.

Unless *Malachy* didn't know?

Happy thought.

"I saw your shingle when Graham hung it up. I wanted to stop in and say hello. How are you, Scout?"

That voice.

She couldn't tell bass from baritone, but it was deep and unforgettable.

Perhaps he hadn't hugged her in welcome because becoming a cop had cured him of being a hugger. He *had* been a hugger. They'd both been friends with Danny Kilbourne, slightly honored to be liked by the youngest graduate of Trinity, in Dublin. A PhD candidate, a native of Ireland, teacher of English 101. But Danny never graduated from Trinity, and he wasn't even Irish; his accent entirely put on, part of the fake person he'd invented. *I wasn't the only one taken in.* Danny, her ex-partner, for want of a better title, had hoodwinked the University of California.

Danny and Malachy had kept in touch, at least for a while. Maybe they'd stopped. Maybe neither had spoken a word to the other since the last time she'd seen them in each other's presence, more than a decade ago. Malachy hadn't come to their wedding. Danny had told her he wouldn't come. Anyway, didn't she want to keep their wedding small, intimate?

Actually, *he* had.

Well, the reason for that had become clear in the end.

"I'm fine. How are you?" She stepped out onto the stoop and squinted at the insignias on his uniform.

He cracked a smile, a ghost of one she remembered.

"I thought you were saving the environment or something," she said. "Isn't that—I know it's what you studied." Because she'd taken classes with him, momentarily steered away from her own stars.

"I took law enforcement training because I felt it would help me get a job as a ranger."

This was actually a logical route to a post with one of the federal public lands agencies.

He shrugged and concluded, "But I found out I liked doing this."

Now that she saw him *as* a state trooper, it seemed a surprisingly good fit. "Come on in," she said.

He'd been staring at her face.

"You look diffcrent," he said abruptly.

There was nothing to say to that. She turned away and heard him follow her inside. She began stripping plastic off the furniture, and he produced a Leatherman tool from a pocket and helped.

"You look like you're from the city," he elaborated as they sat down, he on the couch, testing it out, scrutinizing the blue upholstery. Then his eyes shot up, studying her face.

"Well, Cro-Magnon Girl isn't in style." She tried to sound amusing, but inside she was frozen. How horrible to be sitting with an intelligent handsome man, a man who could give any movie star a run for his money, the kind of face women dream about waking up with, and feel...nothing.

No, that wasn't true.

Not nothing.

Her guard had gone up, which meant she felt plenty. This wasn't a professional meeting. Scout silently insisted that this was why she instinctively protected herself. Malachy wasn't a client. He was someone who could, in the context of a relationship, betray trust.

I'm a mess, she thought. How lightly her partners had suggested—without *really* saying so—that there was something wrong with her personal reaction to men, the personal rather than professional reaction. For five years, they'd been delicately hinting at it. Cautiously, like people balancing pillars of stacked china teacups.

She didn't hate men. It wasn't that.

And when they were clients, she didn't fear them, fear that they could hurt her heart.

He said, "I never thought you looked like Cro-Magnon Girl."

There was nothing to say to that either.

Granted, he'd seemed to like her once. A one-night stand on the beach in Santa Barbara, where they'd been at university together. But the romance hadn't gone anywhere—except back to strictly platonic friendship. When Scout had seen his girlfriend, the surfing champion, she'd realized that she'd misinterpreted his behavior. Malachy had been the first man she'd believed she couldn't live without and the first she'd discovered she actually could live without.

She noticed his eyes taking in her left hand. If he didn't mention Danny, *she* certainly wasn't going to.

And if he'd heard what had happened, he wouldn't be tacky enough to bring it up, would he?

He said, "Did he have to go to jail or anything?"

So much for her faith in Malachy's sense of delicacy. She sighed. "Not the last I knew. But I don't keep tabs on him."

"You didn't have to get a divorce, did you?"

"No." After all, she and Danny had never been legally married.

"I felt responsible, when I heard."

Scout widened her eyes. "How could you possibly bear any responsibility whatsoever?"

"Your brother and I were friends. You trusted me. And Danny and I were friends. I knew him better than you did. I knew something wasn't right."

"Unless you knew he was already married, your reticence is forgiven."

He laughed. "That's what I remember about you."

"What?"

"Your sense of humor."

"I got to keep it in the settlement." This was another thing she did, according to Dana and Victoria; she used humor to separate herself from men, to stay untouchable.

"You must have needed it."

"I'm so glad you stopped by to discuss that painful period in my life. Have you suffered, too, since we last met?" She hadn't meant to say it. She stopped herself from putting her hand over her mouth, from showing any sign of regret over abusing her freedom of speech.

But the way he watched her now seemed predatory.

"You didn't tell your family," he said.

Did she blanch? She felt faint. *Fake it.* "Whatever gives you that idea?" She could hardly believe that after ten years, she and Malachy were sitting together in her new office in McGrath, Alaska, where he shouldn't even be, because he should've grown up to play golf and drive a Lexus in Pasadena, California.

Unlikely though that outcome was for a person who'd grown up in sight of Siberia.

"Because I talk to Holden every once in a while. I asked him how you were and he said, 'Fine,' and in the course of that conversation I realized he had no idea that Danny Kilbourne was a bigamist."

"Did you enlighten him?" Because if he had, her twin had done a good job of hiding his knowledge of the facts. They *did* e-mail regularly. And she *did* intend to see her brother while she was in Alaska. To see him— and to help him, if she could, because it saddened her to think of him imprisoned by shyness, a victim of their remote upbringing.

Malachy shook his head. "I didn't tell him."

"Why not?" She sounded cold, but she couldn't stand it that Malachy knew the truth, not just about Danny but about the fact that she hadn't been able to face telling her family.

"Because you hadn't." He stared at the wallpaper.

"I know," she said, about the wallpaper, as though that had been the topic. "It's crooked."

"Is this a new business?"

"New to McGrath, not to me."

"Tell me about it." His gaze turned both aloof and

piercing. He used to look at her the same way long ago, as though thinking, waiting, listening, reserving judgment.

"Just what it says on the shingle. I'm a psychologist. So are my partners." Good grief, her voice was wavering. As though she was still eighteen and infatuated. "Mostly, in places like this, I end up providing life-coaching for men who are seeking partners. People tell me their goals. I encourage them, help them recognize and navigate obstacles. If they want more success in relationships, I tell them the things their respective partners are unwilling to tell them."

His black eyebrows crowded together in a look of puzzlement. "What—you tell them how to dress and talk?"

"Oh, much more than that."

"Which fork to use?"

"Definitely more than that."

"Say I wanted to sign up. What would happen?"

Scout scrutinized him. The uniform—blue shirt, gray trousers, holster, gun, the whole thing—became him, although she still couldn't quite accept the reality of Malachy MacCullagh, tall, sexy, untamed wildness, as a cop.

"Seriously," he said. "What would I get?"

"A discount."

"Excuse me?"

"Well, you're attractive, employed, not an alcoholic?" She phrased only the last as a question.

"Never touch the stuff."

"You'd attract women who want to use our service, so we'd be eager to recruit you and would give you a discount."

"How much? I mean, how much does it cost?"

"Well, we have different packages. I haven't had time to unpack my materials. I literally just got here. But for instance, someone who wanted coaching… Well, for life coaching only, the price is five hundred dollars a month. That's the rate for McGrath, Alaska. It's eight hundred in California. I also offer counseling at sixty-five dollars an hour. And the same as a marriage and family therapist. Again, that's the McGrath rate."

"You think people here have that kind of money?"

"I know they do. Do *you* think I would've come here without researching the community thoroughly?"

His lips twitched. "So, say I was a…client, what sort of advice would you offer me?"

"For free?"

He shook his head, smiling, but she also saw in his gaze something she remembered, a sense of wonder about her, as though he found her unique and fascinating. She'd mistaken it for attraction, when all he'd wanted was her friendship because he'd found her interesting.

"Well," she offered, "since I don't give free advice, we'll create the hypothetical situation that you came in here because I'm the only single woman in McGrath and you knew me at one time and you think you have a chance. I would tell you it's probably not the best move to start off by asking about my separation from the bigamist I never actually married because he'd already married someone else. Did you hear about The Student, too, by the way?" If it weren't for The Student, she might never have learned about Danny's wife. She'd thought *she* was Danny's wife before his real wife saw the small newspaper announcement about his engagement to The Student. There had been a domino effect, involving Real Wife's private investigator, whom Scout had spotted following Danny. She'd suspected—silly her—Interpol or the CIA persecuting Danny because of his former—nonexistent—involvement with the Irish Republican Army. *I'll never be that naive again* still wasn't much consolation for learning that her nonhusband, housemate, and bed partner was already married and also planning to not-marry again. He was carrying on with Scout, Real Wife and The Student simultaneously.

Perhaps Malachy couldn't grasp why she hadn't told her family the truth, but she was nearly certain that just about any woman who'd found herself deceived by a bigamist would feel much as she did. Mortified. Yes, her father especially and Holden to a lesser degree might shake their heads over the fact that she hated hunting and had once peed her pants in fear of one of her dad's lead dogs, but *this*... She supposed it came down to her own belief that they'd feel, if not actually say, that she'd gotten what she deserved, as though people who chose to live Outside could expect such misfortune.

She was curious, though. How much had Malachy heard? *Did* he know about The Student, The-Nineteen-Year-Old Student?

Malachy let his chin drop. Undoubtedly, that meant yes. He opened his mouth, and she thought he was going to apologize.

She was wrong.

"I did come in to see you because we were friends and because your brother and I were good friends and because I felt bad about Danny. But I also think I need the services you're offering."

"*You* can't get a date?"

"It's not that." He gazed at her thoughtfully. "If I tell you something now, is it confidential?"

This was not what she'd expected. It was the last thing she'd expected. Did he need counseling? "I really can't counsel you or do psychotherapy with you. I mean, you're someone I know. It's too close. It's not ethical or professionally correct."

"Can you keep this to yourself?" he repeated.

"Of course."

"I don't care about the ethics. I think you might be able to help me."

"*I* care about eth—"

"I've found the woman I want to marry. I'm absolutely sure. And I need help closing the deal."

CHAPTER TWO

"No." She didn't have to think about it. "I'm not Yenta the Matchmaker. We do have a dating service as *one* service we provide. People who wish to use the dating service pay an initial fee, and we videotape an interview, prepare an ad for them for our Web site and magazine. Then they can contact people they're interested in dating through the Web site or the snail-mail center. Each client does his or her own work, with the help of life counseling if he or she desires. And, as I've said, this is just one facet of the Harmony Agency. We're psychologists, and each of us works independently as a clinical psychologist, too." Certain she'd closed that book firmly, she admitted, "I'm fascinated, though. I'd love to know more about this—as a friend." And she wanted to see the woman who had inspired such a fervent desire for matrimony in Malachy.

"I understand why you can't take me as a...client. But don't you have things I can read?"

The invitation was there, to ask about the woman, to ask why she didn't want to marry him. But the situation was very iffy.

"The Harmony Agency does not link anyone with another particular person. We just don't do that. It wouldn't matter who you are. At some point, there's very little controlling who falls in love with whom."

He leaned back on the couch, stretching out his arms, taking up too much space. "I don't suppose you'd help me as a friend?"

"What do I get out of it?" She knew how that sounded, knew also that her Other Persona had abruptly taken over. She was, on a level she could not even feel, let alone control, deeply afraid. The love channels were shut down, and she could not reopen them.

But they could open without her permission.

"What if I set you up with your own team of dogs and a sled?"

"Try and remember that you're talking to a person who, if she wanted such a thing, would prefer to handle the details herself." *Considering that I was forced to help with the family trapline before you learned your times tables, Trooper MacCullagh.* "In any case, I wouldn't describe myself as a dog-lover."

"That's a disability."

She rolled her eyes. "Okay, I like dogs. I just don't like having my hands bitten by sled dogs."

"Not all dogs make a habit of biting."

"Having a team is a labor of love, and I'm not in love with the idea. All right?" She also wasn't planning to remain in Alaska long-term. She'd be here for a year or two, help Holden, if she could…. Because her twin needed her help, even if he didn't know that. She could draw him out of his solitude, make it impossible for him to escape relating to others. Some small gatherings with a few friends. Maybe group camping, where he could feel confident.

"You won't take money?"

She shook her head. "The whole thing sounds like something that could land me in serious trouble."

He glanced around the interior of the building and said, "So what you offer is really like—" he seemed to search for a comparison "—long-life oil filters. Cellulite cream."

"What the Harmony Agency offers *does* work," she replied.

He raised dark skeptical eyebrows. "As evidenced by?"

"Happy marriages. Happy relationships. Happy friendships. Better dating experiences. But we don't promise to help anyone secure a relationship with a particular person."

"But you must have…" He stopped. Frowned. Thoughtful. "Don't you have a general program for improvement?"

Scout sighed. "I can't do it. You and I have a relationship." Blushing, she said, "I mean, we know each other."

"And there is that issue of the first time. Yours," he said.

"Another thing I hoped delicacy would discourage you from mentioning." She swiftly moved on. Scout just didn't like to remember the innocent and hopeful young woman she'd been—a child, really, believing that love between men and women worked out the way it did in fairy tales. And since then she'd become calloused, and that was sad, too. She smiled, smiled because she was past being in love with Malachy, or infatuated with him. Over it. "So, who is she, anyhow?" That left no doubt that she was asking as a friend. Simply a friend.

"Mary Clarke."

"Oh."

Mary Clarke, two-time winner of the Iditarod.

She was beautiful, one of those women blessed with a combination of athletic ability, cover-girl-caliber beauty, and notorious Alaskan toughness and independence. There'd been days in her life when Scout would have paid good money to possess the last. She remembered that Mary Clarke lived in the bush not far from McGrath. "And she knows you're alive?" Scout tried to keep the twitching of her mouth to a minimum.

"We've been seeing each other for a little less than a year. So you'll help?"

"No." Scout shook her head, laughing. "I *can't*. Don't you understand?"

"For fun."

"Where's the fun for me?" she couldn't stop herself from wondering aloud.

"Satisfaction, then."

She gave that all the response she thought it deserved. Then, something else occurred to her, something that should've been there from the first and probably had been—she'd just ignored it. "Why the desperation on this issue? Aren't you getting everything the normal red-blooded male desires?"

His eyes were still for a moment, and from that she knew he would lie—or at least withhold the real answer to her question. Strange, her sixth sense about some behaviors had become unfailing; lying, for instance, she always recognized. This was only since the catastrophe of Danny Kilbourne. After five years of oblivious nonmarriage to a pathological liar, she had suddenly learned to see every untruth.

He shrugged. "I want a family."

It wasn't a suspect answer in itself.

"Let me guess. She has eighty-three sled dogs and would rather have twice that number than a baby?"

"No. No. It's not that."

"You have a rival."

He sighed, and she intuited that in less than thirty seconds he would stand and make an excuse to go.

"No." He looked at his watch. "I shouldn't keep you from unpacking. You just got here. Anyhow, this doesn't work. What you do here." He stood up.

She *knew.* She knew what he was doing. She knew that he was baiting her and she was too smart to take the bait. "Fine. Go ahead and think that."

"It's one thing to give hope to a bunch of strangers," he said. "Different to take money from someone who knows your family, someone you've known since you were eighteen."

Through Holden, he knew her parents. How much did he see of any of them?

"It's *unethical* for me to accept you as a client," she said from between her teeth. It came out a hiss. "I can't do it, all right? I'd be risking my license." That might be an exaggeration, but not a gross one.

"You mean, you can't help a given woman fall in love with a given man. You can't improve his chances at all."

"That is false. I could definitely improve his chances." She had spoken rashly. "Yours, that is, if it's you and if she isn't married to someone else or in another committed relationship or—" She didn't want to sound as though she was backpedaling. "It's for *professional* reasons that I can't do it."

"Do it as a friend," he suggested. "Let's have a friendly wager."

"Why?" Her voice had grown shrill. "What would I possibly gain?"

"Isn't there something you'd like to have?"

Scout considered. She had found that in general she could have what she wanted if she decided to get it. Money. A relationship, *if she wanted one*. Which she didn't. "World peace," she said.

He ignored that.

"I'll think on it," she told him.

"I'm good with a hammer." He eyed the floorboards, the wallpaper. "Good with interiors and exteriors."

If I want something done here, I can hire someone or do it myself—the last rather badly.

"Sure about the dogs?" he asked. "Sweet dogs."

She hadn't lived with a dog since she'd left Alaska. She couldn't adopt a team of dogs and then leave Alaska. Maybe one dog, a pet, that she could take back to California. But sled dogs were working dogs. They wanted to pull sleds. And she couldn't—or wouldn't—*stay* in Alaska. Nonetheless...

"I have an idea." A small smile formed on her lips. She felt it, enjoyed it. "Here's a trade. I can try to help you become the person Mary Clarke wants to marry. In return, you can attempt to do what my parents couldn't."

"Which is?"

"While I'm forced to be here, you can try to make me like Alaska. And you can try to help me fit in."

His expression turned thoughtful. "That's a tall order."

"Yes."

"Will you follow my instructions?" he asked. "Will you be a willing student? That's the only way you'll learn to love the place where you were born."

"With one caveat. You know I've lived in the bush. It didn't take. Ordering me to skin furry animals and can high-bush cranberries won't do the trick. You'll have to try something new."

"You've got a deal."

"Why am I suddenly afraid?"

"Needlessly," he assured her. "But you are going to have dogs."

"Sled dogs?" she asked without enthusiasm. "Remember what I said?"

"I've met your family's dogs, Scout. That isn't what I had in mind."

"My family has an *excellent* kennel," she exclaimed in outrage. "They're working dogs, not Iditarod dogs or sprint dogs. So, needing relationships with humans isn't part of their makeup. That's true of most native dogs in Alaska." The vehemence of her defense surprised her.

Malachy's lips twitched.

She snapped, "What do you know about them? The other side of the Kokrines isn't your jurisdiction."

"Sure is. Anyhow, I've been to your folks' place many times."

"To see Holden." Anxiety and irritation soured her stomach. Maybe Holden didn't need her help after all.

Malachy refocused. "In any case, sprint dogs are what you're going to have."

Sprint dogs? Hyper dogs with goofy smiles and a total inability to be still for two consecutive seconds? "I don't know if there's room in the yard." There was a chain-link fence of some kind. How far it extended, she had no idea, but it was high.

"There's room," he said.

"Fine. But I'm a miserable dog driver. And I'll need equipment. A sled. Everything. I already have plenty of expenses without dogs. All of that aside, it's impossible. I'm not planning to stay in Alaska. What's going to happen to these dogs when I go?"

"You can sell them. Or I'll take them."

"Sure, just shift them from one home to another willy-nilly."

"We're not talking about a German shepherd, Scout. Sled dogs are bought and sold and traded all the time. You know it as well as I do. They don't feel it like pets do."

"How do you know? Have they told you that?"

"Sled dogs want to pull sleds. The musher is secondary."

Scout suspected he was right. After all, what she'd always found strange about sled dogs—her father's dogs, anyway—was that they didn't seem to need people. "I intensely dislike falling down in snow and ice," she said.

"We'll try to keep that to a minimum."

She snorted. Wrecks were a fact of mushing.

Her dog-driving experience was helping Holden and her father run an eighty-mile trapline with big-boned, slant-eyed dogs, some of them positively snotty, none of them with an agenda of friendliness. Her father, she thought, looked down on racing as frivolous—and in his eyes it didn't get more gratuitous than sprint racing.

"At least," she said, almost to herself, "that'll provide an opening to work on *your* half of the deal. I have to meet this woman, and maybe dogs are the best way. I'll bet she has puppies coming out of her ears."

"Distance dogs. But you're right. Worth looking."

"I don't suppose you have sprint dogs."

"I do. My job doesn't allow for running the Iditarod or the Yukon Quest, but the local sprint races are fun."

Malachy watched her. Was that hope he saw in her eyes? If so, what was the hope?

But he knew Scout, knew Holden, had met their parents.

In college, Scout had seemed resigned to *not* fitting in with the rest of her family. She used to remind him, I'm not like Holden. *I'm not good at living in the bush.* But even Malachy had to admit that her father's taste in dogs veered toward undomesticated packs. *My dad,* Scout had maintained, *likes to do everything the hard way. And the hard way isn't my way.* In one heart-to-heart she'd told him about the isolation in which she'd been raised. *It made us complete social misfits. When we went to high school in Fairbanks, it was a joke. We didn't know how to be normal.* She and Holden had been "a disaster" at school, and every time they'd returned to the bush she'd felt she *needed* to do so, needed to hide from the other world. And because she'd recognized the need to hide as unhealthy, because she'd refused to acknowledge that there was something she *couldn't* face, she'd flung herself Outside. There, she had determined to befriend other humans and learn to communicate with them. Instead of knowing only family—and what was wild.

Malachy wondered if she remembered confessing these things to him. He remembered because of his own Alaskan upbringing, so different, yet with its own problems.

It was when Holden had come to visit her in Santa Barbara that Malachy had met Scout's twin. He and Holden were still great friends, always talking about dogs or fishing or flying.

But Scout had never told Holden about Danny's being a bigamist, and Malachy couldn't figure out why.

"I hope you don't think I'm going to buy dogs from you," she said. "This liking Alaska business had better not cost me a pile of money. And no money's going from my pocket to yours over this trade."

Hearing herself, Scout was appalled. Had Danny turned her into someone who actually came out with remarks like this?

Yes. Danny and the stupid Camaro. Danny and the sailboat. Danny and how they need to buy the fill-in-the-blank expensive thing he always needed—instead of whatever *she* wanted.

Malachy said, "*I* wasn't going to charge you for dogs. I was going to give you a couple of puppies I think have real potential. But I imagine you'll want some from other sources, too. Shall we agree to make your happiness in Alaska a joint venture?"

It sounded kind.

Almost intimate.

What a man might say to a woman he liked in *that* way.

Malachy did not like her that way. He liked Mary Clarke that way and was doing things for Scout so he could become the husband of McGrath's foremost musher.

"So," she asked, "when can I meet Ms. Clarke?" She'd have to get to know the woman to discover why she didn't want to marry Malachy.

"I was going out there tonight. I could bring you

along and introduce you, tell her that you're new in town and want to meet people."

"Let's tell her I want to look at dogs."

"And in the meantime," he offered, "I'll check out your yard, see about some housing for them."

If the situation had been different, Scout knew this would've bothered her. But Malachy's interest in Mary Clarke gave her a margin of safety. She wouldn't have to put energy into chasing him away from her; he was in love with another woman.

"By the way, Malachy—"

He glanced up.

"Have you *asked* her to marry you?"

Again, she thought he'd lie. In fact, for seconds she was almost sure he would.

Then the feeling dissipated.

"I've hinted at it," he admitted, frowning. "I've said, 'Don't suppose you'd want to settle down and spend our lives together?'"

"And she said?" This was going to be bad. If Mary's response had given him the slightest encouragement, he wouldn't be consulting Scout now.

"She said, 'Not with anyone with two legs.'"

Scout tried to see the bright side of this answer. It meant that Mary Clarke had nothing against Malachy specifically, nor against men.

Just all humans.

"Well," she said, "*that's* not too bad."

"I thought the same," Malachy told her in all seriousness.

Good grief. Men were capable of reading encouragement into almost anything. But she'd agreed to help him, and in return he'd agreed to help her like Alaska. It was a fair exchange. Each project had the same likelihood of success—almost none.

"I'll need to know everything about your relationship with her. I don't mean intimate details. Just how long you've been seeing each other, if she's seeing anyone else, that kind of thing."

"Right."

"But you have to understand that the Harmony Agency comes first. I have to make this office…well, livable. Pleasant."

He glanced at his watch. "My shift ends at four. How about if I come back and help you here? Then, we can go look at dogs."

Plenty of daylight left. This was the land of the midnight sun, after all. She'd have to get used to that again. In the back of her mind, Scout also remembered the phone message from Dana. Her family now knew that she was in Alaska, a short flight away. But although they might be puzzled that she hadn't let them know she was in Alaska, it wouldn't occur to them to feel hurt. They hadn't understood why she left.

Now she'd come back to Alaska, to McGrath, which might seem like the middle of nowhere to Dana and Victoria, but was the hub of all civilization compared to where—and how—Scout had been raised.

From her door, Scout watched Malachy climb into his state trooper SUV. She wondered how much territory he covered and how much of it in that vehicle. The roads around McGrath didn't go very far. Undoubtedly, he had his pilot's license. She hoped that his plan to teach her how to love Alaska would not include her sitting in the pilot's seat. If it did, he could forget it. She was happy to be a passenger.

Scout decided to unpack a couple of boxes before answering her phone messages.

Malachy was willing to help her set up her office, hang wallpaper, refinish floors, go to extreme lengths of physical labor, not for the chance to spend time with her but because he wanted her guidance in wooing Mary Clarke, who had won the Iditarod. And he wanted to *marry* her—although she'd told him in so many words that she was only living till-death-do-us-part with dogs.

So maybe he actually *didn't* want to marry her. If Malachy MacCullagh really wanted to be married, have a family, all of that, he'd set his sights on a woman who wanted the same things.

Scout began unpacking brochures, which she arranged on the coffee table. She would use this room as a waiting area and one of the back rooms as an office for counseling.

There was so much to do that she'd forgotten the time when a knock came at the door and she saw Malachy's silhouette outside the glass. She let him in. He'd changed into blue jeans and a plaid flannel shirt. Out at the curb was a pickup truck with dog boxes on the back but no dogs.

"Tell me how you'd like it to look in here."

Scout led him back to the room she'd earmarked as an office. They briefly discussed options for the floor and walls.

"I can have the wallpaper off and the walls painted in three days."

"With what? Graffiti?"

He gave her a look that suggested her sarcasm was unattractive.

"Sorry," she said. "That would be great. It's bound to look better than this. Are you sure? I'll buy the paint, but I guess we'll have to get it flown in."

He nodded. "I'll take care of ordering it and have them bill you for the supplies. Will that do?"

"The landlord should pay. I'm going to find out about it."

Malachy nodded, with something like a smile. "As for the floor, it'll be best to do it in two sections. The front of the building, then the back."

"All right."

"You have a back door, so you can see your patients or clients or whatever they are while I'm doing it."

"I hope you end up satisfied with what *you* get out of this trade."

His dark eyes slanted toward her face. "I hope so, too."

"Come to think of it…" Scout half closed her eyes, thinking.

"What?"

"Well, I'll know better after I meet her. Some women don't find a man interesting until they've seen him with another woman—until, in short, they're in danger of losing his attention. Other women see a man's interest in another woman as the ultimate turn-off. In other words, why bother with a guy when he likes someone else?"

"Which are you?"

"The latter," she said, deciding not to ask why he wanted to know. The question—and its answer—could gain her nothing except, possibly, humiliation. "But what's important," she told him, "is which Mary Clarke is. I don't suppose you know?" She squinted at him.

"A little competition might not hurt."

"She's competitive, after all," Scout reasoned. "But you've got to *know,* Malachy. I'm not sure what I can do if she says, 'Phew. Well, that's him out of my hair.'"

He chewed his bottom lip, pensive. Then he focused on the floor. "Why don't I get started on this? I went ahead and brought the sanding machine."

"Well, I hope the landlord appreciates your generosity."

He didn't answer, and her intuition went into overdrive. Her contract was with the Realtor, not the landlord, whose name she hadn't been told. "Who owns this place?" she asked.

His tight-lipped smile answered.

"Why on earth did you buy it?" she demanded.

"It was cheap."

"Then you can buy the paint," she said, "and everything else. You really would've let me pay for the paint, wouldn't you?"

He nodded.

"I don't know why I expected better of you. But, at any rate, thank you for making the place nicer."

"Thank *you,*" he said.

"I haven't done anything yet. And I can't guarantee anything. You're already involved with this woman, though. Correct?"

"Yes."

Surely she heard no hesitation in that reply. "That should make it easier." It made sense to learn whatever she could from Malachy. "Your relationship is exclusive? She's not seeing anyone else?"

There was definitely a pause this time. "No."

She darted a quick look at him.

Malachy reached for the handle of the front door. "Let me get that sander. I'll bring some drop cloths, too. You can cover the furniture again."

There was something he wasn't telling her, but Scout suspected she wouldn't find out what that was until she met Mary Clarke for herself.

HIS SHIFT WAS OVER, had been over when he'd stopped to see Scout. He'd intended from the start to propose to her that he work on the building. After all, he was the landlord, and he had been her friend.

He'd been a bit more.

Her brother, of course, didn't know about this. Malachy doubted Holden would mind, but he felt, in retrospect, that he had not behaved as chivalrously toward Scout as he might have.

It had been very nice. He remembered that. Certain other details had become blurred with time. He just remembered something profoundly wholesome—almost nourishing—about making love with Scout Berensen, about sleeping with her all night on the beach. In some ways it remained, for him, the essence of love, tied up with youth and innocence and an uncomplicated life.

Not like Mary.

He'd told Scout the truth, however. He wanted to be married to Mary Clarke. To him, Mary was exotic. She hated that she'd been born elsewhere than Alaska, that she'd grown up in a suburb Outside. Malachy found this touching.

He didn't understand her, and that intrigued him, too. He could spend the rest of his life learning about her.

But as he drove home, his thoughts returned not to Mary—or to his own disquiet at Scout's reaction, her obvious doubt that Mary would ever accept him—but to Scout. She did look different, and he was sure most of it was because of things like foil highlights and microdermabrasion, neither of which Mary Clarke would ever experience. He knew about these things because he'd always listened to women, listened to people.

Mary didn't listen much, and aesthetic enhancements interested her as much as, say, astrophysics. She liked dogs and challenging her body and mind and spirit, and winning. She loved to win. Sometimes she seemed invulnerable. Her only insecurity sprang from having been born and raised in the Lower 48.

But she didn't take to teasing about it.

She didn't like to be teased at all.

He thought of Scout's tall, strong body in her city clothes.

Her nonmarriage to Danny Kilbourne had nothing to do with Malachy, and she seemed to have taken it in stride. But she'd never told her brother and her parents the truth. Malachy knew her parents and knew her, so he could imagine why.

THREE HOURS LATER, Scout had organized her files in the filing cabinets and arranged her living quarters upstairs—including an antique dresser and metal-frame bed Malachy had brought from another building he owned in downtown McGrath. She sat in the passenger seat of Malachy's Toyota as he drove the three miles to his place, on the good (for the Alaskan bush) road between McGrath and Ophir.

"You probably prefer not to take any dogs tonight. But you can if you want. I'll build you doghouses out back. We can make them like mine, which you'll see in a minute. I have one long shelter with walls dividing it. It works pretty well."

Scout thought ruefully of everything she once would have read into riding in Malachy MacCullagh's truck, going to see his dogs, getting dogs from him and his puttering around her home—even if he was the landlord.

Now she read nothing into it.

He was looking after her in his own fashion as an unspoken, unasked-for favor to her brother, perhaps a private penance for having allowed her to marry a man he could not possibly have known was no good.

He lived in a one-story log house. Dogs were staked out in the yard, in front of three long sheds that were arranged in a giant C. Scout heard hysterical howling, barking and baying as he shut off the engine.

The front door opened, and an older man stepped out behind a black dog with huge pointed ears and a white spot on its chest. The man's luxurious, gray hair swept back from a weathered, sharp-featured face above a royal-blue button-down shirt and gray canvas trousers. He gazed with interest at the truck.

Scout stepped out, eyeing the dog. It sat and wagged its tail and yawned, apparently awaiting her attention. "Hi." She let it sniff her hand, then petted the animal and straightened to squint at the man.

Ice-blue eyes took in her form as he nodded once.

"Scout," Malachy said. "This is my father. John MacCullagh. Scout Berensen."

"Nice to meet you, Scout."

She could barely contain her curiosity. She'd never known much about Malachy's background, only that he'd grown up on the coast somewhere and was half-Aleut.

John MacCullagh followed them out into the yard to a separate kennel, fenced and protected by plywood, with a separate doghouse.

Puppies, about eight or nine weeks old. Combinations of black and white, some with mostly black masks.

Scout's eyes fell on a fat white puppy, all white except for its black mask. Its light-blue eyes appeared to be rimmed with eyeliner.

Puppies are a nuisance. I don't need this in my life.

There were only four.

"Terry came to pick up Black Feet," John said.

Malachy nodded, clearly pleased to hear this. He glanced at Scout. "What do you think?"

"I think they're puppies."

John MacCullagh seemed to be fighting a smile.

"Nine and a half weeks," Malachy confirmed.

"You've already taken your pick, I assume."

"The black one," he said.

Black with those same blue eyes. Malachy would have checked all their gaits and tried to assess attitude. Scout knew how to pick good pulling dogs, but it had never excited her. She'd always wanted to pick a dog she *liked* rather than one with brilliant conformation and an outstanding gait.

Malachy opened the kennel gate. As Scout slipped

in after him, the puppies jumped up at the legs of her pants. "Where's the mom?"

Malachy pointed toward the doghouse, where a bitch stood up and stretched, watching Scout, interested but not overprotective.

This was not how her father's bitches had behaved with puppies on the ground.

"I'll leave you two to negotiate," John said. He made his way back through the other dogs, pausing to examine the feet on one, fill a water bowl for another.

"I figured," Malachy said, "I'd let you pick a puppy and give you a couple of other dogs from these same lines. They're from Kotzebue. I don't know where their racy looks came from. Definitely some Siberian, but there's other stuff in there, too. They're fast, and they're energetic."

"I noticed." The fat white puppy sat on her boot, and Scout scooped her up. One ear was raised partway; the other flopped over. "You're a little fatty." She rubbed the dog's tummy, and the puppy squirmed right-side up.

Malachy made a face. "That one has house dog written all over her."

In other words, house dog, not racing dog. Fine by Scout. "I've always wanted a house dog."

The look he gave her was startled, but he asked no questions. "You're welcome to her. Any of them but the black one. A Welcome-to-McGrath present. Take two, if you like."

"I think one puppy and the other two dogs you're offering are plenty." After all, she needed to see Mary Clarke's dogs. "What does your dad do? Or is he retired?"

Malachy had crouched to play with the puppies, who

jumped at him, jockeying for position. "He works with the dogs, breeds and sells them, and he runs an Internet site that sells native artwork."

"Did he do something different while you were growing up?"

Malachy nodded and stood. "Bring your friend—" he gestured at the puppy "—if you want, and we can go look at the other two. You'll need a four-wheeler for summer training. We have one you can use. If you like it, you can buy it from us, but in the meantime it's yours to use as long as you need."

"Thanks." Carrying the heavy, squirming puppy, Scout followed him out of the kennel.

He'd been evasive about his father, and she remembered that from long ago—and how she'd yearned to know the truth behind the mystery. But she'd never learned whatever it was that Malachy hadn't wanted her to know about his childhood.

And now, she'd matured enough to realize it might be something that he'd never tell.

CHAPTER THREE

SHE RODE HOME in Malachy's truck with the puppy in her lap and the other two dogs—smiling, silly dogs named Ax and Sky—in the back. Scout couldn't believe they'd come from Kotzebue. She thought of Eskimo dogs as being like her father's.

Malachy nodded at the puppy. "What are you going to name her?"

"Estelle."

"Estelle?"

"Like in *Great Expectations.*"

"Nothing like naming her after a nice woman."

"You've read it." Scout flashed him a congratulatory smile.

"That's a ridiculous name for a sled dog."

Scout knew he was teasing. "All literary names are ridiculous," she responded. Having been given one herself, she could make this statement. But the puppy was going to be Estelle, and that was that. "Anyhow, she's a house dog."

"She might *decide* to be a sled dog. They do that sometimes."

"Well, if she wants to pull sleds, I'll let her. Where did you grow up?"

"Unalakleet."

"Has your dad always lived in Alaska?" She was being nosy, but she didn't care.

"No."

So much for that line of questioning. If she wanted to know more, she'd have to be more specific, but Malachy had subtly discouraged probing. It took nerve to walk over his silent cues that he preferred to drop the subject.

Her Alaskan upbringing told her to let it rest, not to press, not to be nosy.

But she'd been Outside for many years, and Alaska's values weren't necessarily hers. "How did your folks meet? You mom was Aleut, wasn't she?"

"Right." They had reached her place, the building he owned, and Malachy parked near the fence in back. He'd brought stakes and chains for the dogs. "These two are used to being outdoors. They'll like it better. Besides, you don't want all your dogs inside."

Malachy stole a glance at Scout's large but graceful hands on the white puppy's fur. *Estelle.* He thought of the question she'd asked.

No reason not to answer. Except that he made a habit of not answering this one.

He turned off the engine and opened his door.

When he and Scout and the dogs were inside the fence, and the two sled dogs were sniffing for old smells and the white puppy was trying to pick fights with each in turn, Malachy forced himself to speak. "My father was a Catholic priest in the Aleutians. My mother was eighteen years old. They fell in love, and because she was pregnant with me, I think, the Church was willing to let him quit. They used to be more lenient then. But my parents had to move far away. That was part of the agreement, even though it meant my mother was leaving the islands and her village and her family and everything she knew, her whole support network. My father says she wasn't happy in Unalakleet and that he regrets obeying the Church by leaving the islands. Anyhow, she left us when I was about three. Went back to the Aleutians. That's all." The words sounded matter-of-fact but unreal to him. He never said these things. "Is telling you this going to help me get engaged to Mary Clarke?"

That's all, Scout echoed in her mind. "Only if it's made you behave in such a way that she doesn't want to marry you." Which seemed more than possible. Abandonment by mother could become a major issue with grown men. That didn't mean, in Scout's opinion, that it excused a variety of unhealthy behaviors designed to avoid future abandonment. Those included, but weren't limited to, choosing unavailable lovers, sabotaging a relationship once commitment was achieved, infidelity, abandoning one's partner...

"It might have," he admitted.

"Or if you've chosen her because, for some reason, there's no way in hell she'll marry you, which liberates you from actually becoming committed."

"Do you talk like this to your clients?"

"No. Mostly I listen. But you're *not* a client." That couldn't be said too many times. "I'm saying things to you I sometimes *wish* I could say to them."

"Are you the matchmaker?"

Scout whirled. A man leaned against the outside of the fence. He had a goatee and shoulder-length hair that had been blond and was fading toward white. He was neither tall nor strongly built. He wore a Hawaiian shirt and army fatigues.

She went to the fence. "I'm Scout Berensen, and I work for the Harmony Agency, yes, but we're not matchmakers."

"Good." He grinned in a vaguely appealing way. "Because I don't need one. Hey, Trooper." To Malachy.

Malachy must have responded silently, with a wave or a nod.

"Just thought I'd introduce myself. I'm Serge Snow."

His name sounded like a musher's energy drink. "It's nice to meet you," she answered, for form's sake and because he might have money that could become the Harmony Agency's.

He stared at her building with a far-away look in his eye, an expression Scout immediately pegged as culti-vated. "No, I've never had trouble meeting women. They come on to me. But you'll have plenty of business. A lot of men up here haven't done their homework."

Meaning you have? Scout glanced behind her, but Malachy seemed to have gone inside, leaving Ax and Sky chained to their stakes and Estelle wandering free. The puppy ambled over to Scout's feet.

"Well," said Scout, picking up Estelle, "I'd better get back to work. I'm still moving in. Thank you for saying hello."

"If you need anything, just ask. The Pork-Fryes know me."

Scout managed to control her features at this name for the Realtor and his wife.

Without missing a beat, Serge added, "In McGrath, I'm the guy who can get it for you."

Wondering if this translated into employment, Scout waved goodbye and turned her back. Tired.

Tired because there were too many predators in the world—which wasn't necessarily to say that Serge Snow was one. But many counseling sessions with female—and certain male—clients revolved around teaching behaviors that reduced vulnerability to predatory people. There was no such thing as invulnerability. Scout had known better than to say or do anything that could be interpreted as encouragement by Serge, who never had trouble meeting women because they came on to him, who had done his homework and was the guy who could get it for her.

With Estelle in her arms, she headed for the back door, which she'd unlocked when they returned. She went inside to find Malachy studying a section of floor he'd sanded earlier.

She set Estelle down, and the puppy began to sniff, then came to sit beside Scout's legs. "Do women come on to Serge?"

"In my law enforcement capacity, I have had to ask Serge not to make unwelcome advances to three women in McGrath, by which I mean not to touch them without their consent. I'd say he's harmless, but he bugs people." He changed the subject. "When I refinish this floor, the fumes are going to drive you out of here for a few days. You'll be all right upstairs, but when do you want to start scheduling appointments?"

"I thought I'd give myself a week."

"Good."

Estelle wandered across the floor toward the

furniture, and Scout watched her. Abruptly, the puppy sprinted back. "When can I meet Mary?"

"Oh, we were going to do that tonight, weren't we?"

"You have plans with her, I think?" Scout asked.

His habit of not answering immediately was beginning to get to her. What wasn't he telling her?

"Let's drive over and see her sled dogs," he said at last. "Estelle can come. We'll put her in one of the dog boxes when we get out to look at Mary's dogs."

"*Do* you have plans with Mary for tonight?"

"She won't be surprised if I come by."

"Does that mean you have a standing arrangement of some kind? Malachy, I can't help if you don't tell me what's going on."

To her surprise he paused where he crouched to examine the floor, then sat, leaning back against the wall.

Scout lowered herself to an adjacent stretch of sanded hardwood, wanting to take off her boots but leaving them on in case they really were going to Mary Clarke's in a couple of minutes. Estelle climbed over her legs, then over them again.

"Last week," Malachy said, "she told me, 'You're just not the most important thing in my life.' And, you know, I understand. That's why I like her. She's her own person, and she's driven. She's mature. She's not some silly girl who falls in love with the wrong person for the wrong reasons. She's a woman."

Scout rubbed her jaw. It struck her that Mary Clarke sounded a bit like her, and that the two of them might actually become friends.

But there were still some facts to clarify. Already today, one man had assured her that he had no trouble attracting women, that they came onto him, et cetera, and Malachy might be equally capable of holding a very subjective viewpoint.

Her phone rang.

The system came with caller ID, which announced the number aloud.

The mechanical male voice called out a local number.

A voice said, "This is…um…Martin Moss. Please call me back. I'm interested in…your services. I want to place an ad, that is."

At least he doesn't think I'm a matchmaker—or a prostitute.

"I have a couple of boxes for brochures that I need to hang outside," Scout said to Malachy.

"Martin Mosquito."

"What?"

"He studies mosquitoes. That's what he does."

The phone rang again.

"This is Serge. I think I might be able to do some things I could trade for aspects of your program. I'm open to learning more about relationships. We never stop growing. If you need bodywork, for instance, we could work out a trade…."

Scout managed not to roll her eyes, which would've been her reaction had Malachy not been sitting there watching her face.

She decided to ignore the voice on the answering machine, which was still talking, about meditation and getting together so he could help her get "connected" in McGrath. She asked Malachy, "Do you consider Mary Clarke your girlfriend?"

The question shouldn't have required so much thought.

"She's not seeing anyone else," he finally answered. "She sees me sometimes, and she doesn't mind if I come by, but she's into her dogs. The dogs come first."

"Anyhow," said Serge, "I just wanted to reiterate my welcome to you. I hope you make McGrath your permanent home. And if there's anything at all you need…"

Malachy cast a look toward the phone.

"What?"

"Nothing." He pressed his head back against the wall. Serge continued talking.

Estelle whined and yawned but didn't sniff the floor as though she needed to go out.

Scout looked at her watch.

Mercifully, the machine beeped, ending the message. She stood. "Maybe I can get more information from Mary."

"Good idea." He rose, too. "I don't ask her how she views our relationship. Not often. When I hint at it, she just tells me she has a full life and I'm one part of it."

That, Scout decided, was the most hopeful thing she'd heard about this relationship that Malachy hoped would culminate in marriage.

SHE SUPPOSED the two mud tracks that led to Mary Clarke's home qualified as a road, but she was glad she wasn't driving. "I'm impressed Estelle hasn't gotten sick in the truck."

Malachy briefly eyed the puppy, who now rested her head on the open window.

"Does Mary Clarke have puppies for sale?"

"Probably. Plus a few can't-grows she'd give away." These did not sound like dogs that would make a winning sprint team. But sprint dogs were smaller than distance dogs, and if most of Mary Clarke's dogs were built for distance…

When she'd grown up running dogs, she'd had more success running those that were from the same lines, establishing some symmetry in a team. That made it easier for dogs to maintain the same speed and made for compatible gaits. She saw the dogs first thing as Malachy pulled up outside the long low cabin. Mary Clarke's dogs were husky mixes with lots of thick black fur. Many had white socks and white on their faces and chests.

They barked and howled at the arrival of Malachy's truck. As far as Scout could see, dogs and doghouses edged three sides of the cabin. She imagined Mary Clarke had about a hundred dogs.

The front door opened, but the woman who emerged only waved a disinterested hand at Malachy's truck as she headed out to her dogs. She either hadn't noticed that Malachy had a passenger or didn't care. She also seemed not remotely interested that he had arrived.

I have my work cut out for me. "You're sure she knows you exist?"

"Ha ha." Malachy considered, then added, "She knows." One reason he'd never given Mary up as a lost cause was his inner certainty that if he ever moved on, she would suddenly display a host of responses she'd never shown before. Possessiveness, jealousy, determination to have him back. But he preferred not to have to break up with her and start seeing someone else—a dishonest move that could hurt the new person unnecessarily—to help Mary discover that she really loved him.

He knew she loved him.

She just couldn't be bothered to do anything about it.

Scout opened the passenger door and climbed out. Without consulting Malachy, she put Estelle in one of the dog boxes. The puppy whined and cried at the separation, then jumped up and put her head and paws to the round window. She was adorable.

Scout walked beside Malachy toward the woman in the yard. As they neared, it struck Scout how petite the musher was. Small and beautiful—and the kind of Alaskan woman Scout had never managed to be.

Mary grasped a shaggy black dog by the collar. It jumped on her, then pulled her forward, tail and whole body wagging as she moved it to a different stake than the one where it had been chained. She glanced at Malachy and seemed to notice Scout.

Not pretty—stunning. Very curly golden hair, sharp features, turquoise eyes that Scout seriously doubted were enhanced by contact lenses.

She and Malachy would make a gorgeous couple.

They could produce gorgeous children together.

They could raise them in true Alaskan fashion.

The children would be born at home.

They would have about six.

All that had to happen was for this woman to take her eyes off her dogs and notice that a fabulously handsome man—*employed, nonalcoholic,* added the Harmony Agency representative in Scout—was crazy about her.

But Mary Clarke appeared to prefer her dogs to Malachy.

Her affection for Estelle aside, Scout couldn't imagine liking dogs quite that much.

Though she wasn't overfond of most men, either.

"Hi." Having chained the dog to its new stake, Mary crossed the yard, her strides long and energetic. "I'm Mary," she said, holding out a hand to Scout, completely ignoring Malachy. No hug or kiss of greeting, no glance that would have marked them as lovers.

"Scout Berensen."

"Scout and I went to college together."

Malachy, Scout thought, could do a superb impression of a man doing an inadequate job of explaining why he was driving another woman around in his car. There was no reason for him to feel guilty, but he *sounded* guilty.

If I was Mary, he'd be out of my life in a heartbeat.

Interestingly, Mary gave Malachy the first look of real romantic attraction that Scout had seen from her. Maybe attraction wasn't the right word, but this wasn't a proprietary look, either. Simply, Mary seemed intrigued by Malachy's behavior. Intrigued with the confidence of a woman who knew she could keep her man in line.

So they are lovers. Scout couldn't imagine why Malachy would have invented that scenario if it was untrue, but she'd begun to think that he had, in fact, invented it.

Why did I agree to have anything to do with this situation? Because I wanted to love Alaska?

Nonsense. She'd long ago come to terms with being who she was rather than who her parents had raised her to be.

Loneliness?

There was more to that possibility than she wanted to examine. She didn't want a boyfriend or lover, and even wondered if maybe she was incapable of maintaining a romantic relationship. Such relationships presupposed respect, and she had a poor track record of feeling respect toward men.

She'd worked so hard, for so many years, to maintain a marriage with a man who was, frankly, mean to her—only to learn that they weren't actually married, after all. How was she supposed to explain that to her family, anyway? To her humorless father, whose obsession was with living off the land, living on as little of everything as possible, using everything that came their way. And a mother who followed his lead, sometimes without appearing to have a thought of her own. And to the brother who seemed unable to establish even rudimentary relationships with other people.

The last of those was going to change, if she had anything to say about it. And she'd come back to Alaska, in part, to have that say.

Malachy spoke then, distracting her from thoughts of her brother's social life. "Scout's getting a team together. A sprint team, actually. She wondered if you have any can't-grows around who might make good sprint dogs."

"I might. Have you ever driven a dog sled?"

"I grew up north of Kokrines. I helped my family run a trapline until I went away to college." Why this need to make herself sound so competent?

You gave her a truthful answer, Scout. You can drive a sled.

"But you want sprint dogs?"

Mary seemed amazed that Scout could have found any work more interesting than running that trapline.

"I don't have time to train distance dogs." Instead of,

If one of your dogs so much as looks at me wrong, I'm out of here. "I'm a psychologist. I'm setting up an office here in McGrath."

"Undoubtedly, *that's* something we need, not that you'll have many takers."

Scout gave a slightly more expanded description of the Harmony Agency.

"Well, that actually might be a success," Mary declared. "With the men, anyway."

"Exactly the population she plans to fleece," Malachy explained.

Scout threw him an injured frown.

Mary bit back a smile. "Let's look at dogs. I have one puppy who's five months and I don't think he's ever going to catch up with his littermates. Truthfully, I don't think he'd make that great a sprint dog, either. Too mellow. He's more of a pet type, but you can see how you feel about him."

The dog was topaz-eyed, with the thick black-and-white fur and ever-so-slightly turned up nose that seemed characteristic of Mary's lines. When Scout sank onto the ground, he sniffed her shoes and pants but without great enthusiasm. As Mary had indicated, he seemed reserved.

Then he climbed into Scout's lap and curled up.

Oh, my.

"You can have him. But bring him back—within a month, please—if you decide he's not going to work out."

"Does he have a name?"

"Pigpen. I named this litter after *Peanuts* characters."

"Does he know his name?"

"Actually, he answers to it. He'd make someone a great house dog. I'm just not sure he'll ever be a sled dog."

Scout agreed with Mary that Pigpen didn't seem to have the temperament of a sled dog, let alone a sprint dog. But she didn't think Malachy's plan for her to love Alaska necessitated her *rejecting* a puppy like this.

What about her own plans, though? If she returned to California, any house dogs would have to go with her.

"I'll try him out," she said incautiously. "Thank you. Any others?"

"I have a few I would sell that would make good sprint dogs."

"How much?"

"Let me introduce you."

Malachy said, "I'll let you two talk. Want me to take the C team out for a short run on the four-wheeler?" he asked Mary.

"If you keep taking them for *short* runs, they'll never be good for anything except the C team," Mary replied tartly. "Whatever. Yes, it's fine." She did not say *thank you*. Scout suspected that she felt she was doing Malachy a favor by letting him anywhere near her dogs.

Malachy's mission took him to the far end of the yard. Scout glanced at him once as he began to line out tugs and harnesses. The noise in the yard— yelping, howling and barking—reached such a crescendo that any possibility of conversation between her and Mary vanished.

Mary, however, far from focusing on the dogs she planned to show Scout, watched Malachy through narrowed eyes, clearly ready to pounce if he made any move not to her liking.

As a professional relationship counselor, Scout was intrigued. Malachy apparently didn't mind Mary's bossing him around, which wasn't what she, Scout, would have predicted.

Usually, men who exhibited the behavior Malachy was showing with Mary—falling in love with a dominant woman—had very powerful mothers. But Malachy had known his mother only a short time.

Don't bother figuring him out, Scout. You're not getting paid for it. You're not getting paid at all. And the project is to learn how he can convince this woman to marry him.

It seemed a long time before Malachy pulled out of the yard on a four-wheel all-terrain vehicle pulled by eight sled dogs.

When he was gone, Mary gave a sharp growl, and the rest of the dogs quieted. Some of them lay down. Others licked empty food bowls.

"Sorry about that. I have to watch him. Once he put two of my wheel dogs in the lead position." She shrugged, then said abruptly, "So why did you decide on McGrath as a place to open an office?"

For a moment, Scout felt the gaze that had rested on Malachy as he hitched the dogs. Wary, suspicious, distrustful.

Immediately, she regretted agreeing to the idea Malachy had proposed. She hadn't thought through to the fact that this plan would involve deceiving Mary Clarke, who seemed nice and interesting, someone who could be a friend to her, Scout.

"We've been looking at Alaska for a while." No deception there. "My brother mentioned McGrath, and it fits our profile for a small office. Also, my family's here." She wouldn't say that was an attraction but it *was* part of the truth. "My brother's my twin." *Who's turning into a dysfunctional recluse*... She didn't add it, and it wasn't precisely what she felt. Only that the way they'd been raised left some obstacles to be overcome. She needed Holden to see that, too. Not for her sake but for his own.

"He's a friend of Malachy's," Mary observed. "Your brother. Holden, right?"

Scout blinked. "Right." Mary knew who Holden was? Did she think Holden had suggested McGrath because...because... *No, Holden wouldn't try to get Malachy and me together.*

"Malachy doesn't want me to go to counseling with him, does he?" Mary asked.

"If he does, he hasn't mentioned it to me." Oh, this was so much like lying and so unprofessional. Even her temptation to tell Mary that she *couldn't* see Malachy on a professional basis would be a kind of lie, because what exactly was she doing?

Playing games.

Childish games, no less.

Damn it, Malachy, why did I agree to this?

That was a question she didn't want to examine too closely. "For friendship's sake" wasn't the all-inclusive answer she wanted it to be.

"You *do* know that he and I are seeing each other? Not that it matters." Mary shrugged again. "I barely have time for anybody and, to be perfectly honest, I'm better with dogs than men. I mean, I'm thirty-six. I'm past the point where I'm good at saying 'How wonderful you are!' to someone who just isn't that wonderful. You know?"

Oh, how Scout knew.

"I mean, Malachy *is* wonderful," Mary said so quickly that it was almost one word rather than a sentence.

"Is he?" Scout asked.

"You haven't seen him for a long time?"

Scout shook her head. "Make no mistake, I would've cut off my right arm for his attention when I was eighteen."

Mary said, "Sometimes I don't think I was ever eighteen, if that's what being eighteen means."

"It was an exaggeration. My way of saying that when I was eighteen, I believed him to be perfect."

"Did he prove you wrong?" Mary seemed to genuinely want to hear the answer. Also, she seemed far too decent for Scout to continue with Malachy's scheme. She'd have to tell him the deal was off.

"No." Scout lifted one shoulder. "It's just what I thought when I was eighteen."

"You and I should get together some night," Mary suggested. "Sit down and discuss the superiority of dogs."

"I'd love that." Of course, Mary didn't know that Scout was not a lover of all dogs and that she was already dying for the company of someone who wanted to discuss Pilates and cute shoes. But the invitation was nice.

Yes. She'd have to tell Malachy that the deal was off. Because she sensed that Mary would like someone to confide in, probably about Malachy.

On the other hand, she could just *tell* Mary what Malachy had asked her to do. But that would be a betrayal of a different kind.

One of the cardinal rules of adult life, professional and non-professional, was not to betray confidences. Anyone's confidences.

Well, she just wouldn't repeat to Malachy what Mary

said to her—unless Mary gave her permission. She *had* done this before, more than once. She'd seen two different people in her practice as a psychotherapist, listened to each talk about the other, and had never revealed that she'd even met the person being discussed.

"Anyhow, let me show you some dogs. A couple of them I'd sell for a hundred dollars each. I just want *something* for them because I do feel they have potential as sprint dogs. But there's one I'm selling for five hundred, and you probably don't want to spend that much money at this point. It's a question of gait. You've got to see him move. This animal can really run, and he's all there, if you know what I mean."

Scout did. It occurred to her that she was going to be buying dog food, giving immunizations, cutting toenails, sewing booties, investing time and money in these dogs.

Of course, Malachy had said they'd do it together. Should she consult him now? And what would Mary think of that?

Maybe she *could* spend five hundred dollars on one fast dog. Yes. Why not? She wasn't sure she could remember her father ever actually paying for a dog, let alone big bucks—although he'd certainly sold some for good money. Sometimes Holden had found dogs at the Anchorage and Fairbanks pounds and flown them to their family's property. He and her father had bred what they considered the best intact dogs, and their kennel's reputation had grown.

Holden. It would be nice to see him, to talk with him—if not with her parents.

Tonight, when she returned to her place, she'd call

them. She'd tell them she was in McGrath. She'd tell them about the dogs. She'd talk about refinishing the floor. These were things they'd understand.

She followed Mary around the exterior of the cabin, and Scout met the dogs Mary had mentioned. She bought the expensive dog, paying in traveler's checks, not having opened a local bank account yet. McGrath had a small branch of the Bank of the North for its five-hundred-plus year-round residents and for visitors at peak seasons—summer and Iditarod time.

Mary wrote down her phone number, told Scout to call if she had any questions, and helped her load the dogs into some of Malachy's dog boxes. Seeing Estelle, she said, "I like that puppy. I'm not sure she'll ever be a sled dog, but there's something about her."

Scout opened the box and gathered up Estelle. The puppy became ecstatic, wriggly, hysterical, licking and squirming in her arms. "That's how I feel. I wanted her right away."

"How much did you pay for her?"

Oh, dear. "Well…" Scout thought fast. "We worked out a trade, of sorts."

Mary did not ask the nature of the trade. "He's mentioned you before." She made that point again.

Why would Malachy tell Mary about a female he hadn't seen for ten years, especially when that female had never been the most important person in his life?

"He said you were his first friend who was a girl and you taught him that love wasn't always about jumping into bed."

"It would've been if I'd had anything to say about it. Back then, I mean," Scout answered hurriedly. There was no need to mention what had eventually happened. Sharing sleeping bags. Et cetera.

Mary grinned. "I guess I do remember that aspect of being eighteen." She heard the four-wheeler returning. Mary's dogs began barking and Scout's new family members, in the dog boxes, joined in. "It's been great meeting you, Scout." She paused. "You probably had the kind of childhood I really envy."

And would've been good at. "You didn't grow up here?"

"Kansas. I've been here fourteen years, but I still feel like an Outsider half the time."

Twenty minutes later, as Malachy guided the truck back over the two ruts that were Mary's drive, Scout said, "She seems *really* nice. I like her. To be honest, I have some discomfort about what I've agreed to do."

"You think she'd be making a mistake?"

His take on the issue surprised Scout. "No. I just meant I'm not going to deceive her. If she tells me things in confidence, as a friend, I can't tell you those things. You realize that, don't you?"

He said nothing.

She glanced at his profile.

"I think that's why I asked for your help," he said. "I've always understood you. And I've always believed you understood me."

Awareness spilled through Scout, a sensation more imagined than physical, a bracing awareness, a swaying of impending disaster—a horror that his words held magic and that she no longer believed in magic but *wanted* to. After Danny, she was no longer innocent and only wished she could be. She'd never truly been married, yet she'd learned how challenging marriage is. But the harder lesson she'd learned was that she couldn't always trust what she wanted to believe.

So she chased the goblin warnings out the window of his truck and sat there in silence for too long, trying to think of a single thing to say.

CHAPTER FOUR

SCOUT'S FIRST TWO WEEKS in McGrath flew by. Having her own dogs was different from living with her family's kennel. Estelle liked to lie down beside the bathtub whenever Scout had a bath. And somehow, Scout had ended up letting Estelle and Pigpen onto the bed. Her father would *never* have allowed that.

But she found herself feeling fond of even the five outdoor dogs, the sled dogs who *weren't* house dogs. For instance, she now saw them as vulnerable instead of as predators—with her as prey.

Then there was the moment when Bobby, the fast dog she'd bought from Mary, first kissed her.

Suddenly, he wasn't a stranger. He was *her* dog.

Estelle hated being left behind when Scout ran the other dogs with the four-wheeler, so Scout set up a special box for the puppy in front of her own seat. Soon she had a routine, and not one dog had tried to bite her. She was tempted to let them all sleep in the house, although she knew it would be a bad idea. What if they fell in love with her and she couldn't leave them when she returned to California? Worse, what if she fell in love with them—loved them more than she already did? So Estelle and Pigpen got the preferential treatment.

I can't get any more dogs, she told herself again and again. *How will I let any of them go?*

But what if she remained in Alaska?

I didn't come here planning to stay.

But now that she was here, she found she didn't hate it. Not really. McGrath wasn't like where she'd grown up. Everything seemed different.

What was most different was that she liked having dogs.

She'd established a schedule: Clients four days a week, sometimes as late as 7:00 p.m. Three men had signed up for Harmony's full service. Four others had placed ads on the Internet through Harmony and in their magazine. And one couple and a family with a troubled adolescent had come in for counseling. She ran her dogs seven days a week first thing in the morning or in the sun of the arctic night. It was pretty in McGrath and she liked following the tails of happy dogs, which was the last thing she'd ever expected to enjoy.

In the interest, he said, of making her warm, comfortable and happy in Alaska, Malachy had shown up every day before or after his shift to fix and paint. He'd also constructed a shed of separate kennel areas for her dogs and provided suggestions for where else she could obtain excellent sprint dogs. Scout said she didn't want any more, but he thought she might like to race and felt she should have more for that. Unfortunately, two of the prospective sellers were clients, which meant she couldn't get dogs from them but couldn't tell Malachy *why* they were unsuitable.

Scout had done far less to keep her part of the bargain. She and Mary had both been too busy to get together yet, although they had tentative plans to share a bottle of wine and some salmon that coming weekend. Probably Mary would open up more about Malachy then.

She'd probably say all the things Scout couldn't tell Malachy unless Mary said she could.

The fact was, her own role in this deal seemed very complex, and she could hardly bear to imagine Dana's and Victoria's faces if they heard what she'd agreed to do.

But it couldn't be *professional* suicide, because she wasn't acting in a professional capacity. She was just helping out a friend who wanted to marry another friend. And he was helping her like Alaska.

Malachy, in uniform, leaned against his patrol vehicle in her driveway when she returned that Thursday morning from running the dogs. She had put Bobby, the pricey dog from Mary Clarke, in lead, as usual. He didn't seem to be a great leader, but he was the best she had at the moment and definitely her fastest dog. Ax and Sky ran behind him.

She let the dogs pull her past the SUV and all the way into her yard, where she began unhitching them and turning them loose in their new kennel as Malachy joined her.

"Something strange has happened," she said. "For what might be the first time in my life, I want it to snow. Maybe."

"Now, that's wholehearted enthusiasm. Can you do a ride-along with me today? I have to go to Nome to speak with a probation officer."

"You have one?"

"Ha ha. It's about a local kid who's spending the summer there. Needs to be out of McGrath for a while. I figured we could visit the pound, maybe pick up a dog or two for you."

"You can take dogs with you when you're working?"

He shrugged. "We'll throw them in burlap sacks. They'll be fine."

By air, then. Of course.

This was her day free from clients, although she'd agreed to see one of her regulars, Martin the mosquito man, this morning. He'd already met a woman on the Internet through Harmony. They were corresponding via e-mail and had spoken on the phone, and he wanted Scout's in-person advice about some aspect of this budding relationship.

"I have a half-hour appointment at eight. I'm free after that." She tried to ignore her guilt that Malachy was doing still *more* for her and she had yet to have a long heart-to-heart with Mary Clarke.

"I'll pick you up at quarter to nine," he said, crouching to pet Estelle who, out of her box on the four-wheeler, ran free around the yard giving the other dogs the business. He squinted at the puppy as she ran away to tackle Ax. "She might turn into something yet."

"She is something."

The look he cast her was enigmatic—affectionate and vaguely pleased.

It would be nice to see snow, she reflected. She hadn't seen any for a few years, not since the first and last time she'd gone skiing at Lake Tahoe. Preoccupied with her guilt that she'd done no more for Malachy's cause, she asked, "Have you seen Mary?"

"Funny you should ask."

Scout said, "C'mon, Estelle," and started for the house, glancing at Malachy, who joined her.

"I decided not to go by her place for a while, to see if she noticed me not being around."

That Mary wouldn't notice seemed, to Scout, a realistic concern. "Did she call or try to get in touch?" Scout climbed the steps to the back door and opened the screen.

"Yes. Last night. She called and asked if I had a new girlfriend."

"Ah." Scout digested this.

"I said I'd just been spending time getting this place in shape."

Scout supposed this was just the sort of answer to worry Mary Clarke if Mary was worried about Scout as competition for Malachy.

"And?"

"She suggested she and I take part in the spelling bee Sunday night. It's a benefit for the preschool."

"I thought there was no preschool. The real estate guy told me it failed."

"No. Graham meant that the preschool and day care that was in this building failed. There's another preschool now."

Scout made herself shut down her professional-unprofessional fascination with Malachy's pursuit of Mary the Musher and asked, "Can anyone take part?"

"Anyone with five dollars."

"This is what I've missed most about Alaska. Culture."

"She also asked if I wanted to come over tonight and drink wine and play chess."

Scout considered this. "She likes chess?"

"She knows I like it."

"Do you always win?"

"Against her?"

"Yes."

"Always," he answered.

Scout had never known Malachy liked to play chess. "How long have you been playing?"

"Since I was a kid. My father and I used to play."

A slight diffidence colored his manner as he mentioned his father. Did Malachy blame his father, somehow, for his mother's leaving them? After all, she'd had to move away from her family and culture because the Church had dictated it.

Scout didn't spend a long time thinking about it. She held to the belief that nothing that had happened in her life so far had caused her lasting harm and figured it was probably the same for Malachy. People had to get over the past and move on. She could blame her parents for the social naïveté she'd shown at eighteen, or she could thank them for trying to teach her to be self-sufficient in challenging physical circumstances. She preferred to do the latter.

When it came to Danny, however, she wasn't yet so free. The bigamist ex-husband tended to linger in her consciousness after she would've preferred him to be gone.

The fact was, if she hadn't found him profoundly sexy, lovable and brilliant, she wouldn't have fallen in love with him in the first place. She'd been in love up until she'd learned that he wasn't actually married to her but to someone else.

Finally, she said, "So you have a date to drink wine with her and beat her at chess."

He nodded.

"I don't think you need me," Scout said happily. "You're doing really well on your own."

"Remember the magnitude of the goal."

"We can talk about this some more on the way to Nome," Scout told him. "I want to know if she's opposed to marrying you."

"I'll see you in an hour or so."

Scout glanced at her watch and realized she needed to hustle if she was going to look presentable for her client. "Right."

"So I ASKED HER if she'd like to visit," Martin said. "I told her I'd buy the ticket."

"What did she say?"

"That she'd buy her own ticket. She doesn't like being under obligation to anyone, she said."

Scout waited. He would explain his trouble with this in a moment. As she and Martin both knew, the woman was following Harmony's guidelines regarding gifts. Hopefully, she'd be smart about accommodations, too.

Martin pushed his glasses up on his nose. Thin and about Scout's height, he wore his brown hair in a long ponytail and his beard untrimmed. He was a mosquito expert doing a long-term research project on Alaskan mosquitoes. His ability to foot an airplane ticket for a prospective girlfriend came from family money; he had a trust fund. As her new clients went, Scout rather liked him. He was forty-five and had been married once for three years. He detested his father.

"I think," he admitted, "that she wants to come up here and shop around. For men."

The female in question was an electrical engineer employed in California's Silicon Valley. Scout suspected she was quite independent. "How do you feel about that?"

"Well, I'm not real pleased, to tell you the truth. I feel a bit used."

"Tell me why."

"I kind of feel like she's using me as an excuse to come to McGrath and check out who's up here. She's going to stay in a hotel, and she said she'd like to spend some time with me but that she'd like to feel free to do whatever else she wants as well."

Excellent, Scout thought. Sometimes she felt Harmony's most important service was teaching people to protect themselves. "That sounds straightforward."

"I know there's no real reason I should object. I might not like her company, either."

"True."

"And she's following the agency guidelines—I know that. But I feel as though she's just going to be the new woman in town and I'll have the same chance as any other guy."

"Is that so bad?"

He looked thoughtful. "I don't know. Up here, sometimes I think we all get a bit...desperate. I don't like feeling desperate."

Scout felt one of those flashes of compassion that seemed to ease the rough edges of her job. Here was a person admitting to feelings with which she could empathize. She felt connected to the human race, felt the success of being able to relate to others and mirror their feelings for them.

She smiled. "Have you written back to her since she communicated all this?"

"No. I wasn't sure what to say."

"She seems sensible to me," Scout told him. "As you

said, she's following the guidelines, and she probably sees why those guidelines are a good idea. She may just be making sure that if you don't enjoy each other's company, neither of you feels stuck with each other."

Martin squinted under bushy eyebrows flecked with gray. "I didn't think of it like that. You're right. I'm just freaking out. Thanks."

"It's something that can make you nervous," Scout told him.

Martin sat up slowly and peered at her through his glasses. "Have *you* ever done it?"

"Done what?"

"Had a mail-order relationship, an e-mail relationship, any of it?"

"No. One of my partners met her husband by e-mail, though, so we're believers."

He eyed her suspiciously. "How long have they been married?"

"Five years. Maybe six?"

He continued to look thoughtful. Then, abruptly, he nodded and rose. "Thanks," he repeated. "Thanks."

"So," said Malachy, "is Mary opposed to marriage or just to marrying me?"

"I don't like leaving Estelle behind. She was upset."

"No one would ever know you grew up with dogs. Are you this attentive to your clients, by the way? I was going to answer a question you asked."

"Yes. Right. But you're not a client. I *am* more attentive with clients. Of course. Look, let's just go back and get her."

Estelle, Malachy translated. "It's good for her to be

in a kennel. The other dogs are nearby, but none of them can get her."

"Which is fortunate, because you and I both know they'd pick on her."

"She does her share of picking on them. I don't believe in coddling sled dogs," Malachy answered, continuing on the road that led to the airstrip used by the Alaska troopers.

"We agreed she's a house dog. Malachy, wouldn't it be good to accustom her to flying?"

"I thought you said she was a house dog. Even if she was a sled dog, she'd be a sprint dog. Why should she have to fly?"

"Because she might have to sometime. Humor me. Pretend it has to do with my biological clock."

He glanced at his mirrors. "If you answer one question."

"What?"

"*Does* it have to do with your biological clock?"

"Malachy!"

Smiling slightly, he turned the car.

ESTELLE RODE in a burlap sack in the back of the police plane. Scout's headset was in contact with Malachy's. She could hear all communication and talk to Malachy if she liked. She hadn't expected to fly again so soon after arriving in McGrath, but she savored the trip, picking out the Iditarod Trail as Malachy identified landmarks below. The price of fuel had affected air travel in Alaska, too. There were fewer planes airborne, and travelling in a four-seater with just one other person was a luxury.

In Nome, while Malachy went to his meeting, Scout

walked by the sea. At noon, they met at a diner where he treated her to halibut and received suspicious and not particularly friendly looks from some locals and familiar greetings from others.

"All right," Scout said over the red-and-white-checked tablecloth and foam plates of food. "Tell me— is Mary willing to live with you? Is it just marriage to which she objects?"

He stabbed at the fish in front of him, spearing the flesh with his fork.

A suspicion seized her. "Or are *you* the one with objections to living together?"

"Not exactly. It's just not practical."

"Does this have anything to do with your father?"

"In what way?"

Yes, then. She simply waited.

"Well, he wouldn't be thrilled, but he wouldn't be completely opposed either. He still goes to Mass but accepts that I don't. Still, the fact is, I own the place where we live, and he lives with me."

Scout nodded, understanding. "And Mary owns her place."

"Exactly. So living together would require enough of an adjustment for all of us that it wouldn't be too different from being married. We'd need to be just as sure."

"You are that sure, though." It was a question, but she didn't phrase it as such.

He didn't speak right away because, she decided, he was swallowing. "Yes."

"Your father likes her."

Slow response. "He agrees she's good looking."

Scout shook her head.

As THEY ENTERED the pound, Scout told Malachy, "I have enough dogs. I'm going to have trouble leaving them as it is when I go back to California."

"You won't go back to California." He peered through some chain link at an overweight black lab mix and murmured, "Hey, buddy."

"God, I can't stand this," Scout said. *You won't go back to California.* "All these dogs."

"Right. Let's save some lives."

Why had Malachy said she wouldn't go back to California?

Was he correct?

The idea of that shocked her. She followed Malachy's lead as he eyed prospective additions to her team. She didn't need his help. She'd gone with Holden to pick sled dogs from one pound or another many times. But she was distracted by the thought that maybe, possibly, she'd come home, that maybe she'd actually come to Alaska *looking* to come home.

She'd definitely come for Holden, though, to pry him from his solitude, to share with him what *she* knew—she, the relationship expert of the Harmony Agency whose so-called husband had turned out to be a bigamist and a pathological liar. *But I believe in relationships. I believe that people relating to other people is the most important part of life.*

I have to call Holden, she thought—as she'd been thinking since her arrival in McGrath. But speaking to him meant speaking to her parents.

Malachy liked the gait of a spotted bitch that looked like a cross between some kind of southern hound and an Alaskan husky. The tan-and-black bitch's eyes were almost lemon-colored, and she barked at them aggressively before Malachy took her from her kennel on a lead.

"Now, that's personality," Scout remarked as the bitch snarled and leaped at a neighboring kennel.

"Maybe she'd teach you to love dogs in a new way."

"If you like her, you can have her."

Malachy did—and Scout picked out a blue-eyed bitch, all yellow and white fur, a fluffy husky-type mutt, and named her Sylvia, after a dog in a play by the same name. But the black-and-tan clearly considered herself the baddest bitch on the block. As they walked the dogs back to the airplane, both were pulling hard on their leads, a good sign in a potential sled dog. With the scrappy bitch, whom Malachy decided to call Ices, trying to get at Sylvia, Scout said, "I'm not sure my heart's in the racing thing."

"You don't like my new dog?"

"Teaching me to like dogs like that would take much longer than you and Mary becoming engaged. Fortunately, it's not what you signed on for."

Malachy had Ices on one lead, while Scout held Sylvia. Malachy kept checking his wristwatch.

Scout, listening to the sound of the sea, so close, said, "Do you have to be back by a particular time?"

"I…was planning to meet someone—at the airfield."

"Ah."

She suspected the truth, even before she saw the plane. She knew the call numbers of that Cessna 185. It was the plane in which she'd learned to fly—badly— and she saw the thick unruly mop of hair half standing up from her brother's head as he stalked across the tarmac toward them. He was all long limbs and awkward angles, but Scout knew that his looks were deceiving. Holden had a way with wild animals, had once coaxed a wolf bitch near enough to touch. He could fix any piece of machinery that was broken, build a shelter from almost nothing in any kind of weather.

At least her parents had gotten half of it right.

"Are you angry?" Malachy's voice came low beside her.

"No. I've been thinking about him all day." She tried to stop herself from asking. And couldn't. "You didn't tell—" Stopping too late.

"No."

And his free arm surrounded her shoulders, his hand gently squeezing her.

It was comfortable. Natural.

Her stomach swooped. Ices tried to take a bite out of Sylvia, just as Scout thought, *Oh, no*.

But not about the dogs. Or Holden.

Keeping Sylvia out of reach of Ices was a welcome distraction. The last thing she needed was a stomach-swooping reaction to Malachy MacCullagh.

He was now grabbing burlap sacks from the plane. He bagged Sylvia first, expertly.

"Hey, sis." Holden had reached them. He gazed at her, frowning. "You look different."

Scout was beginning to resent that adjective, but she gave her brother a one-armed hug. His shyness had never extended to family, and he counted Malachy a friend. But Scout had seen him outside the world of those he knew and had witnessed his being in the company of others for hours at a time without uttering a single word unless it was practically pried from him.

Sometimes, he managed to pull this off with an air of aloofness that made him seem snobbish rather than shy. Other times he blushed or stammered, and the truth was known to all.

But she'd sensed in his e-mails that he'd become resigned to life alone, to dying as a bachelor. She'd also sensed his frustration.

"Did you have business in Nome?" Scout asked as he grabbed Ices with experienced hands to help Malachy bag her, too.

"I do. Good-looking bitch." He asked Malachy, "Where is he?"

"His probation officer's driving him over." Malachy told Scout, "I'm guardian to a boy from McGrath. He lives with my father and me during the school year. He's going to stay with your family and learn about real work until he comes back home in September, for school."

I bet he'll love that. Of course, to be fair, he actually might. "Why?"

"His probation officer and I decided that some time off the grid is probably a good idea before he returns to McGrath. A confidence-building wilderness experience—" he gave a small sigh of irritation, about what, Scout couldn't guess "—away from McGrath."

"It was confidence-*destroying* for me," she muttered.

Holden didn't raise his head, didn't look at her, yet she knew that he'd heard.

Malachy studied her face. He was Holden's friend, a friend of the family. It shouldn't have surprised her that he thought her family would be good temporary caregivers for this teenager. "How old is he?" she asked as the two men loaded the bitches on the plane where Estelle had awakened and was crying.

"Thirteen."

Scout teetered between being impressed that Malachy had agreed to assume responsibility for the boy and curious as to how it had come about. She freed Estelle from the plane and slipped a lead on her. Estelle peed on the tarmac without delay. "What did he do?" Scout asked. "To have a probation officer, I mean?"

"A few things."

She could tell that both Malachy and Holden knew the details, but neither of them was forthcoming.

"What's his name?" she asked.

"Jeremy," Malachy said.

"What are you going to do with that?" Holden asked his sister. He meant Estelle.

"I think she's going to be a sled dog. She might even turn out to be a leader." She'd never said this before, even to herself. But it annoyed her that just because Estelle was goofy and cute and sweet, Holden assumed she couldn't pull.

"A sprint dog?"

Malachy must have told him the kind of team they were putting together. To his credit, he only sounded fifty-percent skeptical.

And to Malachy's credit, he didn't reveal that she'd called Estelle a House Dog within the last six hours. Well, who said Estelle couldn't be both?

"Please don't make fun of my dogs," Scout replied with dignity. So Holden and her parents were going to help take care of a juvenile delinquent, undoubtedly teach him to do all the things she'd learned—maybe even spinning. Both her parents spun, dyed with plant dyes, knitted, crocheted, all of it. Both of them sewed.

It made her happy to see Holden. For so much of her life, they'd been best friends, playmates, everything. He had *cared* that she wasn't good at certain tasks. He had *cared* when she cried. She remembered camping trips with the dog sled, maintaining the trapline, flying...

"When will I see you again?" she asked.

"Why don't you come home for a visit? He'd bring you." Holden indicated Malachy. "You could both come. Pick berries. Or fish."

Which they could do just as well in McGrath. Again she remembered just who had suggested a McGrath office. Now Holden seemed to assume that she and Malachy were constant companions.

We nearly are.

Depending on how often Malachy slept at Mary Clarke's, it was possible that he spent more time with Scout than with the woman he wanted to marry. Well, at least Mary had noticed, and her response had been to want to be with Malachy. That was all to the good, and Scout discounted her swooping feeling. A man like Malachy MacCullagh was not for her.

As for Holden's invitation—she detested the inevitable distance created by the secret she couldn't stand to reveal to her family. What if she *did* tell them?

They would reflect that it couldn't possibly have happened if she'd stayed in Alaska.

But she couldn't avoid them just because of Danny. That would be a way of letting him win.

"I will come home," she promised Holden. "It's not a

good time now. I still have too much to do for the business, but in a few weeks I should be able to get up there."

"That is never going to be a sled dog," her brother said.

Scout scooped Estelle, almost too big now, up in her arms. "You can't judge a book—"

"Oh, yes, you can," her twin answered.

Malachy gazed at Scout, an arrested expression on his face.

"What?" she asked.

He only shook his head, his brown eyes thoughtful and smiling.

Why do I have this thing with him?

How strange that long ago he'd become her first lover. They'd only been together like that once, though they'd made love three times then, and Scout had thought of three as a sacred number, as perfect as the experience. The whole night was hallowed in her memory.

An SUV bearing the seal of the City of Nome drove onto the tarmac and parked. Scout saw the native driver. A young teenager sat in the passenger seat.

He opened his door slowly, lethargically. He was skinny, dressed in black, his hair peroxide-white.

He fits in here about as well as I do.

The officer with him was brisk. He shut his door sharply, nodded at the boy. They approached the group at the airplanes together.

Malachy's charge had many piercings, including a stretched circle in the middle of one earlobe and a barbell through one eyebrow. He wore boots, Doc Martens. Malachy introduced everyone.

Then Scout left them and stuffed Estelle into her

burlap sack and put her in the back of the plane with the other dogs. *Snow,* she thought again. But winter was months away. Instead, this was mosquito season. She'd learned early to at least try not to scratch at bites. Tried not to be driven mad by clouds that sometimes reminded her of a dark shadow following her.

They'd driven her mad anyway.

She heard Jeremy and Malachy talking, Holden saying little, and then Holden and the teenager headed for the Cessna.

While Malachy did a walk-around of the police plane, Scout sat in the co-pilot's seat. He had brought her today because Holden would be here. Did Malachy think it was sad—read, pathetic—that she seemed to have nothing to do with her family even though they lived so close by?

Did he think she should tell them about Danny? If so, he'd never said as much.

When he climbed into the plane, secured the door and took the pilot's seat, she said, "Thanks."

"For what?"

"Well, thanks for asking me to come along today, so I could get Sylvia. But I meant, thanks for arranging things so I could see Holden. I've wanted to call him."

He didn't ask why she hadn't. "You have a pretty nice family, Scout."

She wondered if she heard reproval in his tone. In any case, she said, "I think so, too."

They didn't speak after that, Malachy unwilling to voice his thoughts, which weren't about Danny Kilbourne or about Scout but about Jeremy—and Mary's reaction to Jeremy.

For him, there'd been no question. The decision he'd

made had been the only decision he could make, the only decision he could make and remain himself.

He hadn't expected better—or worse—from Mary than that she'd be irritated. Anything that complicated her schedule, which revolved around dogs and conditioning, was an irritation. He didn't fault her for it. But he wasn't willing to change who he was or had to be to accommodate *her* refusal to change. He didn't need her to change—but he did need her to accept him as he was. And he'd never been raised to become a mere consort to a self-involved professional athlete.

Why do you want to marry her, Malachy?

He told himself he wanted to marry her because he loved her. But Jeremy was a litmus test. If she couldn't accept that his life wasn't simply going to revolve around her profession, her desires, then there really was no future for the two of them.

He didn't want to find out that was so.

But increasingly, he feared it was. And he had no idea how he was going to get his doubts across to Scout without a certain disloyalty to Mary. He didn't consider her small because of her feelings about Jeremy. He didn't believe her selfish because of it. But in some way that he would never say aloud, even to his dogs or his own reflection, her attitude did make him pity her.

And he could think of nothing more insulting.

CHAPTER FIVE

THE FOLLOWING EVENING, Scout rode a used bicycle she'd bought from the owner of McGrath Hardware and General Supply out to Mary Clarke's house for their date to drink wine. During the ride, she divided her thoughts between the mosquitoes she told herself to ignore and her discomfort with what she was about to do.

She should've simply asked Malachy if she could tell Mary the truth. But Malachy had other things on his mind. He'd stopped by Scout's place after answering a call to a domestic at a place where he'd been before on nearly identical calls. He and Aaron, the local constable, suspected the male resident had a drug lab in another house in town. Unfortunately, the judge didn't believe it was a realistic possibility or that there was probable cause for a search.

Meth labs can be easily broken down, Malachy had said. *And someone really has to see something.*

The man Malachy suspected of manufacturing methamphetamine had befriended Jeremy in the past— which explained Malachy's sending the teenager north. At the end of the summer, the man and his girlfriend would head for Colorado and the ski industry there.

When Scout reached the end of Mary's road, Mary

had just finished feeding her dogs, who set up a chorus of welcome—some friendly and some less so—as Scout drove into the yard. Mary waved to her and told the dogs to be quiet, which they heeded.

Her thick, curly golden hair was pulled back in a loose ponytail, and Scout thought again how beautiful this Iditarod winner was. With something like shame, she recalled her own feelings of excitement and interest when Malachy had dropped by her place just hours before, apparently just to talk. But this was who he wanted, a beautiful woman who'd won an endurance slog that rivaled the Tour de France in difficulty.

Mary's back deck fronted a tributary of the Kuskokwim River. Citronella pots tried to discourage mosquitoes as she and Scout sat in Adirondack chairs eating baked brie and garlic on sourdough toast, cheese and crackers, grapes and slices of apple and drinking chianti from heavy, pale-blue glass goblets. Mary asked Scout if she was being pursued by McGrath's "tribe" of bachelors, and Scout replied, "They don't seem particularly tribal to me. They're all so individualistic. You know what I mean. Profoundly American."

Alaskan.

Mary laughed. "I do know what you mean. The Declaration of Independence serving as license to be weird."

"Maybe. That guy—uh, Serge—keeps trying to be helpful, but that's about it. I can't date clients."

"*That* man needs your help."

Scout made no reply, and Mary said, "When I first came here, I got involved with him for a *very* short period of time. Trust me, he'll drive you crazy. He'd drive anyone crazy. I think he's sort of attractive, and unfortunately he thinks so, too."

It was almost an invitation to step down her path of deceit. "I suspect you're better off with Malachy."

Mary's mouth twisted in a way that could have conveyed anything—anything except passion for Malachy MacCullagh.

This is the crux of the matter. She's going to tell me what I need to know to help Malachy. Scout mentally crossed her fingers. If only Mary didn't ask her to keep what she said confidential.

"This is something I've told him, too," Mary said, "so it's not like I'm telling you a secret. I'm just not sure he's the one. I love him. He's a lovable person. But I think I need someone more…dominant. It's not that he's *passive.* Or weak. It's just that I'm very bossy. I'm the pack leader here, with my dogs, and I tend to treat men like that, too. And Malachy kind of goes along with it. Except when he decides to do something *his* way, he's not exactly a team player."

"What are you looking for in a man?" Scout asked, truly curious. The question was one she'd never been able to answer satisfactorily herself. How would she describe the man of her dreams? Occasionally, she and Dana—Victoria was married—made lists of qualities they wanted in a mate. Victoria critiqued the lists.

The first traits on Scout's list were:

—*not a bigamist*

—*not married*

—*employed*

—*not an alcoholic*

—*nonsmoker*

—nonbully

It seemed to come down to things she *didn't* want.

Mary seemed no more certain. "I don't know. Obviously, I don't want someone pushing me around. I mean, that was Serge's problem in a way. *One* of his problems. Belligerence and button-pushing. If he sensed you were stronger than him, he'd pick a fight or try to dictate something ridiculous that no self-respecting woman would accept. He'd have you believe he's a pussycat who understands women, but what he really is, I'd say, is a little man with a Napoleon complex."

"How long were you with him?"

"Off and on for a year. But at first, for a couple of months, I was really in love with him and we were together all the time. He can talk a good story, and I believed all this stuff he said about himself."

Been there, done that, mass-produced the T-shirt.

"He's a jerk," Mary finished.

Scout thought of asking if Mary was *in love* with Malachy but decided she didn't want to hear the answer, whatever it was. If Mary wasn't in love with him, Scout was going to fail—probably. She'd have to convince Malachy to move on, if he wanted to get married. If Mary was in love with him—*I don't want to hear about that either.*

Well, she could say this much: "He said he's asked you to marry him."

Mary shrugged. "Never with a ring. I have a friend who's been proposed to six times, and she says it doesn't count if there's no ring."

"I'm so glad I have no friends who've been proposed to six times *with rings.*"

Mary laughed.

Scout thought about proposals that didn't count. *Actually, it doesn't count if he's already married and neglects to mention the fact—before or after the ceremony. Then the marriage doesn't count, either.*

Thankful that her own relationship history remained secret, she said, "So you'd marry him if he had a ring for you when he asked?"

"Oh, I didn't mean that. I just question his seriousness. You know, if guys are serious, they try to do things right—the details, I mean. And Malachy has never, like, taken me out to dinner and asked me. He's taken me out on dates, but it's never been as though it was a real proposal."

"I think it was."

Mary eyed her. "Did he put you up to this?"

"In a way."

"Well, *I've* wondered," Mary said, "if maybe he's interested in you."

"He has definitely never asked me to marry him."

"Have you ever been involved with him? I don't mean to pry. I just want to know."

Scout killed a mosquito. "I wouldn't call it involved, and I'm sure he wouldn't. No. And it was a very long time ago."

"That you weren't involved."

Scout laughed, laughed yet felt disinclined to explain. The night she'd spent with a much younger Malachy on a beach, both of their bodies clumped with tar from a moonlight swim, curled together in joined sleeping bags, the woodsmoke from the campfire forever in her hair, everything Malachy had said and clearly felt—all of that had subsequently evaporated. Yet her love and desire for him had not ended. Not for a long time, not until Danny Kilbourne came along, behaving as though she was the most special woman on earth.

When she might have settled for being the only woman presently in his life. For being his only wife.

"I had a crush on him," she said.

Apparently, nothing Malachy had told Mary contradicted that, because Mary showed no distrust of the statement. Scout wasn't sure whether that realization pleased her or not.

"Anyhow," Mary said, "it used to seem like he was on the phone or in my presence or running my dogs *all* the time. Not as bad as Serge—"

Serge again.

"—but I wanted more time alone. Then you came along, and it's like he's disappeared."

"Is it better this way?" Scout asked. She thought it was the obvious question.

Mary frowned. "Not really. I mean, once I started thinking maybe he was going to end up with you, I wasn't real thrilled about that, either."

"Well, I live in the building he owns, and he's been doing a lot of work on it. He's just investing in his property." Did she really believe that?

Mary didn't seem to. "And helping you get a dog team together. I get the feeling you're his latest project, and I can't figure it out."

"I think he feels bad for me because he knows I'm not thrilled about being back in Alaska, again." Scout wished she could call back those words.

Mary stared at her.

"Growing up in the bush sounds cool, but it wasn't easy for me. I like living in the city."

"And you came *here* for a job?"

Scout shrugged.

"These days I don't even know if I'm his lover," Mary admitted. "He acts like he's lost interest."

If he had lost interest in Mary, there could be only one explanation. But Scout couldn't accept that he'd lost interest in Mary. He still talked about Mary.

But not very much.

He talked more about Scout's dogs, Scout's new home, Scout's family, Scout's business and how the building could be changed to accommodate it. And he asked questions.

Scout realized this with growing horror. Two weeks ago, he'd told her he'd met the woman he wanted to marry and that woman was Mary Clarke. He'd enlisted Scout to help him secure a promise of marriage from Mary Clarke.

Does he want me now?

And if he did, what did *she* want?

He's Mary's.

Mary had forfeited him.

And Scout had known Malachy long before she'd met Mary. All was not fair in love and war—but this *was* fair. Or fair enough.

Though it couldn't possibly be true that Malachy preferred her to Mary Clarke.

Scout said, "So let's talk about dogs. Which are your best leaders?" Her interest was only partly feigned. True, Mary's dogs reminded her a bit too keenly of those she'd grown up with. But she'd never known an Iditarod winner.

"Well, I have several good ones." Mary seized the topic eagerly, and they went out to her yard, and Scout met Lakota, the bitch who'd led Mary's team to an Iditarod victory, and Thorlo, who often ran beside her. Lakota was in season and isolated from the others in a separate kennel.

It was while Scout greeted the eager husky mix that Mary asked, "Are you attracted to him now?"

It was a bit like having warm water thrown over her head. That unexpected.

This was not a question Scout felt comfortable answering candidly, yet lying would *really* feel like lying. She managed a reassuring smile. "I resigned myself to not having him a long time ago."

"Yes, then," Mary said. "You're his type, you know. More than I am."

"What do you mean?"

"You were born here. I can live the rest of my life here, and it won't make a difference."

"Did you catch the bit about my not loving Alaska?"

Mary made a dismissive gesture. "I don't know. Nobody seems good enough for him to stay with. He's gone through a few women."

That was new information. "Malachy wants to marry you," Scout repeated.

"I'm not sure he really does." Mary stole a glance at Scout. "Do you know about the foster child?"

"Jeremy?"

"Yes."

"Malachy didn't say he was a foster child."

"No. It's more permanent than that. He promised the great-grandmother. Jeremy's. I don't think Malachy legally adopted him, but it's like that. He's his guardian till he's eighteen. Anyhow, Malachy never even talked this over with me. Is this the behavior of someone with a realistic view of marriage?"

"How do you feel about it?" Scout asked. "About Jeremy?"

"I'm not the maternal type. Also, I'm not crazy about the idea of having a delinquent around. I mean, he tried to kill someone. Yeah, it was a fight, but he's an angry little dude."

Scout hid her surprise. She'd been contacted by someone from the district court about her willingness and ability to do court-ordered counseling sessions and evaluations. She'd readily agreed to the former, but she'd confessed she had little training in forensic psychology. The government would be willing to finance further training for her, and the idea interested Scout. It also pleased her that she was receiving adequate work in McGrath. If the McGrath office thrived, the Harmony Agency would open in another location, probably Anchorage.

Yet if the court referred Jeremy to her, would she be able to treat him? It seemed a little complicated, especially since she knew Malachy so well.

I do know him well. He's my best friend here.

And that, too, was like warm water—but flowing through her. Comfortable and uncomfortable both.

Scout said, "If someone is hoping to marry you, it does seem reasonable to ask how you feel about sharing responsibility for a thirteen-year-old."

"No kidding. It's not a deal-breaker for me, but I'm pretty busy, and I'm gone a lot. I think work can be good for kids. The kind of lifestyle I have might help. He could take care of dogs—if I trusted him, which I don't yet. It's a bit complicated." She shook her head, blond curls bouncing. "I'll confess, I got a bit ticked off."

Scout sympathized. Clearly, Mary had genuine reasons for not agreeing to marry Malachy, at least not until some issues between them were settled.

"So are you back in Alaska for good?" Mary asked, and Scout suspected she was hoping that wasn't the case.

The only explanation for that was one Scout felt should encourage Malachy. Mary saw her as a threat. And if she saw Scout that way, it meant she valued what was threatened.

When Scout got home, if it wasn't too late, she'd call Malachy and tell him.

And ask why he hadn't consulted the woman he wanted to marry about something as important as becoming guardian to a teenager who'd tried to kill someone in a fight.

SCOUT GOT HOME in time, but she didn't need to phone Malachy because she found him in her house, putting the finishing touches on a replacement woodstove. The old one, he said, hadn't been safe, and this one should provide more heat.

Ignoring the question of why he seemed to be spending every minute of his free time working on the building where she lived and worked, Scout told him as much as she could about her visit with Mary. Finally, she asked him about Jeremy. "She says you didn't talk it over with her."

He climbed down from the ladder he'd been using to check the seals on the stove pipe and sat on a lower step.

"Have you ever known people with whom it's better to present a *fait accompli* rather than ask their opinion?"

"I'm not sure 'better' is the word you're looking for. How about *easier?*"

"Easier, then."

"Fine. It was easy. But if you want to marry her, I think you have to share decision-making with her."

"Is this the kind of thing you tell your clients?"

"As a matter of fact, yes. For instance, if the two of you were married, and you decided to buy a new thirty-thousand dollar vehicle—I see this one a lot, by the way—she'd have the right to be more than a bit annoyed if you didn't discuss it with her first."

He fixed her with his dark eyes. "So you and Danny discussed things?"

"More to the point, Danny and I weren't actually married. But the fact that he was married to someone else was something I wish he *had* discussed with me. First."

"Right, right. But you did live with him. Did he discuss things with you before he did them?"

"No, and you notice we're not together anymore."

He grinned suddenly, wolfish. "I notice."

Scout almost shot at him, *You're not attracted to me, are you?*

But he'd laugh at her.

And what if he was? She hadn't been able to get involved, truly emotionally involved, with any man since Danny. She'd lost so much trust, and she didn't expect Malachy to change that—especially if he was capable of making massive decisions without recognizing that he needed to consult his life partner.

"I knew Mary would try to dissuade me if I asked her

how she felt about Jeremy. Also, this came up on the spur of the moment, and I agreed because it was a crisis. His mom's rarely sober and not too stable, to put it mildly, and when he got into trouble—and it was serious—"

"I know what it was," Scout said. "Mary told me."

"Exactly what did Mary tell you?"

"That he tried to kill someone in a fight."

"He *almost* killed someone in a fight. I won't insult you by asking if you can appreciate the difference."

She could. And she heard his anger toward Mary. "Perhaps I misunderstood her."

"I doubt it." The undercurrent in his voice told Scout they might have hit on the real problem between him and Mary. Maybe. "Anyhow, his great-grandmother said she couldn't keep him in line. She asked me. It was— she's an elder." He added this lamely, as though he was slightly ashamed to admit that he'd been swayed by such a fact.

"Athabascan?"

"Yes. Her granddaughter was married to Jeremy's father, but they divorced, and his father died two years ago. He was a commercial fisherman, and he drowned. Anyhow, Jeremy's great-grandmother is a good lady, and she was at her wits' end."

"Which is the house where you think there's a drug lab?"

"The cabin over by the beaver pond."

"Can't those places explode?"

"Yes."

At his tone, she said, "Sorry to bring it up…"

"I meant to tell you where it is, anyway, so you'd stay away."

Scout squinted at him. "What kind of signs do you look for? What would the judge consider probable cause?"

"I have some brochures with photos in the car. I'll bring them in later."

She changed the subject. "Do you know Mary's ring size?"

He nodded, sober.

"But you haven't bought a ring?"

"I always thought she'd want to pick it out herself."

"Have you ever told her that?"

"It's a difficult conversation to have with a woman who says she'd rather have puppies than babies and prefers sleeping with her lead dog to a man."

Scout suddenly felt exhausted by the two of them, inclined to tell Malachy that if he wanted to marry a woman who was so lukewarm toward him, lukewarm with some reason, he'd need to pull it off himself.

"So, she'd say yes if I proposed with a ring?"

"I have no idea," Scout told him honestly. "You said Jeremy lived with you?"

"The last two months of the school year—and he will again in the fall."

And Mary, he seemed to be saying, *needs to accept that because it's a done deal.*

Again she wondered if he'd been trying to sabotage his relationship with Mary by not discussing this with her. But they hadn't been engaged, hadn't been living together.

"It's worked pretty well," he said. "My father had Jeremy working with him, repairing equipment for the trapline. Not that Jeremy has an approachable personality. But my father likes…having a ministry." Malachy's look had grown cool, but the remote tone in which he'd made that statement was like a NO TRESPASSING sign.

Exactly the sort of sign Scout had learned to ignore.

"You and your dad must get along pretty well to live together."

"I'm sure he offers it up," Malachy replied, standing and abruptly collapsing the stepladder, turning it on its side to take with him.

"You mean…" Scout paused, frowning. "What *do* you mean?"

"Sorry—a Catholic thing. It's hard to explain. What I mean is he's not a complainer. For most of his life he's been in a position where he had plenty to complain about, but he'd made his bed, quite literally, so he's never complained."

"That sounds saintly." Sort of. What it really sounded like was passive aggression. "What would he have complained about?"

"He would've preferred to remain working as a priest. He's still a priest, of course. They don't take that away. But he wanted the job and the life. Doing what he does for the parish here isn't the same. It depresses him, I think." Scout thought for a moment. McGrath had a small, pretty Catholic church. She'd heard that a Catholic priest flew in every other week. "How do you know your father feels that way if he never complains?" Scout asked.

"I know. I just know. Let's leave it at that, shall we? He had a life he believed to be higher than the calling of husband and father. But it would've gone against who he was, who he is, to turn his back on my mother and me. Then my mother left, and after that it was just the two of us. He's ended up being celibate anyhow."

Scout thought this over. "Would they let him go back? Since you're grown up?"

"Go back because his marriage didn't work out? I don't think so."

He had the ladder in his arms and was headed for the door. He'd always been so secretive about his family background, and it touched her that he was talking with her about these things at all.

"Will you come with me to choose a ring?" he asked Scout.

To help him choose a ring for Mary. "Surely you can do that without my help. I'm not sure she'd want me to help, Malachy. Truthfully, I think she's a bit worried."

"Good," he said, his voice surprisingly cold. "She doesn't have to know that you helped me pick it out."

What came to mind suddenly was Danny, giving her that gold ring with the emerald. It reminded him, he'd said, of Ireland. She shuddered at the knowledge that all the time they'd been together, she had been living with a chimera—just a representation of a human being. All the stories about his brief time in the IRA, his childhood in Belfast...

Scout dragged her mind from the topic. She hadn't been harmed by anything he'd done, not really, not at the deepest soul level, and not physically. She was changed, yes, but she'd moved on, and she liked her present life. As for buying Mary's engagement ring with Malachy—why not? It wasn't like *she* wanted to be married again. This way, she could enjoy the fun aspects of a relationship vicariously.

"Okay," she agreed. "I'll do it."

SCOUT HAD DECIDED to participate in the spelling bee.
She dressed with special care, using the wobbly, tilting,
walnut-framed mirror Malachy had brought for her use
in the upstairs apartment. The light was weak, but she
managed to tweeze her eyebrows. She might be back in
Alaska, but she would try not to "let herself go," as
Dana had put it.

Not that it mattered. What she saw looking back from
the mirror could not compare to Mary Clarke's natural
beauty, a beauty that burst from her. Perfect bones, a
sculpted chin, plenty of eyelashes, shapely eyebrows.

Scout thought, *But there's only so much I can do.*

In California she'd learned to do it all. She had learned
that believing herself to be beautiful resulted in some
kind of beauty. Furthermore, in California she'd learned
to dance—all kinds of dancing, for hobby and fitness—
and that had boosted her grace and self-confidence.

But she could not compete with Mary Clarke.

I don't want to compete with her, do I?

She had chosen flared jeans, low-rise hip-huggers,
and a long-sleeved light-pink T-shirt imprinted with the
words GIRL SCOUT. It had been a gift from Dana and
Victoria. Her screen name and e-mail address were girl-
scout, so the shirt was particularly important to her. In
a private rebellion against the past, against what Alaska
had once meant to her and as a symbol that she'd moved
beyond it, she wore her most elegant Dansko shoes,
open-toed and faintly ridiculous for the bush, and a pair
of triangular silver earrings sparkling with fake gems.
She might not be as beautiful as Mary, but she would
be noticed. She felt stylish and sure to attract men she
didn't want.

The spelling bee was being held at the community center, a utilitarian building constructed with government funds. Rustic, wooden exterior, practical surfaces inside. The evening's moderator, Frank Scholl, was one of Scout's clients. Frank had gone for the full package, including weekly counseling, Internet and magazine profiles, everything. Scout doubted he'd lack for interested women. Sensitive about his completely bald head, Frank was a bush pilot with a marten farm and much more attractive than he believed himself. Not in his favor was that at forty-five he'd never managed to make a relationship with a woman last more than three years.

Scout walked over, checking her cell phone messages on the way. She had two text messages. The first was from Victoria: *AK is good mrkt. Shr u wont stay? Think on it.*

The second was from Holden: *Nice 2 C U, Strangr. Come HOME.*

Did that scream loneliness? Or desire for her to be reunited with her parents? There hadn't been a falling out. That wasn't the problem.

As she reached the center, she switched her phone to vibrate and put it away.

"Well, I see *you've* decided to show up."

It was Serge, and Scout felt renewed astonishment that Mary Clarke had ever maintained a relationship with the man. In her acquaintance with Serge, Scout had found him to be interested in one thing—the wonder of being Serge. He swung open the door for her.

"Thank you," she murmured.

"You're welcome. I was raised to treat women right."

"Good," she said. *He is not a client, he is not a client, he is not a client...*

"*And* to excel at word games," he added. "My family had spelling bees all the time when I was growing up, my parents both being PhDs."

"Was it fun?" Scout asked. Where had he grown up? Her curiosity was tempered by the probable length of the answer to that question. Better not to ask.

"Torture. I'm dyslexic, so there was a lot of pressure, but I've overcome that. I do a lot of process on it."

Scout kept her expression neutral.

A hand touched her back, between her shoulder blades.

She started.

Malachy.

Warmth flooded her, and then she saw Mary beside him. A Nordic goddess.

"Well, well, well," said Serge.

Could Malachy feel her trembling? Or feel the air around her heat up because he'd touched her? Did he somehow *know?*

And *why* had he touched her that way?

He's attracted to me.

It was that simple. She knew it as fact.

"You look good in pink," he said.

Was it her imagination, or was Mary annoyed at this compliment? Scout reminded herself to give Malachy advice on the wisdom of complimenting other women in Mary's presence. Though maybe, in this case, it would serve a purpose. Maybe that was why he'd done it.

"I," said Serge, "am an old hand at spelling bees, as I was saying to our new matchmaker."

She resolved to save her breath.

Malachy's blue flannel shirt brushed her arm. He could have won a role in one of those movies that needed a handsome native American. But now that she'd met his father, Scout began to see more of John MacCullagh's Irish features in his son.

About sixty people, the youngest an infant, the oldest a woman with a walker, crowded the room.

Not everyone was choosing to participate in the spelling bee; some had come as spectators. But Scout followed directions to join the line that was forming, which Malachy and Mary also joined. Mary eased in behind Scout, perhaps so that her date would not. She inclined her head to one side to say in an undertone to Scout, "Is he trying to make me jealous?"

"I think so."

Mary rolled her eyes. "You know, after a certain age—about sixteen—they don't really mature."

As though to illustrate the point, Serge held forth in a loud voice about the processing he had to do on being dyslexic in a family of geniuses.

"Get over it," Mary muttered in an aside to Scout. "Like anybody had a perfect childhood."

Scout refrained from comment, but she allowed herself a smile.

"Frank said he's going to your agency," Mary added.

Scout *couldn't* respond to this. She said, "Do you think I can drum up more business by being here tonight?"

"Everyone in McGrath already knows about you."

Scout remembered again the unsettling choice before her, a choice that wasn't truly a choice. Mary was becoming her friend. Malachy *was* her friend. Malachy wanted to wed Scout's new best female friend. Malachy wanted Scout to help him pick out the engagement ring he would present to Mary.

If she and I are friends...

But Malachy was a very old male friend and a much closer friend of Scout's than Mary was.

As they stood together, Mary whispered to Scout about many of the people in the room, male and female, adding to Scout's store of local knowledge.

"That's Jenny Curtis. She's the primary school teacher, but she's only been here a year. I'm surprised she came back. She thinks it's too cold, she hates mosquitoes, and she says there are no interesting men. Well, who can disagree? That's Andy Case. Have you met him? He's got some nice sprint dogs. I can take you over some day. Someone told me he's got a litter on the ground. And Eyebright—yes, she renamed herself that. Actually, she ran most of the Yukon Quest last year. Malachy was seeing her for a while, then did his usual number of getting bored."

No one had mentioned this "usual number" to Scout. But Mary had alluded to it when Scout had visited her cabin. Something about his "going through" women.

"He's not bored with you," Scout told her.

"Watch what happens if I ever commit to him. Oh, that's Jeremy's—you know, *Jeremy?*—that's his great-grandmother, who talked Malachy into being a foster father or whatever he is. Granted, he could hardly say no when she asked. She's an incredibly strong woman." Mary paused. "Strong in *every* sense. I helped her and her cousin with their nets one year, and they were faster than me—*and* stronger. It almost seemed supernatural to me. I mean, she's got to be eighty, and Willa's no spring chicken, either. Willa's got dogs, too, but she doesn't mush anymore. Afraid of breaking a hip, she said. Believe me, I don't think she's really afraid of anything. Well, I take that back. They're both afraid for their families, especially the kids. They talk a lot about how the old ways were better, and they're right. Even Jeremy's only, like, an eighth Athabascan, he was raised with that family. But what happened with him would never have happened back then."

Scout heard a derisive snort. She threw a glance at Malachy.

"*My* maternal grandfather," he said, "got shot in the leg during what I can only describe as tribal warfare."

"The Aleut are notorious hotheads," Mary insisted, with surprising certainty. Scout wouldn't have made that statement, and it seemed unlike Mary, respectful of all things Alaskan, longing to fit in.

She's picking a fight with Malachy.

But that couldn't be true.

"Anyhow, all these kids care about," she said, "are snowmobiles and rifles. I tried to get Jeremy interested in putting his own team together, maybe trying to make a sled, which I've never done but have always wanted to try "

This was news to Scout. So Mary had attempted to befriend Jeremy—or that was how it sounded.

"He didn't want anything to do with it. He doesn't like me," Mary concluded. "I think he's a bit sexist."

Scout gave her an interested look and didn't check Malachy's face for confirmation.

"I mean, he respects his elders—some—" Mary did look at Malachy. "But not his mother. She's an alcoholic, and I hear she's pretty easy with what she does for booze."

"Where does she live?" Had Malachy told her? Scout couldn't remember.

"Well, she used to live here. In the last year or so, she's been seeing this total lowlife. I don't even know his name. Malachy does. But she's off in Anchorage now. She lives there a lot of the time. It's sad."

"Yeah, you cry about it every night," Malachy said.

Mary appeared shocked by this sarcasm. Scout *was* shocked, although he'd said what she herself had been thinking.

Mary changed the subject. Frank, the moderator, wasn't bothering to take names. Probably everyone in the room was known to everyone else—everyone but Scout. He became Mary's next topic. "Frank's one of the better men in McGrath. Not my type, though. It's a pity he's your client. I guess that'll rule out a lot of guys."

"Not in the market," Scout answered.

"There's Brodie Kerr. He's an alcoholic. Also, he's a hunting guide, and I know he takes game for his clients. He gets all these rich dudes from Texas and Wyoming or whatever, and they all want trophies. His ethics are sketchy, at best. And he hits his dogs. I haven't caught him at it—I'd take him on myself, believe me—but you can tell someone beats those animals. I just want to see him do it during a race."

Then his career as a musher—a racer, at any rate—would be over.

The spelling bee began. The beginning words weren't terribly difficult. Scout got BRIDGE, Mary SCULPT, Malachy FRIEND. Serge successfully spelled ORIGIN. He jumped place in the very long line to say to Scout, "Have you ever done this before?"

"I've never been in a spelling bee, no," she answered.

"Hey, I wanted you to know that if you need more harnesses for your dogs, some recently came to me. I'd be happy to share. Maybe we could work out a trade."

Mary looked more than irritated; she seemed angry. Because he was someone she disliked behaving in a way she disliked?

"I'm set for harnesses. Thank you." Scout guessed that "trading" with Serge could become a very complicated business indeed.

"Also, I can do many modalities in bodywork. If you're interested."

I'm not. Once, she would've said it. But here, now, with Mary looking on as though Serge were a particularly loathsome slug, she restrained herself. "No, thank you." She turned to watch the next person, Jeremy's great-grandmother, spell her word VALUABLE.

Martin the mosquito man spelled THESPIAN, and a girl, junior high by the look of her, went down on TERMINAL. Her friend, the next contestant, spelled the word correctly.

"Embarrass," prompted Frank to Scout.

"E-M-B-A-R-R-A-S-S."

He turned to Mary. "Pedant. Example: She moved away from the man she despised, believing him to be a pedant."

Possibly an allusion to Serge.

"P-E-D-E-N-T."

Buzzer.

Mary groaned—and flushed. Scout, knowing that a competitive soul flourished within that beautiful exterior, felt for her and gave her a smile of commiseration.

"Pedant," said Malachy. "P-E-D-A-N-T."

Serge spelled VULNERABLE.

Later, Scout saw a certain inevitability. Serge fell out early on PARASOL. Martin went down on MORIBUND. Others had dropped long before him.

She and Malachy remained.

One word after another. She considered misspelling a word intentionally, just to end the drama.

"OCCURRENCE," offered Frank to Scout. "A misspelled traffic ticket was a rare occurrence, because they were printed by the state."

The spectators laughed appreciatively.

"Occurrence. O-C-C-U-R-E-N-C-E."

Buzz. Damn.

Malachy spelled the word correctly.

And it was over.

She offered Malachy her hand, and Frank presented him with *The Oxford Dictionary of Etymology*.

As Scout accepted Serge's congratulations, disengaging her hand from his, Mary slipped her own hand through Malachy's arm with a very obvious yawn.

"Oh, let's go cuddle up," she told him, her head on his shoulder.

Scout knew this was not for Serge's benefit. It was a message to *her,* and it surprised her even as it made her wonder if she assumed too much to count Mary a friend.

With a deliberately sleepy look, her head still resting, in territorial fashion, on his shoulder, Mary added, "Oh, Andy says he does have a couple of puppies for sale. Want me to go with you and help you check them out?"

"Thank you," Scout answered, her mind full of the picture of Mary and Malachy *cuddling up*. "I'd like that."

"See you soon," Malachy told her, his eyes not on hers but inside hers, saying something she couldn't understand.

Was it apology? Regret?

Or pity.

Serge said, "Would you like an escort home?"

She glanced at him. *I do not have to be childish at this moment. I do not have to do something that will cause me future difficulties simply because I want to make Malachy jealous.* Why should he be jealous? Serge was a pain, and Malachy was going home with the Iditarod winner. "I can find my way, thanks," she told Serge.

"You never know." He wiggled his eyebrows. "Granted, it's the perfect evening for those who are afraid of the dark—" since it wouldn't get dark "—but there might be a line of suitors waiting at your door. Things could get complicated. I promise I won't do anything inappropriate."

Why was she so sure that his idea of *inappropriate* was miles from hers?

"Serge," Malachy said, "Scout and I have known each other a long time. You could almost say we're family. So why don't you behave as if I'm her brother?"

Serge straightened, a look of challenge on his face.

"Family," repeated Mary in a flat voice that reminded Scout, unreasonably, of Ices growling.

Malachy seemed not to hear.

"Fine," Serge said. "I think your *sister* is old enough to make up her own mind without your input."

"And she did," Scout said. "Good night, everyone." Ducking, she hurried through the people in the community center, waving good night to familiar faces.

CHAPTER SIX

SHE DID NOT SEE Malachy for almost a week. Mary must have laid down the law. Or maybe things were going so well with her that he no longer needed additional help. At first, his sudden absence filled Scout with tension. Part of her hoped, she supposed, that he was staying away because he *was* attracted to her, perhaps because he felt himself in danger of succumbing to her charms. Then she flattered herself that Mary saw her as a real threat. At last, it occurred to her that she missed Malachy.

And when a week had passed since the spelling bee, she congratulated herself on how little she cared about him *that* way, in any way but as a friend of her brother's and an old, quite casual friend of her own.

When Andy Case, the bearded musher from the spelling bee, asked her to dinner at his house, Scout accepted. He wasn't a client, he loved dogs, he was intelligent and employed as a forester with the state.

He lived in a prefab house in town that he had custom-insulated and aesthetically improved. The interior was clean; Scout didn't count the shed hairs of his lead dog, a friendly husky cross, majestically tolerant of Estelle, whom Andy had invited Scout to bring. He had a large television and an impressive collection of interesting DVDs and VHS tapes. She felt a sense of comfort when he mentioned that he'd been divorced for three years. The deal-breaker had been Alaska. He wouldn't leave; she wouldn't stay. The marriage had lasted five years. He was forty-two.

Not bad, Scout thought, pleased to find herself assessing him not as a client but as someone she might become involved with. Nonetheless, the issue of place could come between her and an Alaskan determined to remain in Alaska. *Would I stay for Malachy, if he loved me?*

She tried to keep such thoughts at bay, but as she and Andy ate salmon and rice, delicately seasoned with lemon and herb, she kept thinking of the difference she'd feel if Malachy sat across from her.

Some sense of animation seemed absent between her and Andy. He'd probably make a good friend, being sober and thoughtful and interesting. Someone to watch movies with.

Why can't I feel?

It was the question she'd been asking herself since her nonmarriage evaporated into the nothingness it was.

The only answer was that she knew now that she *could* feel.

She had felt recently.

She felt every time she thought of Malachy. Her discipline at not thinking of him was laudable, but had her feelings changed?

I feel. I like someone. Someone I can't have, but even unrequited love must be progress.

Alaska wasn't the place for her anyhow. Yes, Malachy was doing his best—more than she'd done for him regarding Mary—to make her enjoy Alaska. Yet she couldn't be sure how much of her present contentment, and she was surprisingly content, had to do with feeling that she was finally fitting into what was ultimately, someone else's idea of who and how she should be.

"Rumor has it you and Malachy are old friends."

Her pulse reacted to the name.

She shrugged, savored another bite of salmon. "We knew each other in college, and he's a good friend of my brother's."

"I think you've got old Mary worried."

Scout made a face as though this suggestion was unworthy of notice. She awarded herself extra points for not asking what made him say that; to ask would be to feed never-expressed wishes of her own. She'd never expressed these wishes because she didn't know what they were, and she didn't want to know. She didn't want to know because Malachy had plainly said that he wanted to marry someone else. She realized he hadn't turned up to take her shopping for Mary's engagement ring. Which was, frankly, a relief. "I can't imagine Mary worrying about anything less important than the health of her dogs." Andy couldn't take this compliment as ambiguous, but she decided to clarify. "I think she's very much her own person with a positive sense of her own worth."

"I knew what you meant."

Everyone agreed Andy Case was handsome. No pretty features. Just rugged Alaskan good looks on a bigger frame than Malachy's.

"But she should worry," he remarked.

"I'll take that in the generous way I'm sure it was intended," Scout said. "Thank you."

"Women up here get pretty cocky about being *it*. Then they realize that it's a tough existence. I think they harden up a bit. My wife didn't. I guess that's why I never fell out of love with her."

This was a new take on that nebulous person Scout had spent a fair bit of time believing she had *failed* to be. Cocky. Someone who "thought she was *it*." She pulled her attention back to Andy's last words.

"You refused to move out of Alaska to make her happy. You call that not falling out of love?" Scout heard how accusing she sounded. "Sorry. I know place of residence can become a huge issue between people." *Oh, how I know.* A big enough issue, in fact, that neither her parents nor her brother had ever considered moving elsewhere.

"It's not just an address. You stay up here long enough, it becomes part of who you are. Moving to Florida—Florida, mind you—I'd have had to be someone different."

"I can see you running a dive shop," Scout said. "Either that, or I have to present the opinion that you weren't actually in love with her. Being in love means being unable to be apart. Well, it's not that simple—but I think missing Alaska would be less painful than missing her."

"You're a romantic," Andy said. "And I had you pegged for a cynic."

"You're one of the few."

"Then most people figure the matchmaker or dating consultant or marriage counselor—what have you—has stars in her eyes?" he asked.

When in fact she has a cash register for a heart, Scout thought.

His look was wise but considerate, too. "I think you're a lot more romantic—and maybe more vulnerable—than you let on. And, back to Sara, missing her *was* painful. But pride is an ingredient in the equation, too."

Scout could believe that. "Do you still talk?"

He shrugged. "We have."

"What does she do?"

"She's a park ranger in the Everglades. It kind of fell into place for her. She says she's happy. She's not seeing anyone."

Interesting. Scout did *not* consider herself a romantic, whatever Andy said, but his marriage didn't seem quite the thing of the past that he'd implied. Of course, divorced was divorced, and divorces were painful. Scout hadn't personally known any couple to reconcile after one, but that didn't mean it never happened.

"I need to run dogs," he said. "I used to do the long races, but work interferes now, so I've switched to sprint races."

"There are trees in Florida."

"I'd have work. But could you give up dogs?"

She couldn't help laughing. She gave him the encapsulation of her childhood experience with dogs, her decision to move to California, what had kept her there, what had brought her home. "I like the dogs I have now," she said. "In fact, I *love* them, which was practically against house rules the way I grew up. I love their whiskers and their paws and their eyes and their moods. I love how they behave with each other and how they behave with me. But I consider all my dogs pets. Pets who like to pull."

When she walked home just after ten with Estelle,

who had made friends with Andy's friendly lead dog, she found an Alaska state trooper's vehicle in front of her building.

"On nights, now?" Scout asked as she approached his window in the summer evening light.

He nodded. "You and I are supposed to pick out a ring," he said.

"Come on, Malachy! You can handle that on your own." Discoveries she'd made in the company of Andy Case—namely, that she was strongly attracted to Malachy, that she *felt* something for him—had influenced her. How willing was she now to promote Malachy's relationship with Mary?

But that's what you agreed to do. Whether or not you fell in love with him yourself wasn't part of the bargain, and it still isn't.

Anyhow, she wasn't in love. If she was in love, she would've been miserable for the past week.

But was that true? Life went on.

In any event, this put paid to the notion that her feelings for Malachy were returned. If his intentions toward Mary had changed, he would've told her, Scout. And he wouldn't be planning to shop for an engagement ring.

She said, "What's wrong with inviting Mary to look at rings?"

"That you won't be there."

Scout's heart skipped. What did he mean? She knew what he meant, but what could she say? She waited.

He said, "Mary and I have had a parting of the ways."

"So you don't really need to shop for a ring," Scout clarified.

"Correct."

"Want to come in?"

"I'm on duty. Want to go for a ride-along?"

"Only if Estelle can come."

"We're dog-friendly."

As he slowly cruised McGrath's dirt roads, he remained silent.

Scout said, "So what happened? Was it that scene at the spelling bee? With Serge?"

"No."

Malachy couldn't tell her. Getting back to Mary's house that night, realizing he couldn't even kiss her, unsure why. He no longer trusted himself because just weeks before, his heart had been certain that she was the one for him. They'd been lovers, and he'd believed himself in love.

But he hadn't been.

"I wonder," he said, "why I didn't tell her about Jeremy before I made my decision. I keep thinking about it. Basically, my father never wanted to be married to my mother—"

If he'd been a client, she wouldn't have interrupted, but he wasn't a client, and she wasn't his therapist. She was someone completely different with him. "How do you know?" she broke in, almost angrily.

"He wanted to give his life in service to the Church, to God. That was the choice he'd already made, and he was fulfilled in that choice. I'm sure he got involved with my mother because it was something he wanted in a very momentary way."

"You've just made several assumptions. Unless your father has said these things to you in so many words?"

Malachy shook his head. But he didn't need to win

the argument, because he *knew*. He knew his father, and convincing Scout that his father would have preferred to live as a priest would change nothing. "Anyhow, I decided I *did* want Mary and I chose Jeremy so I'd have to lose her."

"That's convoluted, but I think I know what you mean."

"But it's not true. I just wanted to save myself the trouble of an argument, because nothing she said would've changed my mind about taking him."

So he hadn't intentionally sabotaged the relationship. He'd wanted to avoid conflict.

"What have you been doing for the past week?" Scout asked. "Spending time with Mary?"

"No." Eyes on the road, sweeping the surroundings as he turned onto McGrath's highway, the stretch of asphalt leading to Ophir, he said, "Have you noticed that I'm attracted to you?"

Scout thought through several replies before answering. "It has occurred to me that you are."

He laughed without pleasure. "It's occurred to me, too." He pulled over and looked at her very directly. "I'd like to do something about it."

THE RADIO CRACKLED in the background as he kissed her.

Scout clung to his shoulders, afraid of the earthquake of desire sweeping through her, flushing her blood, her skin, everything.

She didn't worry that she wasn't as beautiful as Mary Clarke. That no longer mattered. This man wanted her as she wanted him, and she knew it.

She also knew, with her entire being, that what moved between them now was the stuff of which lifetime commitments were made. They were friends and would be lovers, as they'd once been, but with greater intensity, greater commitment. With permanence. Nothing would stop or interrupt what they shared.

In books and movies, perhaps, people who fell in love and wanted each other and were free to be together still managed to find ways to be apart, but relationships were her area of expertise, and she knew it was only in fiction that such unrealistic situations prevailed.

Soon, he was simply holding her, a mutual gladness swimming through both of them, uniting them in comfortable certainty.

"Is Mary going to hold this against me?" Scout asked.

"Oh, definitely."

"Ah." She didn't like the answer, everything it implied. She didn't need an enemy or a neighbor who felt that Scout had stolen her man. Yes, Malachy and Mary had split up, but Scout was a big part of the reason. A reality that might be bad for business. Mary liked to talk; Scout had seen that for herself. Who could guess how she might describe this?

Abruptly, Scout remembered something Mary had said at the spelling bee: *Watch what happens if I ever commit to him.* The very thing that had concerned Scout during Malachy's pursuit of Mary. Now, Scout couldn't help noticing that once commitment seemed within reach, Malachy had fallen out of love with Mary and in love with someone else. And Mary herself had predicted this.

Don't psychoanalyze. Dana had once warned her that if she did that with every man she'd met, all men would fall below her personal standards.

Every person, she figured, could name some trait in a partner that would be a deal-breaker in a relationship. She could name more than most, in part because she'd learned that living alone wasn't the most horrible thing in the world. Her first would have to be deception. And if her partner showed any real interest in straying, that would be intolerable as well. Both of these were unacceptable to her because she had lived them.

Malachy won't be able to commit.

The seed had been planted, not by Mary Clarke initially but by her. Malachy had been abandoned by his mother when he was three, and he would go to great lengths to avoid future abandonment. *Psychoanalyzing again.*

One thing was certain. The deal-breaker bad trait for Scout was not a man's fearing abandonment. If this turned out to be Malachy's flaw, she could work with it. If she got the chance.

"Have you spoken with your mom since she left?" Scout asked.

He straightened slightly against her, not quite tense but definitely alert, his mood changed by her question. "No."

That wall again. The wall with its sign that said KEEP OUT.

Scout ignored the sign. Again. "Why not?"

"Because she obviously doesn't want to see me."

"How do you know that?"

He started the SUV again. "Did you have a date with Andy Case tonight?"

"There are no secrets in McGrath, I see. It was more like dinner with a friend." A temptation arose within her. She knew its pitfalls. She could hold Malachy's interest almost indefinitely by never letting him feel secure in her love for him or commitment to him.

But how long could she do that?

A year, max, Scout figured. More important, she didn't want to play. An adult male ready for a lasting relationship would seek a woman who wanted a lasting relationship with him.

Exactly what Malachy had not done. Until now.

She fastened her seat belt. "You know what's going through my mind?" she said as he made a U-turn and headed back toward McGrath.

"Tell me."

"I think you have a pathological fear of actualizing commitment." She could practically see his disdainful expression. "I think Mary was ready to commit to you, and you promptly fell out of love with her. Before she could fall out of love with you."

"Oh, that's nice. Did you put Andy through this tonight?"

"Of course not. I just met him. Anyhow, this has nothing to do with Andy."

Malachy pulled his vehicle to the side of the road and looked at Scout. "Will you marry me?"

He was trying to prove something.

A sensible person, she thought, would point out that a week earlier he'd wanted to marry another woman. In light of this, it was difficult to take his proposal seriously. No doubt he counted on her to react in this sane fashion.

What could possibly be the point of calling his bluff? To find out if it *was* a bluff, of course.

Then I can tell the whole story to Dana and Victoria.

Minus the part where she'd agreed to help him get Mary Clarke to accept his proposal.

"Only," she said, "tomorrow."

He stared at her for a moment.

"If we do it tomorrow," she clarified, ready to laugh and say, *Just kidding,* or *April Fool's* or whatever would reassure him that she hadn't taken leave of her senses and had no intention of binding him to a spur-of-the-moment proposal.

She would have done that, too, if her pride hadn't been forced to take the next blow, the almost imperceptible tightening of his jaw. It made her angry. A marriage proposal wasn't something you offered like an after-dinner mint.

His eyes held her face. "Fine. Would you like your family there?"

He couldn't be serious. *He* couldn't intend to go through with it.

What should've been one of the more romantic moments of her life was beginning to feel like a game of chicken.

Well, she wasn't going to lose at *that.*

"Yes." She lifted her chin, telling herself that she felt like a hag of ancient legend securing the promise of a handsome knight, a promise based on honor rather than love or attraction. Telling herself that she felt as untroubled by this as that mythically hideous bride-to-be because she knew her knight.

But she couldn't stop herself from throwing Malachy a lifeline. "Your father won't object? He won't want you to have a Catholic wedding? They take a long time to prepare for, I understand."

And what would she do, Scout wondered, if he ran flat-out for this escape route?

"He knows that what I want—what you and I want—is the important thing here."

Undoubtedly. Of course, he doesn't know that you reached this decision over the long reckoning of a single heartbeat. Still, she wasn't going to bail. Not yet, anyhow. For casually asking her to marry him, he should be forced to endure at least a few more minutes of panic. "Can he perform the ceremony?"

"Can but won't. His refusal to break faith, no pun intended, with the Church's rules is what made my mother leave. I think she missed her family, but the Church had ordered him away from the Aleutians, so away he went."

Surprised back into rationality by his completely serious response, Scout thought briefly of Andy and his ex-wife, Sara, who didn't like Alaska. And Mary Clarke's emotion associated with not being born here. *Place.*

She remembered her meeting with Holden at the airport in Nome and felt a longing for her own family. "You're probably right," she told Malachy. "But why didn't she take you with her?"

"That's the big question." He turned out onto the road again.

A dirt bike bounced out of the trees onto the asphalt, gunning onto the highway before them.

"Excuse me," Malachy said politely, turning on the dome lights and the siren.

CHAPTER SEVEN

THIS IS INSANE. I've got to put a stop to it.

It was eleven thirty, and Malachy had just dropped Estelle and Scout off at Scout's house.

I can phone him on his cell. I can call it off.

Anyhow, the truth was that if she *did* marry again— marry anyone—she wanted a real wedding, not a repetition of the "intimate ceremony" she'd shared with Danny. She wanted to tell the world that Malachy MacCullagh—or *whoever,* she added quickly to herself—wanted to marry her. And wasn't that what a mythological hag would do? Wasn't there a story about a famous knight marrying a hag who eventually became beautiful, and didn't she *demand* a big wedding, refusing to feel ashamed of being ugly and yet marrying the man who was most desirable?

Of course, it was silly to even have these reflections because Malachy didn't truly want to marry her. It was all a bit of a joke. Wasn't it?

As Estelle wandered through her office and flopped onto one of the dog beds Scout had bought for the downstairs, Scout picked up the phone. She had messages, but before checking them she dialed Malachy's cell.

He answered. "Yes, my betrothed?"

Her heart jammed in her throat. In fact, for a moment she couldn't talk. She'd planned to say, *I want a big wedding.* But that would carry on the whole charade. *No, I have to address this.* "Malachy—" *I wasn't serious.* But could she say that? Was it true? "I don't want you to rush into this. Just a few days ago, you wanted Mary Clarke for your wife. Tonight you asked *me* to marry you. So I understand that you were being impulsive." *I sound pathetic,* she thought. Well, so be it.

He didn't speak.

"You're off the hook," she clarified.

More silence.

She answered with the same.

"Are you breaking our engagement?" he asked.

She answered carefully. "I question your…gravity. To be perfectly honest, I felt you weren't serious when you proposed."

"Were you serious when you answered?"

He seemed unafraid of her reaction.

But now she was afraid.

"I should've asked at the time," she said, "if you were serious."

He didn't reply.

She'd said enough.

"It wasn't impulsive. Whenever I began thinking about Mary—about a wedding, kids, day-to-day life, even buying a ring—I realized that you're a better friend and that I would enjoy your company more."

Not romantic, Scout decided, but sensible. And, in a way, flattering.

"I am serious," he said. "If you're willing to make a life with me, I'd like to make a life with you."

She breathed. She trembled. Estelle, at her feet, whined.

"Then," she said, "I want a wedding. A big wedding."

"Ah."

She heard a smile in his voice.

"In that case," he said, "we'll use tomorrow to find a ring."

She hugged herself, as open and vulnerable and terrified as she'd been at eighteen.

This means staying in Alaska. You know it does. You've listened to the story of how Andy Case's marriage collapsed—over the issue of place.

She told herself with a cheeriness that felt entirely false, *I like Alaska now.*

Did she like Alaska just because Malachy was around, paying attention to her, being kind?

Though she'd spent some time fantasizing about running her dogs with a high-quality, very fast sprint sled, she'd spent as little time as possible remembering the cold. Remembering moment after moment when existence had felt like a constant matter of fighting for her life. When she'd felt too small, too weak, for Alaska, the state of her birth. What had changed? That she now had a flush toilet and her own shower with an adequate hot-water supply? That she had money to get to Anchorage for highlights and a good haircut if she wanted?

Maybe. Maybe that was enough.

Maybe Malachy was.

Some time after she and Malachy had hung up, neither saying the words *I love you,* just bound in their incredible agreement, she pressed the button to retrieve her messages.

The first was from Martin, saying that his long-distance

date would be arriving the following week. He hadn't called Scout's cell phone—she'd gotten no calls while she was out—so his need to talk wasn't urgent. The cell phone was only for emergencies, in lieu of an answering service. The next message began, "Scout, this is Danny—"

"Shit," she whispered. "Shit, shit, shit."

"I found you through Harmony. I'm in Anchorage, actually. I've come up here to see you. I've changed. I've gone through some major life changes, and I just want to talk. In person."

Who the hell told him I was in Alaska? But no one had to tell him. It was on the Internet, on the Harmony Agency Web site.

He gave her his cell phone number and asked her to please call him.

"Not in this life," she told Estelle.

It was the last message, and it riled her and stained the night of floating bliss she'd anticipated.

But life felt very real again.

"I DON'T WANT TO go to Anchorage. I'd rather look for rings on the Internet than go to Anchorage. There must be a jewelry store in Nome."

"All right," Malachy agreed. "I see you're convinced that if we go to Anchorage, you'll run into Danny."

"Correct."

"He said he'd changed?" Malachy sounded slightly amused, slightly cynical, the last no doubt due to his experience as a cop.

"Something about major life changes. All I could think of was serial killers finding religion. I'm happy for them and everything, but it doesn't mean we should let them out on the street. So," she said, "if he's changed, I'm happy for him but I still don't want to see him or talk with him ever again."

"Back to the ring," Malachy said as they drove to the airfield. He'd be flying the plane he and his father owned today. "If we don't find the ring in Nome, I'll buy you a temporary ring until we can find the right one. I want to advertise that you're my fiancée, even at the expense of looking cheap."

People could say what they wanted about rings, but Scout thought a future husband *should* feel as Malachy did. Proud to have people know of his fiancée, proud to proclaim their engagement. A ring needn't—and shouldn't—put a couple in debt, but the symbol, a simple and public sign of commitment, was ancient. From what Scout saw at work, men who stalled at a ring were rarely committed—not lastingly. They were after immediate benefits. Although it was no guarantee that a man wasn't an adulterer or batterer, a ring did seem a basic prelude to marriage.

Somehow this was a relief to Scout, because she was unwilling to tell a soul of their engagement until she had *some* ring on her finger. As evidence, she supposed. She wanted people to know. She was just surprised Malachy felt that way.

They saw it at the same moment, in a store called Nome Gold. She was not a wearer of gold, but the ring was white-gold shaped into a naturalistic circlet of leaves and berries, incorporating a blood-red ruby and dotted with tiny sapphires and emeralds, giving life to the leaves and berries.

Small the stones might be, but Scout shook her head immediately, making a guess at price.

"Scout," he said.

"What?"

"I'm only doing this once. If you like it, try it on."

It fit.

They took Estelle with them to the beach. The sky was gray and endless, and Malachy took the ring from the box and put it on her finger.

She said, "Thank you. I love it."

"You're welcome." He did not say, *I love you.*

But wasn't it a sign of love to buy her this ring? It hadn't been cheap. She hadn't been allowed to see the price. He'd paid with a combination of check and what she was almost sure was a couple of thousand dollars in cash. She thought of asking if he was doing it to make Mary jealous. But he could've done that for free.

"I need to ask an indelicate question," she said.

"Ask."

"When was the last time you were…well, let's say intimate, with Mary?"

"That *is* indelicate. But working on the optimistic assumption that there'll be no deceit between you and me—"

"I hope that's a *realistic* assumption."

He smiled. "I haven't slept with her since you've been back in Alaska. Not necessarily *because* of that, on a conscious level. I went on sort of a sex strike when I realized she wasn't sure she wanted to marry me. I decided to distance myself from her and see what happened."

"I wonder if you're the first male in this century who's tried that."

"Ha ha."

Happy, she said, "Malachy, I want to *win* sprint races this year. Let me run your best sprint dogs with mine."

"Shall we move in together?"

"Where?"

"Your place."

"Rent just evaporated! I'm thrilled. Will your father be all right? I don't mind if we live with him."

"You haven't lived with him."

"Or with you." The wind whipped her hair. "Jeremy will live with us, right?"

He didn't answer, but when she glanced up, he was gazing at her.

What struck her, with a wonderful terror, was that he was happy, too. Perhaps as happy as she was.

As MALACHY DROVE HER home from the McGrath airfield, Scout thought ahead to telling her parents the news. Her parents were not fans of divorce—didn't know Scout had never had one because she hadn't been legally married. Which was something else they didn't know. Holden would be happy, but Scout dreaded the ordeal of telling her parents she was engaged.

She wondered if her parents doubted that she was worthy of a good man. She knew they loved her, but they were grudging in their approval and always had been. For instance, even when Holden had taken phenomenal photos of wolves, her father had said very little. No censure, but no praise either. Sometimes it had seemed that her parents were afraid she and Holden would begin to think well of themselves.

In retrospect, it made Scout sorry for Holden in a way

she'd never been sorry for herself. As far as she knew, he'd never kissed a girl, never had a date, was a virgin. Of course, he could've taken to visiting prostitutes in Anchorage, but somehow she thought even that would require social skills he didn't possess.

Which was why, underneath it all, she had agreed to return to Alaska. Because she, as a counselor, as a *relationship counselor,* a woman who ran a dating service, for crying out loud, was ideally placed to help her brother come forth from his chrysalis. It wasn't too late. It couldn't be too late.

And now was the time.

As he pulled up in front of her office, she asked Malachy, "Are you really going to move in?"

"I am. I'll go home to sort out some things and feed my dogs. I'll bring a few clothes and a few dogs and—" his quiet smile "—myself."

Something warm, a liquid magic, suffused her chest and then her whole body. Tonight he would be her lover.

SHE DECIDED to take a bath before calling her parents to tell them she was engaged. She wanted to look and feel as perfect and appealing as possible. She was actually, she thought, in better physical shape than she'd been at eighteen.

All the dogs began barking as she was getting out of the tub. Before she could towel off, Scout heard knocking on the upstairs outer door to the apartment. She used the back stairs only in the morning, when she first went out to greet the sled dogs.

Malachy had a key....

It's going to be Serge or someone like that.

She considered not answering, but her curiosity got the better of her. "Just a minute!" she yelled.

Wearing a towel into the big upstairs room, which had taken on the feeling of a sultan's den with her new selection of huge pillows and rugs, she grabbed a pair of fleecy, low-cut sweatpants and pulled them on, then a camisole. Both were pink, and she remembered Malachy saying she looked good in pink.

She hurried to the door and opened it with the absolute knowledge that she shouldn't because Danny Kilbourne could be on the other side.

He was.

HE'D GROWN, if possible, more attractive. Lush quizzical brows crowned thick-lashed eyes. Laugh lines didn't quite disguise what she now saw in his brown eyes and craggy face, what she hadn't been able to see when she'd married him—a falseness. The manufactured persona of a sociopath. "You can't come in," she said. "I don't want to see you. I don't want to talk to you. A state trooper is due here at any moment, and I have no compunction whatsoever about asking him to make you leave. If you don't stop bothering me, I'll get a restraining order."

This was surprisingly easy to say. She had told the occasional female client that it was the thing to say to problematic and dangerous men, but she'd never been in a position to so herself. Back when she'd moved out of the house she and Danny had shared, he hadn't followed her. In fact, he'd told her she was fat and that he wasn't attracted to her anymore.

She remembered this as she waited for him to leave.

"Scout, won't you just listen to me?"

"No." She shut the door and locked it, breathing hard, her heart pounding with fear and anger. *Why now?* Why at this moment when she was happy?

The dogs had not quieted.

Danny didn't like dogs.

She rushed to the phone and called Malachy.

He was still at home.

"Danny's here. He was outside. I'm not sure he's left. I told him to go away."

"I'll call Aaron, and I'll get there as soon as I can." Aaron was the Native American constable, Malachy's subordinate in McGrath. "Aaron's closer. Stay on the line. I'll use the other phone to call him."

"He's knocking again. I've told him to leave."

"Don't open the door."

A moment later, another voice came on the phone. "Scout? It's John."

Malachy's father.

"Everything okay there?" he asked. "Malachy's calling Aaron."

"Everything's fine." Scout listened to what was happening outside. She thought she heard him descending the stairs. "I think he's leaving."

"Here's Malachy," John said. "And I'm pleased about your news."

"Thank you."

"We'll talk later," he added.

"Aaron's on his way, Scout."

"I think Danny's leaving, though. Or has left."

"That's okay. Aaron will find him."

Scout didn't care whether anyone found him or

not, although there was some benefit to knowing where he was. Keeping back from the window, she lowered her lights, listening to the dogs, who hadn't stopped howling and barking. When they did, she'd know he was gone.

Estelle whined and pressed against Scout's leg. Scout sat on the floor with the puppy in her lap, angry because now she shook uncontrollably, reduced to someone she hadn't been for a very long time. Someone frightened. Someone jumping at noises.

Damn it, you creep, I did not need this, and I will not yield to it.

Danny's threat to her wasn't violence. It was his voice. He had the power of Tolkien's Saruman to seduce with his voice. Not necessarily a sexual seduction. More a persuasion. He'd lost his power to persuade her, but he was capable of wreaking havoc among those around her. She knew from painful experience that you could shout to some people that Danny Kilbourne was a bigamist and a pathological liar until you were blue in the face and they would assume you were bitter because your marriage hadn't worked out. People who spoke to Danny on the street twice a week were convinced they knew him. They vouched for his good character.

She had chosen her first posting for the Harmony Agency far from her past with Danny Kilbourne so that she wouldn't have to deal with acquaintances who somehow came away with the idea that he'd been wronged. Now, years and miles away, he had come looking for her, on the very day she'd become engaged to another man.

You are not wrecking this for me, you swine.

The dogs settled down, and she got up from the floor and went to the window.

Part of her hoped the constable didn't find Danny, that Danny simply left McGrath and she never had to deal with him again. But it wouldn't be that easy.

Damn it. Why did he have to come here tonight and remind me how stupid I was?

She made herself go into the bathroom, apply moisturizer, make herself presentable, *not* tremble. Admire her ring. Remember Malachy putting it on her finger. Their hands together.

Eventually, she heard the key in the lock below and she risked a trip to the front window to peer around the blinds. Malachy's truck was parked out front. He hadn't come in his law enforcement capacity.

But then she heard the door close even before it was opened. Malachy's shape peeled back onto the street, where it joined two others. One of them was Danny. She moved away from the window, wishing she didn't feel ill, wishing herself unaffected by something that had happened so long ago.

She pulled on a pale-blue hooded sweatshirt and went downstairs with Estelle. She left off the lights but was waiting, sitting in the office she used for counseling, when Malachy came inside, bringing a dog, probably his lead dog, Trooper.

Estelle charged out, barking, and Scout followed.

"Hi," he said. "How are you?"

"Fine." She wasn't going to fall apart just because Danny had shown his face again. "Was that him out there?"

"Yes. We told him to leave you alone and suggested he get out of McGrath."

"I'm sure he didn't argue."

"Oh, no. Would never do anything to make you uncomfortable, disturb your inner tranquility, the usual."

Relief washed over her. Danny had tried his charm on Malachy and had failed because Malachy wasn't an idiot and knew how guys like Danny behaved, knew their acts of surprised innocence. Malachy also knew Danny.

To prove her inner serenity to all witnesses, she watched Trooper and Estelle sniff each other and said, "How many other dogs did you bring?"

"Are you kidding? It wasn't on my mind."

That was nice. She didn't have to worry about Danny. Malachy had been ready to do it for her.

"When's the last time you saw him?" Scout asked.

"It must've been ten years. More? I don't think he recognized me. I just introduced myself as an off-duty trooper."

Scout got a bad feeling and didn't know why. She supposed it had to do with her belief that Danny must've seen Malachy enter her place. If he assumed she was involved with someone new, it might encourage him to pursue her, like her own personal natural disaster. She doubted she'd really seen the back of him. Not yet.

Malachy locked the front door behind him and turned the dead bolt. He squinted at Trooper and Estelle. Estelle was trying to invite Trooper to play, with little success. "Think they'll manage together tonight?"

"Yes." Was he truly moving in with her? He'd be with her every night, so the threat of Danny Kilbourne would be nothing more than a specter? "He's never been violent," she said. "But he's kind of a bully. And twisted. You know what I mean."

"A sociopath?"

"I think so. It's amazing that I can trust anyone after living with him."

"It's better," Malachy said, "to know what people are capable of doing and being."

"I'm not so sure. I'd rather not run into anyone like that."

"Oh, they're out there."

She'd seen in her work as a psychologist that most disorders occurred on a continuum. Someone might have four traits required for a diagnosis but be missing a vital fifth. Or the four traits might be so strong that the missing fifth seemed less important.

"I wonder what he's after," Malachy said, shaking his head at the closed blinds as though pondering the mind of the man somewhere behind them.

"I've *always* wondered that. But it's probably money or sympathy, the chance to have me in his psychological power again. To play with me. I don't know what brought him here now, though. I really thought I'd seen the last of him."

"Is there any way he might hope to get money from you?"

Scout considered. "For a while, some time after he left me, there were threats of a defamation suit because I told a woman he'd asked out what he'd done to me. But he was blowing smoke. I won't engage with him, Malachy. I know how to get rid of him, and that's simply to refuse to have anything to do with him and to use the law, which, fortunately, is on my side. He has no legitimate reason to come around."

"That's true. Let's go upstairs. Trooper." He made a sound, summoning his dog.

Estelle romped after Trooper, skidding on the floor and almost falling over.

"She's hilarious," Malachy said.

And I'm nervous.

The past few weeks had reminded her why she was careful never to fall in love. Falling in love, in her experience, brought pain—*and* humiliation. It was painful and humiliating to love a man and not be loved in return.

But Malachy wanted to marry her. Malachy was not a bigamist and would not become one—not that she was likely to run into two of *those* in one lifetime. Being in love with Malachy need not bring pain or humiliation. This time...

Granted, it had brought some pain when he'd seemed to prefer Mary Clarke to her. But that was over.

Upstairs, she lit the bedside lamp, which had a pink globe shade.

Glancing around, Malachy smiled. "Come here, woman," he said.

Her nervousness vanished. He wanted her and they were friends, and there was nothing to fear.

IN THE MIDDLE OF THE NIGHT, he pulled her against him, snuggling close. When he did that, Scout remembered Danny hadn't behaved this way. She'd had lovers who did; she had resisted their caresses because they'd seemed only to want to deprive her of sleep.

But between her and Malachy was a comfort that allowed for both passion and rest. What was more,

Scout detected no sign that he would've preferred to be with Mary Clarke.

In the morning, as they sat on her back steps drinking coffee, she said, "Are you going to put in another room upstairs for when Jeremy comes here?"

"Why don't we give him one of the downstairs rooms?"

Scout thought the arguments against this idea would be obvious. Since apparently they weren't, she said, "It hasn't crossed your mind that we might have a better idea what he's up to if we slept on the same floor?"

"It has." He rubbed his jaw. "He's not going to be easy, Scout. You know that, don't you?"

"You mean, easy to manage?"

"I suppose I do."

"Well, maybe you should fill me in on exactly what challenges you expect. What did he do?"

"Someone insulted his mother, said she was turning tricks, which she does and which Jeremy knows she does. He fought with the other boy and nearly killed him. As for challenges…"

Scout waited.

"He lies."

"Now, there's a trait I really like in a person."

"And—"

Scout watched Malachy's face. He was particularly slow to answer. "He's been diagnosed with something that'll undoubtedly mean more to you than to me. Granted, it was *explained* to me…."

"Why don't you just tell me," she suggested.

"Conduct Disorder?" As though it was a question.

Often considered a precursor to Antisocial Personality Disorder.

"Any fire-starting?" she asked casually.

"No."

"Torture of small animals?"

"No. Not that." Malachy took a long drink of coffee, set his cup on the step beside him. "I'm not an optimist about this kind of thing. I'm not a rescuer. I did this because of the person who asked me, because I knew I was more capable of handling it than she was. I harbor no real hope of turning him into someone else."

"Is he smart?"

"Smarter than I am, unfortunately." The answer was grim.

Scout understood the grimness. Danny Kilbourne was smart. In certain people, smart equalled dangerous.

Smart could equal disaster.

CHAPTER EIGHT

"UNLESS HE'S HAVING the world's most wonderful time there," Scout said, "we need to get him away from my family. Surely you've told him about the dangers of going near meth labs."

"The danger's maybe part of the attraction. Everyone in your family knows what he's like. Holden and I talked about it in detail."

Only twelve hours had passed since Malachy's revelation about the nature of Jeremy Crestone and what could be expected of him. But Scout had thought of little else all day. Admiring the engagement ring on her finger had kept happiness close, even during her moments of concern about Jeremy, but by the time Malachy got off work, it had to be addressed.

Scout didn't respond to Malachy's protest of a detailed conversation with Holden.

"I'm not making light of your fears," he said.

"Good, because I'm telling you, my family might look like the picture of domestic sanctity to you, but my father—" She got a grip on her temper. "Let's just say he can be insensitive in the way he expresses his expectations of people. And I'm not talking about expecting his children to be kind and respectful."

Malachy said nothing.

"For instance," Scout continued, "I cried when a puppy was stillborn. He said, 'Forget about it, Scout,' and tossed what he called the *carcass* into the bush for scavengers. I suppose I was supposed to feel that he'd been compassionate because he didn't feed it to the other dogs. He's not a monster. But I don't like the idea of an unpredictable young person like Jeremy up there in the bush with him and my mother and Holden."

Malachy felt rather than saw the strength of her concern. Tempted to brush it off, he knew better. She was a psychologist; he was law enforcement. High risk meant more than risk to the child. Her family was at risk from Jeremy.

But did Scout mean that Jeremy was at risk from them, too?

"It'll be a couple of days before we can fly up there. We can offer Jeremy the option of coming back here." He studied Scout's face.

He felt contentment at the prospect of building a life with her, yet he knew the strain a kid like Jeremy could put on a relationship. That Scout was a psychologist might not help them at all. In their home life, she wouldn't be acting in a professional capacity. Already, she seemed apprehensive, her face knit with worry.

"I wonder what's become of Danny," she said. "How did he get here?"

"You didn't see him today?"

"No." She squinted at Malachy. "Did you? Did he fly out by any chance?"

"I didn't see. And no, I haven't seen him again either."

"Best-case scenario," Scout said, "your Jeremy could

end up like him. Danny's not violent. He's psychologically scary but not truly sadistic or anything like that. He just got off on having multiple wives." She shook her head. "I can't figure out why he's up here. His story about having changed and wanting to talk is rubbish. This has to be about money somehow. He can't believe I'd have anything to do with him—can he?"

"No doubt we'll find out. And by the way, that's not *my* idea of a best-case scenario for Jeremy."

She smiled, shaking her head again at her own impassioned speech.

The phone rang, and her answering machine came on. "Scout, this is Serge." His voice was loud enough to carry into the kitchen, where she and Malachy were polishing off some salmon she'd baked. "I was wondering if you operate on a sliding scale. As I said, I'd be happy to work out a trade. But I'd like to…I think you can help me with something."

Scout winced. "I have a feeling this is going to be someone else who believes I can fix him up with a particular person."

"In my case, it worked."

Scout didn't reply. She preferred not to remember how recently Malachy had claimed that he wanted to marry another woman. True, Mary had been more keen on Malachy at the point when he'd broken things off with her, but that fact troubled Scout as much as anything.

"I still haven't called my parents to tell them I'm engaged," she said. "Danny showing up put it out of my mind. I may as well call them now."

Malachy nodded. "I'll leave you to it and go out and

check on the dogs." He'd brought six more of his sprint dogs over that night.

Scout went into her office, picked up the phone, and dialed her parents' number.

The answer came with the usual static. Theirs was a radio phone. It definitely discouraged lengthy telephone conversations.

"Berensen," her father barked.

"Hi, Dad. It's Scout."

"Oh. Hi."

He seemed to be waiting, and the silence filled with all of Scout's unmet desires, perhaps the greatest of which was sometime in her life to secure her father's approval. Yet she'd long since decided she didn't really want that approval if it came at the price of becoming someone other than herself.

"Can Mom get on, too?"

"Sure." She heard him say, "Dora. It's Scout."

Then they were both on the phone, and Scout said, "I wanted to tell you that I'm engaged. I'm going to marry Malachy MacCullagh."

The hesitation, the gap before they answered, troubled her.

"Are you happy?" asked her mother.

"Yes." Why their hesitation?

"You're sure it's what you want to do," her father said. No emphasis to make this a question, yet Scout knew it for a question.

"Very much so." Why wouldn't her parents want her to marry Malachy? It almost sounded as if they didn't. "Is something wrong?" she asked.

"Not...wrong," her mother said.

"Right, I'd say," her father muttered.

Scout's apprehension crept to a higher level. "Yes?"

"Well, it's awkward. Danny's up here, Scout."

Horror clawed her throat. Danny Kilbourne was a liar, but he was also a charmer. What did he want from her parents?

"In fact," her father continued, "he'd like to stay at the Moose Cabin."

On the trapline.

Was Danny destitute? Whatever he wanted, Scout knew that it was unlikely to be what he'd told her parents—or anyone—it was.

And Jeremy's up there.

She didn't even know the boy, this teenage ward of Malachy's, yet she feared for him. All the ways in which Danny Kilbourne was dysfunctional could hardly be addressed in a nonstop twenty-four-hour exposition on her part. The picture was too huge.

What immediately crossed her mind was that Danny would need someone to admire him. This was one of the things he'd worked for as a teacher. He'd loved to evoke something akin to worship in his students.

"He's interested in a reconciliation with you, Scout," Dora Berensen said. "He feels he was wrong to take you away from Alaska. He thinks you two have a chance if you live up here, close to us."

Rage, horror and fear combined within her. *I have to tell them right now.*

"First," she said, "he didn't take me anywhere. I decided on my own that California was where I wanted to live and work, and I decided that before I even met Danny."

"It's loyal of you to say that, but he's been willing to admit his part in pressuring you."

Danny had never pressured her to remain in California. He'd never needed to. Scout had a sudden vision of her parents and her brother all falling under Danny's spell, believing him.

"Second," Scout went on as though her father hadn't spoken, "Danny Kilbourne was a bigamist, and my marriage to him was invalid."

"He's explained the circumstances to us," her mother said. "He truly didn't know that his divorce from his first wife hadn't been finalized. He'd received the paperwork without the court stamp."

Of course her parents wouldn't have the faintest idea how divorces actually worked. Scout's voice felt like a piano string, only wound too tightly to make even the slightest sound. "He maintained a separate domicile with another woman the whole time he was with me. And he planned to quote unquote *marry* a third woman. A student no less."

"I can't imagine why you haven't told us this before, if it's true," said her father.

If it's true.

Well, wasn't this what she'd expected? Wasn't *this* why she hadn't told them till now? *Yes, Scout, this is why. Because your own father doesn't like who you are and never has. He's always been too willing to think the worst of you.*

She tried to modulate her voice. "Danny Kilbourne is a pathological liar and a predator, and I'm extremely concerned that he's up there. I wish you'd spoken to me before you made him welcome."

"It would've made no difference."

She knew that tone of her father's.

"This is *my* land," he continued. "I don't need your permission to take someone in. He asked. He's been down on his luck and is trying to change."

Scout wanted to throw something.

"He lied to the University of California about his credentials, Dad." Her voice wavered, too high. "Can you understand the degree of deception that entailed? Forgeries? Falsified references?"

"Look, Scout. The man's never had the chance to prove to himself what he can do right. I'm going to give him that chance."

I hate you.

There would be no arguing with him. Scout wanted to scream, to sob. Suddenly, she was eight years old with her father shouting over her that she damn well knew how to use a knife, that it was time he saw her do it. Dress out that damned caribou.

I can't stand this. I can't stand it. How can my father believe Danny instead of me?

"I understand," she said. "Malachy and I will be up in the next few days to get Jeremy."

"Don't be ridiculous," Frank said. "He and Holden are getting along beautifully."

"May I please speak to Holden?"

"He and Jeremy are out helping Danny at the cabin."

So she couldn't even tell her brother about her engagement.

"I have to go," Scout said. *I have to get off the phone and go quietly insane.*

GET FREE BOOKS and FREE GIFTS WHEN YOU PLAY THE...

Lucky 7

Just scratch off the silver box with a coin. Then check below to see the gifts you get!

SLOT MACHINE GAME!

YES!
I have scratched off the silver box. Please send me the 2 free Harlequin Superromance® books and 2 free gifts for which I qualify. I understand I am under no obligation to purchase any books, as explained on the back of this card.

336 HDL EF4K   **135 HDL EF4D**

FIRST NAME	LAST NAME

ADDRESS

APT.#	CITY

STATE/PROV.	ZIP/POSTAL CODE

7	7	7	**Worth TWO FREE BOOKS plus 2 BONUS Mystery Gifts!**
🍒	🍒	🍒	**Worth TWO FREE BOOKS!**
♣	♣	♣	**Worth ONE FREE BOOK!**
🔔	🔔	🍒	**TRY AGAIN!**

www.eHarlequin.com

(H-SR-10/06)

The Harlequin Reader Service® — Here's how it works:

Accepting your 2 free books and 2 free mystery gifts places you under no obligation to buy anything. You may keep the books and gifts and return the shipping statement marked "cancel." If you do not cancel, about a month later we'll send you 6 additional books and bill you just $4.69 each in the U.S., or $5.24 each in Canada, plus 25¢ shipping & handling per book and applicable taxes if any.* That's the complete price and — compared to cover prices of $5.50 each in the U.S. and $6.50 each in Canada — it's quite a bargain! You may cancel at any time, but if you choose to continue, every month we'll send you 6 more books, which you may either purchase at the discount price or return to us and cancel your subscription.

*Terms and prices subject to change without notice. Sales tax applicable in N.Y. Canadian residents will be charged applicable provincial taxes and GST. All orders subject to approval. Credit or debit balances in a customer's account(s) may be offset by any other outstanding balance owed by or to the customer. Please allow 4 to 6 weeks for delivery.

If offer card is missing write to: Harlequin Reader Service, 3010 Walden Ave., P.O. Box 1867, Buffalo NY 14240-1867

BUSINESS REPLY MAIL

FIRST-CLASS MAIL   PERMIT NO. 717-003   BUFFALO, NY

POSTAGE WILL BE PAID BY ADDRESSEE

HARLEQUIN READER SERVICE
3010 WALDEN AVE
PO BOX 1867
BUFFALO NY 14240-9952

NO POSTAGE
NECESSARY
IF MAILED
IN THE
UNITED STATES

SHE JOINED Malachy in the yard, near the kennel where he'd housed Ices. Ices greeted Scout by snarling at her.

Without hesitation, Scout grabbed a water bucket from beside the gate and hurled it at the bitch. She added a growl for good measure.

Ices whimpered.

Malachy glanced at Scout and grinned. "Well done." Then, "What's wrong?"

Because she was shaking.

"He's up there. Danny." She repeated the whole of her conversation with her parents. "Malachy, we have to get Jeremy out of there. I wish I could take Holden away, too. They're all in danger now, and they're too naive to realize it. Danny's *good,* Malachy," she said, knowing that Malachy would understand what she meant by *good. Good at fooling people.*

He gazed at the kennel, where Ax and Sky were chewing opposite ends of the same moose antler. "Tell me the worst-case scenario. What can he do up there?"

"Sponge, to start with. Get them to sign everything they own over to him."

"Your dad won't fall for that."

"I don't know what he'll do. And I have no idea what Danny really wants from them."

"Truly?"

Scout considered for a minute. "My money."

"You have enough to make that worth his while?"

"Oh, yes." It pleased her that Malachy didn't know this. She'd never suspected him of gold-digging, but it didn't hurt to have her instincts confirmed. "Harmony is very profitable. All three of us—Dana, Victoria and

I—have done very well out of it. Danny must've just learned that I'm a financial success. That's got to be it."

"I can believe it."

"But my parents won't."

"They'll believe a stranger over you? This guy is, after all, your ex—well, not husband—but how could they side with him rather than you?"

"You don't know my father. He thinks I'm soft. He thinks my character's weak because I was such a failure at growing up without flush toilets."

Malachy would never have thought her capable of the distress, the near-hysteria, that he saw rising through her. But he'd seen other women, women shaking in fear as they mopped blood from their eyes while he took away batterer husbands. Right now, Scout reminded him of those women. The violent trembling, the wavering too-tight voice.

He put his arms around her and realized how unused he was to thinking of her as someone who might need his protection. Even when Danny had come to the building, to her back door, Scout had seemed in command of the situation, fully up to chasing him off herself, almost as though help from him and Aaron was just a formality.

She was no longer so self-contained.

He wanted to get in the plane he shared with his father that night and fly up to her parents' land and have a few words with Frank Berensen. His father was a priest—once a priest, always a priest—and as forgiving as anyone he knew. But never would his father have abdicated the responsibility of getting to the bottom of an issue before taking a position against Malachy. Never would he believe someone else over his own son, unless he saw evidence that Malachy had lied.

Of course, Malachy had never made a habit of lying to him. He could imagine that Scout might have lied to and manipulated her family as a matter of survival.

It didn't excuse Frank's present position, however—sheltering Danny, who had done his daughter such a massive wrong.

Malachy said, "Scout, I don't believe Danny, and I never will. I believe you."

"Thank you."

"I'll see if I can trade shifts so we can get Jeremy tomorrow. That place has to be shut down in any case." He meant the meth lab, which cost him sleep. What if children were nearby and it blew up? The chemicals were so toxic and volatile that the Drug Enforcement Agency would have to do the actual evidence collection—and clean-up. "I don't like Jeremy's being around Danny any better than you do. And when we're up there, I'll talk to Holden if you don't feel up to it."

"Why can't they just believe *me?* Holden might." And how that hurt, to have to say that her twin brother *might* believe her.

But no, Holden would believe. He wouldn't interfere with their father's choice, would never fight it. But he wouldn't warm up to Danny, either.

She tried not to remember what Malachy had said about Jeremy. *He lies.*

If only this child who was going to be part of her life would prove to be unlike Danny Kilbourne. If Jeremy was a sociopath in the making… She couldn't finish the thought. She didn't know what she'd do.

CHAPTER NINE

"I'D LIKE TO TALK to your father about Danny," Malachy said the following day as they reached the McGrath airfield.

"No," Scout objected. Though Frank might take Malachy's warning more seriously than Scout's, it wouldn't help her father's attitude toward her. In the wildest, most insecure regions of her mind, it even made her wonder if her father might vilify her so thoroughly, cast so many aspersions on her character, that he might dissuade Malachy from marrying her. But if Malachy came to her defense, her father would probably bond with *him,* and Scout didn't want this to happen, either. She didn't want any man acting as go-between with her parents. If she had to analyze why, it was because that could lead to exactly what had occurred with Danny, that her father would side with her partner against her.

Now, I have no home, she thought. *I have no family. Danny has taken them from me.*

Or had *she* done that, by failing to tell them five years earlier why her relationship with Danny had ended?

"Scout, he's a predator. I'd like to speak to them in a law-enforcement capacity at least."

"It's not like he was charged with anything, Malachy.

Naturally, he was fired, and that made headlines. But he wasn't really married to me, since he was already married to someone else. And the student he married—pretended to marry—was already eighteen."

"Was that how he got caught?"

"Partly, yes. By his real wife. The student's parents were from Montecito, and they put a wedding announcement in several papers, and Kirsten, the real wife, saw it. She hired a private investigator to go after Danny, and that man found me. That's how *I* learned about it. When the news of his bigamy got out, someone looked into his credentials and his diplomas and—well, it was a major scandal."

"Big enough that I heard about it."

"Were you up here?" Malachy was starting his walk-around of the plane, and Scout didn't want to distract him, but she did want to know.

"I ran into someone from school—I don't think you knew him—in Anchorage, and he told me the whole thing."

"Now I wish I'd told my parents. But they might not have believed me even then. I just figured they'd pity me and think I'd been asking for it or something. By living Outside. Of course, what's happening now is worse. I should have told them. But I was mortified. I'm already the family klutz, wasn't good at *anything* we needed to do, you know, in the bush. I was sure they'd say, *Oh, here's Scout, blowing it again.*"

He shook his head but didn't voice his thoughts.

Scout had brought Estelle with her, as she did whenever she could. Her father, if he saw her, would give the dog his most disparaging look, but Scout didn't care. She wanted the comfort of having the puppy with her.

In addition to offering to talk to her father, Malachy had offered to go alone to retrieve Jeremy.

Scout had said, "No, I want to go with you."

She couldn't have said why or how it had happened, but Danny's preying on her family, driving her insane, had actually made her eager to get to know Jeremy. Was it because she didn't want him turning out like Danny Kilbourne?

She just knew that suddenly she cared very much about her situation in Alaska, about the family she'd agreed to help Malachy create.

Jeremy Crestone would be part of that clan.

IT WAS LIKE going back in time. All so familiar. Yes, there were new buildings. But the Kokrines River was the same, unchanging. And she saw no new cabins or additions to the house and kennels. Her father was one for downsizing rather than development, and that rule certainly held on his and her mother's property.

The landing strip hadn't changed either—a bit short, more than a bit scary. Malachy, however, took it gracefully.

Scout's mother came down to the strip. She wore a flannel shirt and jeans, her hair still quite dark with just a hint of gray. When Scout climbed out of the plane, Dora came forward to embrace her, then hold her at arm's length.

"You look wonderful, Scout," she said. "Very healthy and strong."

Scout pressed her cheek against her mother's, feeling affection and, at the same time, the anguish that her mother believed the lies of a man who had done such appalling things to Scout. It was impossible to plead. Not now. Impossible to say, *Let me tell you what happened. Let me tell you everything. This is not a nice person. You don't want him around.*

Because nothing she said would make a difference. Her mother and father had decided to give Danny "a chance."

"Malachy." Dora embraced him, too, and gave him a kiss on the cheek. "I am pleased," she said.

"See?" Scout proffered her left hand.

"Oh, it's beautiful. What's the big stone?"

"It's a ruby, quite a good one. The color's unusually dark."

"It looks so pretty on your hand."

Thank God for this conversation, for her mother's normalcy, her love and kindness in this moment.

The mosquitoes were ghastly, but Scout tried to ignore them. "Where's Dad? And Holden and Jeremy?"

"I imagine they're all heading this way."

They would have seen the plane.

Her father emerged from the trees and waved.

So far, so good.

Scout walked toward him. Frank Berensen was tall and stern-featured. Holden resembled him. Her father said, "You look fit, Scout."

"Thank you."

He hugged her and waved to Malachy. "Going to do some fishing?" he asked.

It wasn't what she'd expected. Of course, her parents wouldn't want her to land and take off that fast. She hadn't seen them for years, for more years than most people thought normal.

"I don't want to be around Danny, Dad," she said. "I'm sorry. You can think what you want and do what you want, but I have a policy of neither speaking to him nor being around him." She wanted to say more, to ask, *Why do you like him now? What makes you think he has anything at all to recommend him? When we were married, you didn't give a damn about him.*

But she suspected that Danny had appealed to her parents simply by wanting to live in Alaska. Perhaps they assumed that if she reconciled with Danny, she'd come home to stay.

But I am home to stay.

Just not at the place where she'd been born. Elsewhere in Alaska. Because of Malachy.

"Well, I certainly hope that's not going to keep you from spending time with your family," her father said, as though he was talking about some other family, some other group of people.

Had he even heard her? She'd told her father plainly that she didn't want to be in Danny's presence, that she wouldn't be in his presence. There were other things to say, but her parents wouldn't hear them either.

Their world allowed only for extreme acts of forgiveness, not for policies of separation or for the possibility that a bad person would stay bad, or the chance that someone they liked would not be the person he appeared to be.

Clarity, though, was important. "I want to spend time with you and Mom and Holden," she said carefully, "but I won't be in Danny Kilbourne's presence. I'm sorry if you don't understand. I'm willing to answer questions if you have any. Please remember that I lived with the man for five years and you've spent very little time with him."

"Scout, when you were married, we did see you together." Her mother had joined them. "And you seemed happy."

"We were *not* married. And he knew it. He had another wife. He spent part of each week with her and part with me, juggling us back and forth with stories of continuing education classes in other parts of the state. He built a whole picture of himself as someone who'd been born and raised in Ireland, which was completely false. He claims he's an orphan, but I don't even know if that's true."

Her mother seemed troubled. Scout watched two forces fight in Dora Berensen. One was a refusal to acknowledge the truly sordid by not hearing it. The other was concern for her daughter. Her mother must know that Scout would never invent something like this.

"He must have been very unhappy," said her mother, "to feel that he had to do that."

"I agree, but his happiness has nothing to do with me anymore. I haven't seen him for years, and I haven't spent even one second wishing I was with him again."

Her father sent a look toward Malachy, who stood talking with Jeremy and Holden. Jeremy had abandoned his black clothes, and Scout knew why. Mosquitoes loved it. His blond hair was undoubtedly an asset up here.

"I don't think he'll come around while you're with us," her father said. "He's very respectful of your feelings, and he's said so. He says he'd just like to talk with you again, to clear the air."

"The last time we 'talked,' he told me I was too fat to be attractive to him anymore."

"You'd just rejected the man!" her father exploded.

Scout stepped back.

An arm, Malachy's arm in blue plaid, reached past her, extended to her father. "Thank you for your blessing, Frank."

As though he hadn't heard her father shouting at her.

Turning the conversation and her parents' attention to fact. A declaration. *I am going to marry your daughter, and she is going to marry me.*

And more. More that her father must have understood. As though Malachy had said, *Surely I didn't just hear you raise your voice to my fiancée.*

Her father stilled. He withdrew his hand. "You're welcome."

Scout turned to see her brother and Jeremy. Both stood near the plane, and Scout walked toward them. She hugged Holden quickly, then put out her hand to Jeremy. "Good to see you again."

His hand was dry, and he didn't meet her eyes. This troubled her less than if he'd looked her in the eye and smiled with charm, the way she'd been greeted by other very dangerous young men. In any event, life and training had taught her that it took a very long time to know anyone.

Had Malachy already told him that Scout would be part of their family? Surely, he'd heard the news from her parents by this point, but it seemed better to say nothing about it.

Holden, however, said, "Your *fiancé* apparently has something to discuss with me." He smirked. "Guess that McGrath office is working out for you."

So Holden *had* hoped this would happen.

"Yes. We want to recruit you."

Her twin blushed, ran his tongue over the inside of his cheek and looked away.

Scout marveled at how her brother, so capable of teasing her, of being companionable and charming among family and a very few, very close friends, could be paralyzed by shyness when meeting strangers. Yet he seemed to have become comfortable around Jeremy. Most people would suppose it was because Jeremy was a teenager, but some adults were just as shy, or even more shy, around teenagers than other adults.

Undoubtedly, her brother had adjusted to Jeremy's presence over time. Had he adjusted to Danny's, as well, or did he manage to maintain his usual extended silence with her ex-partner?

Maybe Danny would just stay away, stay at Moose Cabin, which was, after all, thirteen miles from her parents' place, over difficult country. Snow made travel much easier up here. Her parents did own some ATVs, but Scout wondered if Moose Cabin could even be reached in that way. The river, however, was an option. One of the boats?

Yes, that was how they'd be traveling.

She returned to what Holden had said. "Actually, I could tell you just as well." Danny. She could tell Holden everything now. It was a more pleasant prospect than telling her parents but still not one she anticipated with any pleasure. Unfortunately, now Danny's presence threatened her family. He wouldn't think twice about conning them out of money or assets. If her parents wouldn't listen, Holden, at least, must be filled in. Besides, she had the idea that her brother would be less likely to fall for Danny's charm. Perhaps it was because of the time he spent in solitude and his way with wild animals, but Holden had an unusual ability to see through the machinations of people.

Malachy joined them, and Scout said, "Holden and I need to talk, Malachy. But Estelle's still in the plane. Maybe—"

She didn't know what she planned to suggest, but Malachy said, "Jeremy, let's go get Scout's dog. Yes, I know, the leash—" so the puppy wouldn't be devoured by any of the Berensen dogs "—and go up to the house. Frank said you've done some really interesting carving. I think your great-grandmother would want to see that."

"I doubt it," Jeremy snarled.

Scout glanced at him.

"It's not exactly *native,*" he added. "But neither am I."

"Where were you born?" Scout asked, curious.

"Seattle." The answer was almost defiant. "But my mom's from McGrath."

"Seattle's an interesting place," she said. "When did you move away?" Holden and Malachy were waiting for them, but she wanted this information.

"I was five." He looked haughty. His overgrown features ruled a face that hadn't caught up. The same with huge hands and feet. Some acne. "I don't belong here. I never have. And that's not a crime."

"No, but there sure are plenty of people who'll make you feel like it is," Scout said. She told herself not to read too much into this common ground with Jeremy. If he was as smart as Malachy said, he could use it to manipulate her.

But she had to shut down the psychotherapist in herself, the psychologist who'd done clinical work with troubled teens as part of her schooling. This was not her role in Jeremy's life. For her own mental health and his, she had to remember that. She would be, like Malachy, a guardian, a kind of adoptive parent.

Jeremy didn't answer, anyway. If he cared that she might have experienced emotions similar to his, he didn't show it.

One problem with spending any length of time up here was that it was difficult to retrieve her messages. She planned to try, but she'd called Victoria and asked her to cover with clients in emergencies when she was out of cell phone range—not mentioned that she was engaged, which still felt too new to announce aloud. As Scout was the only clinical psychologist in McGrath, it was the best she could do for now. She'd been exploring options in Nome, conversing by telephone with two different psychologists there, but neither had yet agreed to assist her with Harmony clients.

"I've got to call the answering machine, too," she told Malachy. "We'll be up at the house soon."

She swore at the mosquitoes as she and Holden walked toward the kennels, the dogs providing as good a diversion as any. Scout couldn't help wondering if she'd feel differently about her father's kennel now that she had dogs of her own. What made dogs bad-tempered toward people, anyway? *Abuse* was the simple answer, but Scout thought it too simple. Lack of socialization was more likely. She'd never read a single book about dogs in her life, having spent lots of time around canines and having had no desire to own one herself. Now, though, it might be worth studying animal behavior. She could at least review some Konrad Lorenz. That related to her own profession, after all, and had been part of her education as a psychologist.

She said, "Look, Holden, Mom and Dad aren't listening to me about Danny, but this is serious." She told him. It came out in a disorganized torrent, and it felt hideous to bring it up. One of the hardest things to impress on some clients was how much better they'd feel if they didn't dwell on this or that injury. Everyone had pain in life, but why not live in the present? So it was no pleasure to her to revisit life with Danny.

Holden listened.

Finally, Scout stopped talking and looked at him. They'd reached the kennels, and her twin frowned at a shaggy black dog who was loose in the yard. This dog was probably part of the breeding stock. He eyed Scout but showed no real interest in her. Humans didn't seem to be part of his agenda, which was what Scout remembered about her father's dogs.

Holden said, "I never liked the guy."

And that was it.

He believed her. Her parents might be taken in by Danny, but Holden would not be. Holden believed her without reservation.

He didn't ask the question her parents had, why she hadn't mentioned it before. Scout took it for granted that he could understand perfectly why she wouldn't want to reveal anything so mortifying to her family.

"What's Jeremy like?" she asked, glad to shift subjects.

Holden made a face, but the expression told her little. Maybe he was just thinking about her question. He shrugged. "I haven't been around someone that age since high school."

In town.

Torture, for both of them, especially at first. She'd adjusted. Holden had never liked it.

"He kicked one of the dogs," he muttered.

"What did you do?"

"I told him he could kill a dog that way and never to do it again. Gave him some better options."

Corporal punishment was one of the rules at this kennel. There were a few straps hanging near various gates. Neither her father nor Holden had made a habit of thrashing the dogs, but they weren't above grabbing a strap to answer a bite. Scout thought this was primitive and stupid and would not hit her own dogs. She suspected her father's dogs were sometimes mean because of the way they were treated.

She wasn't a hitter. If that was what keeping dogs in line required, she wasn't going to have dogs.

But it *wasn't* what was required, and she did have dogs. Her dogs occasionally picked on each other—Ax and Sky were real offenders, liking to team up and go after Pigpen, especially. She'd taken to talking back to them in their own language with snarls and growls, which relieved her feelings if nothing else. Also, when she did this, Ax and Sky looked at her in surprise, as though she were an unusually tall canine with the surprising characteristic of having only two legs. Sometimes she thought she detected respect in their reaction. They looked away and got interested in other things.

Scout studied the black dog who was loose. "I still can't warm up to these dogs."

"You don't need to. We feed them. They work. They like to work. It's a good arrangement."

It could be worse, at any rate. And Holden's attitude was very Alaskan. And very like their father's.

"What's Jeremy interested in?" she asked.

"I haven't been able to figure that out. He likes to read. Strange stuff."

"Like?"

"Baudelaire?"

Scout didn't find that particularly strange, just a bit unusual. "What do you think he should be reading?"

"I don't know. Don't ask me. *I* like Baudelaire, but I'm not thirteen."

"What did you like when you were?"

"*Playboy,* when I could get it."

"Like, never?"

"Ha ha, how little you know."

Her brother at thirteen with his nose inside any magazine featuring naked women was something she didn't know about and didn't much want to.

"Dad doesn't like that kind of thing, does he?"

Holden snorted.

Scout understood; their father probably considered pornography an influence from Outside, unAlaskan. He tolerated manual typewriters, which many people would've considered a necessity for someone who thought computers were spawned by the devil. He'd grown up in Kentucky, the son of a coal miner, and had come to Alaska with one thing in mind—living as close to nature as possible.

"He does a better job than anyone I've ever met of inflicting his neuroses on other people," Scout declared spitefully, "and I've met some very neurotic individuals." She didn't mean that she wished her father had a pornography habit. She just felt a wave of old resentment about how she'd been raised—and felt immature for reacting that way.

Holden shrugged.

They were near the house, but before they reached it, Scout saw a familiar figure strutting toward the front porch. "I'm not going in there," she said and abruptly turned around to walk back to the plane. Holden continued inside.

Danny must've seen them, but he didn't look in her direction. He would undoubtedly derive some sadistic pleasure in keeping her from her family. She had to get out of here.

If only Malachy wouldn't linger inside.

But he didn't.

Only seconds seemed to pass before she heard the back door again and Malachy's deep voice saying goodbye to Holden.

As JEREMY FOLLOWED him outside, Malachy studied the teenager. They headed down the porch steps, Jeremy carrying his pack.

"What's the deal?" asked Jeremy.

"What do you mean?" Watching Scout climb into the plane, Malachy tried to contain his own anger at her parents and his much greater fury at Danny, whom he'd once liked.

"You left about two seconds after Danny came in. And he said he didn't recognize you before."

"We were at college together."

"Oh," Jeremy said then, pausing as they walked toward the plane together. "You don't like him because he was married to Scout."

"Actually, I dislike him because he *wasn't* married to Scout." Malachy gave Jeremy an abbreviated history.

Jeremy lifted his eyebrows, seeming vaguely impressed by the extent—and success—of Danny's deception. "That really, like, worked? Neither of them figured it out?"

"Until he tried to 'marry'—" Malachy made quotation marks with his fingers "—someone else, and wife number one saw an announcement in the paper."

"What a clown! Why didn't he skip that part?"

"He didn't do it. His future not-father-in-law did."

Jeremy squinted toward the cedar-sided house. "These people are weird. No offence to your girlfriend or wife or whatever she is—"

"Fiancée."

"—but it's pretty weird living up here. The solar shower and everything. You know, even if they're doing the back-to-nature thing, they could modernize a bit."

Malachy agreed but wasn't going to say so. Strange… Until he'd become close to Scout this summer, he'd never seen her parents as anything but thoroughly remarkable. But Jeremy, coming from Outside and never living anywhere more remote than McGrath—which was pretty remote—took a different view.

"They don't even have a television," the teenager complained. "Let alone, like, *cable*." He stared at Malachy suspiciously. "Is *she* like that?"

Malachy shook his head. "She's been living Outside. She didn't even want to come back."

"Now, *that* makes sense."

JEREMY SAT in silence in the back of the plane, trying to figure out what difference Scout was going to make to his life. He hadn't minded either Malachy or his father, though he thought it was wild that John MacCullagh used to be a Catholic priest. He never let you say that, though. He insisted he'd *always* be a priest, which was obviously not true, like a whole lot of other stuff about religion.

In any event, he was glad to leave the Berensens'. Holden had been all right, but Frank Berensen was an asshole as far as Jeremy was concerned. Also, he wondered why Frank didn't throw Danny in the river or something.

What would he, Jeremy, do?

For one thing, he'd let Danny know that he'd almost killed someone and had *meant* to kill him. Briefly and not in a premeditated way. He'd been enraged. What Rayburn had said about Jeremy's mother was patently true, but nobody was allowed to talk about it. And part of what Rayburn had said *wasn't* true, couldn't have been. Jeremy had told no one what that was. *He called my mother a whore*, should be sufficient explanation for everyone. His mother did not service kids his age. Rayburn hadn't been from McGrath but from Anchorage, and that was where the fight had happened, where Jeremy had almost killed him. If Rayburn's father had been given his way, Jeremy would be locked up—or dead.

If there was a hell, Jeremy was going there, because he'd made Rayburn's father cry. The father of the person he'd tried to kill.

When he, Jeremy, had almost succeeded in killing Rayburn, he'd seen that killing was different from what he'd thought, but still he had meant to kill someone

another person cared about. No one cared about Jeremy.
Malachy was his guardian, but Jeremy knew how things
worked. None of these people cared about him.

Maybe Malachy's father, a little. He didn't want
Jeremy to think he was damned. They had talked about
it, though not directly.

God forgives everyone, John had said.

Jeremy sincerely doubted God was anything but an
idea, or rather, many ideas held by many people. He'd
told John MacCullagh this. John had said, *Jeremy, you're
a very interesting person,* and when he'd said that,
Jeremy had realized that the used-to-be-priest liked him.

But Jeremy would never forget Rayburn's dad crying
or pointing at Jeremy, screaming at him.

*Kids like you should be put down! Some magistrate
thinks you've got a chance, but you ain't got no chance!*

It wasn't the kind of thing you forgot.

CHAPTER TEN

"SCOUT, THIS IS Mary Clarke. I think you and I should get together and clear the air. There are some things I'd really like to say. Call me." *Beep.*

It was Scout's last message, and she shuddered inwardly at the sound of *There are some things I'd really like to say.* Was she obligated to hear whatever Mary wanted to express? No.

Would she call Mary back?

Yes.

Tomorrow.

Definitely tomorrow.

Something about that message, however, kept her from calling Dana and Victoria and catching them up on news—her engagement to Malachy, Danny's appearance, her parents' attitude about Danny. For instance, could she say aloud to Dana and Victoria that she'd told Malachy she would try to help him achieve an engagement to Mary?

It's none of their business.

Malachy had come to her because of the Harmony Agency, though—because he'd mistakenly believed that was what they did *and* that Scout could help him, when neither was true. She'd told him neither was true, but she still didn't like to imagine how her partners would react to the deal she'd made with the man who was now her fiancé.

Dana would say, *I am so not hearing this.*

Victoria would say, *Tell me it's not true.*

Scout told herself again that her behavior had not been unprofessional, indeed had nothing to do with her profession. But she couldn't escape the feeling that, one woman to another, she'd done something underhanded.

She left the machine and joined Jeremy and Malachy in the downstairs bedroom, which was to be Jeremy's.

"Is it okay?" Scout asked.

"This is kind of a weird place. It's not really a house."

"You preferred Malachy's cabin," Scout said, with no questioning inflection in her voice.

His eyes moved from wood floor to high ceiling of pressed tin. "Can I do whatever I want to it?"

Scout looked at Malachy.

"As long as it's not destructive."

"I can paint it whatever color I like?"

"Sure."

Scout smiled. She knew what was coming.

"You'll get the paint?"

"I might make you work for it," Malachy told him.

"I want black."

Malachy shook his head ruefully. "Figured."

"And I want to build a loft. I'll paint that red or maybe yellow." He seemed to be seeing the whole thing on some large scale. He reminded Scout of an artist at work.

"Just consider," Scout said, "that you might find having *all* black walls oppressive."

He eyed the room again. "Maybe."

Malachy had told her everything he knew about the incident involving Jeremy, which had happened in Anchorage. His father had said he thought Jeremy was remorseful but might go his whole life without ever admitting it.

Scout didn't plan to bring this up with Jeremy.

Malachy said that something Jeremy did was steal. He hadn't stolen from Malachy or his father. He stole from peers he considered rich or spoiled, from stores not owned by people who were just scraping by. *It's not okay with me regardless,* Malachy had told her.

Scout knew certain people dealt with anger or anxiety through self-destructive behavior. Cutting, shoplifting, prostitution, any number of self-denigrating practices, brought a kind of calm to minds at the breaking point.

But Jeremy couldn't afford to get caught shoplifting.

Malachy predicted theft as the practice that would be Jeremy's downfall and land him in a juvenile detention center *again.* The three of them, Malachy, Jeremy and Scout, had a meeting in Nome with Jeremy's psychologist the following week. A counseling appointment for them as a family, because Scout was now part of that picture.

The next morning, Serge came in for an appointment. Scout had decided to wait until after this meeting to call Mary. She didn't want to be rattled when dealing with a new client—although she didn't really believe Serge was going to be that. He was determined to get something for as near nothing as possible, and that wouldn't fly.

"I'm not really interested in the dating service," he said. "I don't need it."

"Then how would you like to use this session?" Scout asked.

"I thought we could do some role-playing," Serge said. "I'd like to practice my clinical skills."

Scout immediately felt exhausted. "I don't understand."

"Well, I have some background in counseling, and I'd like to work on my skills as a clinician."

"You have credentials?" Scout asked.

"I have experience in healing."

Scout managed not to put her hand over her face.

After that session, she did call Dana. "I didn't know what to do," she said. "I have never felt so totally helpless as a therapist." What she could ethically reveal to her partner was dictated by circumstances. Certainly, no names were mentioned. "Dana, how would you handle it if someone comes in and says he wants to practice his skills as a psychotherapist and he has no certification, no training?"

"Tell him that's not what you do."

"I did."

"And?"

"He started asking me about my life. He really threw me, Dana." It was unlike her to be so bothered by a client's behavior. "I told him there's no point in our meeting again, since he doesn't want anything Harmony offers." What she was not telling Dana remained a glaring omission. And there were other worries. Jeremy's living in the building, too, was problematic. If he told anyone who came and went from her office, that would threaten her confidentiality. Fortunately, he wasn't listening at doors. She'd heard music playing from his room during her meeting with Serge.

She said, "I have to talk with you and Victoria…about some things. It doesn't have to do with work—"

It all spilled out. Everything but her original deal with Malachy, and then she found herself saying, "There's something else, too. It doesn't have to do with work—exactly—but in retrospect I'm not comfortable with it."

And she told Dana.

Dana said almost nothing during her entire recitation of everything that had happened in her life since her arrival in McGrath.

Dana said, "This is really out there, Scout."

"I *told* him it was absolutely between friends. Just a private deal between us."

"Yes." Dana appeared to be waiting for her to finish the thought.

"Do you think it was unprofessional?"

"I think you made it clear that it was unrelated to your profession. Whether it was personally unwise is, of course, a different matter entirely."

"Oh, it was."

"Because now you're engaged to him."

"And I got this phone message from her…. I haven't called her back yet. I'm just cringing, Dana. I know she's going to say I stole her boyfriend."

"Well, you didn't. You're going to marry him, and it feels right?"

"Totally right."

"Then I'm happy for you. Do you want to tell Victoria all this yourself, or am I free to relay it? I'm meeting her at the gym in half an hour."

"You can tell her. Thanks for being supportive, Dana."

"What else would I be? And I agree, there's a

problem with your residence and office being in the same building. You should at least be on separate floors. Good luck with the kid, by the way."

Scout hung up, took a few deep breaths, then lifted the receiver again and dialed Mary's number.

THEY MET at The Tug and sat in a booth near the back corner.

Mary didn't look particularly friendly, and Scout was struck anew by her good looks and no-nonsense manner.

"Did you intend all along to get him away from me?" Mary's black eyebrows drew together, although she didn't sound accusatory. She seemed to be seeking information.

Scout shook her head.

"I don't know why I asked you to meet me," Mary said. "But nothing like this has ever happened to me before. I mean, I've known other women to be under-handed—more in racing matters than about men. Why didn't you give me some warning? Why did you pretend you wanted to be my friend?"

Scout said, "I didn't *pretend* to want to be your friend. I wanted to be your friend. Malachy's change of heart shocked me."

Mary had a cup of tea in front of her but hadn't touched it. "He told me about the deal you two made. That seems pretty unprofessional. You should know that I'm seriously considering reporting you to the state board."

"Go ahead." She'd qualified with the state board, and the threat angered her. Dana had delineated things for her. She'd been clear with Malachy. She was safe. "It was an agreement between friends, and neither of us felt it was anything different." Scout frowned slightly. "But you're not really in love with him, are you?"

"You certainly can't be. You barely know him."

I know him a lot better than you do, Scout thought, then wondered if she was being overconfident, if maybe she was kidding herself. She didn't answer Mary but saw the other woman's eyes drift to her left hand.

"He bought you a ring and everything," Mary said in a voice of stunned disbelief. "I feel completely betrayed. I mean, he said... Well, he told me he didn't want to see me anymore, and a week later you two are engaged. Don't you doubt his seriousness? Remember what I said about him bailing as soon as things look settled? Obviously, that's exactly what happened this time."

Scout tried not to be affronted. Also, she tried not to take Mary's nay-saying to heart. Her relationship with Malachy was very different from the relationship he'd had with Mary.

She said, "Mary, I didn't set out to steal Malachy from you. The whole thing surprised me. But he and I have known each other a long time. He knows my family. There's history."

"Which comes down to the fact that both of you were born in Alaska," Mary said.

"No," Scout responded. "That's not it."

"Do you know what I'd give to have grown up the way you did?" Mary asked, as if Scout hadn't spoken.

"How did *you* grow up?"

Mary made a dismissive gesture. "Tennis lessons, swim team, Midwestern values."

"I think I might've done better with that," Scout told her, "if it's any comfort."

Mary blinked. "What do you mean?"

"Oh, I just never seemed to fit in with my family. It still feels that way, to tell you the truth."

Mary gazed absently out the window. Without acknowledging what Scout had said, she admitted, "You know, it's my ego that's taking a battering from this. And of course, Serge scooted right over to try to comfort me."

Scout kept quiet. She couldn't imagine any woman having anything to do with a man who was so obviously full of it.

"What do you think of Jeremy?" Mary asked a moment later.

"I like him, but I don't know him yet, that's for sure."

Mary rolled her eyes. "I wasn't really up to that situation. But the fact is, Malachy was a halfway decent boyfriend, which is a rarity in McGrath. Still, he seemed more…" She paused, searching for words.

"What?" Scout asked.

"I need tons of time alone. I like silence. I like just being with my dogs. Malachy wants a family. He'd never admit it, but I think he needs someone who can hear about his job and all that. He's frustrated that there's so little real action in his work up here."

He was certainly frustrated that he hadn't been able to get a judge to issue a warrant to search the meth house.

But Mary's revelations about herself nudged something else in Scout's mind, gave her an idea. Did she dare mention it? *I'm certainly not going to try matchmaking again.* So, into what category did this fall?

"Mary, I know this is probably too soon and not the right time…." She hesitated. "It's not really a matchmaking thing," she began, as though to herself. How could she say this? "I have a twin brother. He still lives with my folks. He's really wonderful and very handsome, but growing up the way we did…"

Mary watched her, waiting.

"He's not comfortable meeting strangers," Scout went on. "I'm not sure he's ever had a female friend, even." She felt indiscreet revealing this to Mary Clarke, whom she hadn't found to be a very closemouthed person. "But you two actually have some things in common. If I got him down here to visit, would you like to meet him? Just…you know. You could be friends if you felt you had anything to say to each other. Or not say. He likes silence, too. And he's incredible with animals. All animals. It's surreal, like he's a magician or something."

Mary gave another slow blink. The tilt of her chin still betrayed the hurt of Malachy's defection, but Scout recognized the interest in her eyes. Mary shrugged. "I wouldn't mind. Is he into dogs?"

"Oh, yes."

They parted not as friends or even on friendly terms but peaceably, and Scout felt that the possibility for friendship with Mary still existed, which pleased her. Also, this was one woman to whom Holden might actually have something to say.

She returned home just as Jeremy was emerging from her office.

They both started.

It was her business office, where she kept her filing cabinets. The door had no lock, because she'd never needed one.

What were you doing? It would sound like an

accusation. She immediately took another path. "Jeremy, I'm sorry I don't have a lock on that door yet. I really need to keep you and Malachy out because my clients' records are in there. It's personal information, and if it was released through me I would be very much at fault and also in danger of losing my license."

He showed no reaction, merely nodded. No explanation of what he'd been doing.

"I think you're mature enough to help on this. Could I ask you not to talk about who comes and goes from the Harmony Agency office?"

"Everyone in McGrath can see who comes and goes from here," he said. "And don't these people put their names on the Internet and stuff so they can find someone who'll go out with them?"

"Not all of them."

He said, "Do you have the Internet?"

"Of course. Do you have a computer?" Was that why he'd gone into her office? To use her computer?

He shook his head.

"I have a laptop I'm not really using. Want me to set it up for you?"

His eyes opened wide for a moment, with a look like a drowning person reaching up to a rescuer. It was no more than a momentary impression, but Scout was moved. She hadn't forgotten the things Malachy had told her about him. He'd nearly killed someone in a fight because the other boy had said Jeremy's mother was a whore.

"That would be okay," he said about the laptop.

"It's in the closet." She stepped into her office. Nothing looked disturbed; if he'd been prying, she couldn't tell What might be different was the position of a thin sheaf of paper. The brochures Malachy had brought her about recognizing a meth lab.

"What were you doing in here?" she asked.

"You won't believe me if I say."

"Try me."

He pointed at the papers she'd noticed. "I saw you bring these in here the other night. I wanted to look at them."

"Why? Have you seen something suspicious? At that house beside the beaver pond?"

"It's not in the *house*," Jeremy said as though it were obvious. "It's in his *van*."

"You saw it? What did you see?"

"I looked in the back window. There are curtains, but one was folded over—"

"Jeremy, you've got to stay away from that place! That stuff could blow up!"

"Don't you want to know what I saw?"

"Yes, but don't go near there again. I don't want anything to happen to you."

He blinked twice, shocked, then walked over to her desk and pointed to one of the photos of a mobile meth lab. "Jars like this with funnels. And something like this."

"We've got to call Malachy." She grabbed the cordless phone. He didn't answer his cell, so she left a message.

Then she opened the small wardrobe she used as a closet and removed her old PowerBook. She'd have to erase files, but that could be accomplished quickly enough.

"Let's go sit in the Harmony office," she said. That was her working name for the larger office, the front room, where she met with clients and explained the agency's services. She then told him that his having a ground-floor room probably wasn't going to work, that her partners objected to anyone having a residence on the same floor as the office.

"But there isn't enough room upstairs," he said. "We should move back to the cabin."

"Malachy's place?"

"It's his dad's too."

Scout switched gears. "Tell me what programs you want. I've got a word-processing program, and Photoshop's on here, too. That's fun. It takes awhile to get the hang of, but you can do interesting stuff with photos."

Malachy came in fifteen minutes later and found them still setting up the computer, Scout showing Jeremy keystrokes to make various things happen, helping him find her favorite computer games, teaching him how to change the desktop picture.

She told Malachy she was letting Jeremy borrow the computer indefinitely.

"Well, he'll have to take a break from it because he needs to write an affidavit describing what he saw."

MALACHY LISTENED to the night.

Beside him, Scout slept softly, her breathing silent, her body still. A written statement from a thirteen-year-old had satisfied the judge that there was probable cause to search the entire property, vehicles and house. They found evidence in the van and house, arrested the couple, then turned the site over to the DEA for evidence collection and clean-up. Jeremy slept downstairs in his room for tonight. Malachy and Scout had agreed they should live with Malachy's father, and John, consulted by phone, had immediately agreed. And her moving out of the upper floor would give the agency more space.

Malachy's chest felt loose, fluttery. This relationship was so different from anything he'd known with a woman before. Usually he experienced something that had an edge of resentment to it, and then he lost interest. But Scout seemed almost to be made for him.

She got along with Jeremy.

She seemed to like Alaska—now. *This* Alaska, which he knew was a very different place from the Alaska of her childhood.

Neither of them had mentioned Danny Kilbourne since they'd returned to McGrath. Malachy wondered if Danny would stay on the Berensens' land through the winter. If he did, it *would* change him. Alaska changed you, summer or winter.

Scout stirred, and he clasped her, suddenly aroused and needing her.

"Malachy," she said, easing against him, natural, fitting.

They were like water together, mated in some river or tide of physical bliss.

Later, she said, "Have you been to sleep yet?"

"Yes," he lied.

"At first, I thought," she murmured sleepily, "that you just wanted to be with me because..." Her voice trailed off.

"Why?"

"I had a theory that you fear abandonment, so when a woman's committed to you and you to her, you find yourself in a position in which you could be abandoned. So you leave before it can happen."

Malachy considered this.

"I think I've left other relationships," he said finally, "because they weren't right."

Was he being honest with himself? Scout sensed that he was. "Do you remember your mother?" she asked.

"Drop this."

She did.

"My father didn't leave me," he said after a long while. "And I'm sure he wanted to."

"I'm not so sure," Scout whispered.

"It doesn't matter. What matters is what he did."

"WE GOT ALONG GREAT," exclaimed Martin the mosquito man. "And she liked McGrath, too, although I have to admit she had some reservations about the prospect of Alaskan winters.

"She'd like to visit again when the Iditarod comes through. That's months from now. But you were right. She wasn't up here looking for other guys. She just wanted to give us both an out if it didn't work out. But we spent practically every minute together."

Martin wasn't the only client to have met someone through the Harmony Agency. One of the men who'd signed up for the agency's full service had gone to Montana to meet someone. As Martin left, Scout felt satisfaction with her work and with the business she'd helped found.

Only that morning, Malachy had asked Scout, "Don't you feel culpable if someone has a disastrous experience?"

"No. We do background checks and encourage practices that protect our clients. But ultimately people make their own relationship choices."

Scout couldn't imagine one of her clients ending up

in a relationship as disastrous as hers with Danny had been. In any case, the Harmony Agency was very clear about the services they provided. *We don't make relationships; we just help people become better at existing in relationships.*

She half expected to hear from Holden or her parents in the next few days and learn that Danny had left. His object, she was sure, had been to get to her—either to cause her pain or to try to defraud her of money. Or both. Once she'd left her parents' home without speaking to him, he would've realized that he could achieve neither of the above schemes. But as far as she knew, he was still there. No one had called to tell her otherwise.

She and Malachy had decided to move to his cabin, but Malachy and John wanted to complete some renovations on it first, to give Malachy and Scout a more private master bedroom. For the time being, they remained at the Harmony office, and Jeremy painted his bedroom black.

At the end of July, he and Malachy had a shouting argument about the dogs. Scout was with a client at the time, and felt embarrassed by the raised voices, although the client was understanding. When the session ended, she went into the back yard.

"They're not my dogs," Jeremy was yelling. "Why should I pick up—"

"Because it's one of your chores this week. We rotate."

"I don't want dogs. Not these dogs."

Scout asked, "What dogs would you want?"

"A Cane Corso," Jeremy said without hesitation. "Or a Neapolitan mastiff."

"They'd be miserable in Alaska," Malachy told him.

"I don't want to *be* in Alaska. Don't you get that? I

don't want to be in this town. There's nothing to do, nowhere to go, and the people are stupid."

His words reverberated within Scout like a stick hitting a drum.

"Well, you live in Alaska, we have dogs, and we all take care of them."

"I'm not doing it." Jeremy turned and walked toward the building. The door slammed behind him, and Malachy and Scout looked at each other.

Malachy followed, and Scout decided to leave it to him. He had to go to work in an hour, and then she and Jeremy could talk, if Jeremy wanted to. But when Malachy left, Jeremy said he was going out and didn't say where. She didn't ask.

Three hours later, the back door, now the house entrance, opened and Jeremy came in, followed by Malachy. He was in uniform, looking tense and harassed. "Don't leave," he told Jeremy. "If you leave the house again this afternoon, you'll have to go to Nome."

That sounded bad.

"What happened?" Scout asked them both.

"Tell her," Malachy snapped at Jeremy. He walked out and shut the door.

Jeremy shifted his eyes, then stalked past her without speaking.

"Jeremy?"

He slammed his door in her face.

Scout knocked.

One of her clients had once summed up children in the following way: *Girls lie; boys know they can get away with telling the truth.*

To their mothers.

"Jeremy, I'm not mad at you, but I just want to know what's going on. Will you please come out?"

Silence.

She waited.

"Jeremy?"

The door opened. "I lifted a DVD from the hardware store."

"And got caught?"

"Obviously."

"You're mad about the dogs," she said.

"Not anymore."

He'd gotten back at Malachy—or channeled his own anger into the act of shoplifting.

"Are they going to press charges?"

Jeremy shook his head. "It's my mom's brother-in-law. He's not going to do anything to me."

"Where's your mom now?" Scout asked him. "In Anchorage?"

"Turning tricks." His mouth formed an ugly, yet oddly shaky, line.

So he said this, although the reason for knifing another boy had been that boy's saying the same thing. But it was different for Jeremy to say it; Scout knew that. Still, she asked, "Didn't you stick Rayburn because he said she did that?"

"No." Jeremy gave her a look of disgust. "He said she did *him*."

As far as Scout knew, she was the first person to hear this version of events. She could appreciate the difference in accusations. She hoped her reaction to what Rayburn had supposedly said showed on her face. She wanted Jeremy to see a certain commiseration there, a sympathy for his feelings on hearing such a thing—but not for his action in attacking another boy.

Jeremy's eyes, that pale gray, avoided hers.

"I know Malachy told you to stay home," she said. "But I think he meant you to stay *with* someone. I want to run over to his house and look at one of the dogs he thought I could run with mine—I'm trying to get more consistency in the team. They seem to fall apart at speed." Part of this was invention. "Besides, I'd like to see how the remodeling's going. Want to come?"

Estelle bounced down the stairs and walked over to Scout's feet, then came forward to sniff Jeremy. She and Pigpen both liked Jeremy, the adolescent boy smell of him and a room that reeked of dirty socks.

He petted her head, and Scout reminded herself that even vicious serial killers could show affection for pets. If only she and Malachy knew what went on inside Jeremy. But they didn't.

John MacCullagh, however, seemed to have some insight. Or so Scout believed.

"I'll come," Jeremy said.

"Let's take these guys and Trooper. Is he outside?"

"Yeah." Jeremy looked unhappy again, perhaps at this reminder of the argument that had preceded his shoplifting.

Scout drove Malachy's truck with the dogs in their boxes.

"I think John misses you," she said. "From what he's said—" admittedly, to Malachy, not to her "—I think he liked having you around."

"I can't wait to move back there. I hate being downtown."

"Malachy said the room's almost ready."

They found John working on his Web site, adding photos of new native carvings for sale. He was helping some local Athabascans on this project.

He stood up and hugged Scout and smiled warmly at Jeremy. "I was wondering when I'd see you again."

"I just came to look at dogs. I can find my way."

"Have a peek down the hall," John encouraged her. "We're waiting for the floor to harden. Here." He handed Jeremy his digital camera. "I have two more pieces to photograph. If one of us holds the light, we should be able to get better shots."

Scout had another client at four, and she left Jeremy at the house with John, explaining that he couldn't be alone because of the shoplifting.

"Fine," John told her. His eyes showed understanding of what she'd done in bringing Jeremy to him. "We've got plenty to do here. Actually, five dogs need their nails cut."

Scout groaned at the thought of that chore.

Impulsively, she hugged both Jeremy and John before she left.

CHAPTER ELEVEN

THE NEXT WEEK, the master bedroom was finished, complete with a bathroom that Scout found luxurious. *You've had enough of roughing it in Alaska,* Malachy told her, grinning as he saw her salivate over the huge Victorian-style tub with sloping sides and the ceramic-tiled shower. *I want to keep you happy.*

She was—as long as she didn't think about Danny, still living on her parents' land.

Scout had been asking Holden to visit for weeks. He, in reply, had asked her to come home again. But she couldn't, not while Danny was there, apparently spending a great deal of time with her father. *His new best friend,* Holden said with disgust in his voice.

It was September they'd moved to Malachy's house, and Jeremy had begun his first week at the McGrath school, expressing boredom and disinterest in his classmates, when Holden finally flew into town. Scout had talked to Mary as soon as she knew her brother was definitely coming and had proposed that Mary choose a dog Scout could suggest as a good addition to Holden's and her father's kennel. This would be an excuse for introducing her brother and Mary. Mary agreed, saying she already had the right dog in mind, a very strong bitch with more staying power than speed.

Between clients, Scout watched for the plane from the apartment window. She heard it in the late afternoon when she was feeding the dogs. She finished hurriedly, grabbed her bicycle, and rode to the airfield.

When the plane landed, the first person out was her father, followed by Danny.

She tensed, her nerves and tendons, everything, strung suddenly tight.

Couldn't her father get the picture?

"Hi, Scout."

Danny. Danny joining her as though they were friends.

"Scout, I just want to tell you I'm sorry. I *have* changed. I had no idea how wonderful your family is."

The false Irish lilt remained in his voice. He'd done it for so long, maybe it had become permanent.

Scout climbed on her bicycle and rode thirty yards away from him. She stopped again and, leaning on her handlebars, took her cell phone from her pocket. She called Malachy.

"Holden just got here, and my father and Danny are with him. I'm going to try and get a restraining order against Danny. I'm not sure I can. The only grounds at this point would be stalking. I've clearly told him to leave me alone, and he's ignoring that."

"Since he's with your parents and living on their land— I don't know. I'm sure you can get a temporary order, but if he decides to fight a permanent order you might have trouble. I'll come on over and have a word with him, too. Do you know where to go for the paperwork?"

"I'll get it online."

"Have you had a restraining order against him before?"

"No, but I thought I might need one so I found out how to do it."

"Did you save that phone message from him, the first time he contacted you?"

"Yes." She'd saved it precisely for this reason.

He's trying to get to me. He enjoys this.

She knew Danny Kilbourne. Others might think him harmless—after all, had his bigamy really hurt anyone?—but Malachy, being in law enforcement, saw the larger picture, saw Danny as a predator who was deliberately causing her psychological pain.

Scout's father only glanced at her before joining Danny.

He's taking his side, she thought.

Did her father think she didn't need her family's love, their loyalty? Did Frank think that Danny needed the Berensens more than she did?

True, Danny had no family of his own—or so he claimed. From the private investigator, she'd learned that he was born in Virginia. But she wasn't curious, couldn't afford to be. Curiosity about someone like that could be dangerous.

MALACHY CALLED AARON and asked the constable to meet him at the airfield.

Danny seemed to be expecting them.

"I just wanted to talk to her, that's all. I thought there was freedom of speech in this country."

"She's asked you not to approach her," Malachy said. "You then contacted her family and have persuaded them to let you live on their land. Now, you've approached her again."

"And I saw it." Holden had come to stand beside them.

Frank Berensen pushed out his chest and said, "I own that plane, and I can choose who rides in it."

Malachy ignored him. "I'm going to write up a report on this, Mr. Kilbourne."

"*Mister* Kilbourne?" Danny said incredulously.

It struck Malachy that he used to see Danny as Scout once had. Engaging. Charming. Danny had intrigued Malachy with his tales of Ireland. Malachy knew he'd at least *been* there. But it hadn't occurred to him, back then, that someone would simply create a false identity for himself.

He thought of John, who'd paid such a high price for admitting to be his father, for asking the Church for dispensation so he could marry. His father had chosen *not* to pretend and had paid a penalty, giving up the work he loved, a price known each day by Malachy, part of the price of his own existence.

But Danny Kilbourne had made up a whole character for himself. Malachy no longer wondered why, because he couldn't understand it. He better understood Jeremy's knifing a peer who'd said Jeremy's mother had turned a trick for him. That at least made a kind of sense. But Danny seemed to need deceit.

He also needed, Malachy believed now, to shift blame, to make others pay; he needed vengeance. Ingratiating himself with Scout's family might yield him financial rewards, but Malachy suspected that what he really wanted was to triumph over a woman who'd dared to tell the truth about him.

A restraining order would take care of some of that problem, but the wedge Danny was driving between Scout and her father could have lasting repercussions. How could a parent be so cruel? Frank Berensen seemed to think he was behaving with charity and compassion. In fact, he was pushing away his daughter with both hands, saying without words that he trusted Danny more than he trusted her. That he *liked* Danny more than he liked her.

Now she stood apart from them all, leaning on the handlebars of her bicycle. Malachy took her a clipboard and pen so she could fill out a statement.

He said, "Hang in there."

"You know, my father never really *approved* of me, but I always felt he loved me. Why is he doing this?"

"I don't get it, either," Malachy answered. "By the way, I ran Mr. Kilbourne, and someone else has a restraining order against him. No one I'd heard of. Looks like she lives in California. Santa Cruz."

"I'm not surprised."

She took pen and paper to write down what had happened, reiterating what she'd told Danny when he'd come to her back door that night months before. "I wanted Holden to meet Mary." She hadn't told Malachy this before and wasn't sure how he'd feel about it.

He raised his eyebrows, showing interest in the idea.

Holden walked over to them and handed Malachy the statement he'd just written. Danny and Frank were striding toward town together.

"What are they up to, I wonder," Scout murmured.

"Nothing good. Danny's looking for a place to deal furs from." Holden scowled.

"In McGrath?"

"It's not even a good front," Holden agreed. "He says he's planning to start a mail-order business on the Internet."

"Tell me Dad's not helping him financially."

"The details are sketchy. Dad wasn't willing to say what's going on."

"This, McGrath doesn't need." Malachy gazed after the two men.

Scout suppressed a shudder. She couldn't live in the same town as Danny, not in a place this small. It was too much to ask. But she'd set up a Harmony office here. She had clients.

She had a fiancé with whom she was living.

And the shared responsibility for a teenager she truly liked.

But if Danny really planned to live in McGrath, could she possibly stay?

I can't let him drive me away. That's letting him win again.

"I'm getting real tempted," Holden said, "to take him on a hunting trip and lose him."

Her brother wouldn't do this. Nonetheless, Scout had reached the point where she'd feel nothing if Danny Kilbourne died. She wouldn't miss him or feel that his absence was a loss.

It was a sad way to think about someone with whom you'd lived as a spouse for five years.

Malachy said goodbye and returned to his vehicle, where the constable waited. Before he drove off, Scout rode her bicycle over to give him a quick kiss. Then she and Holden started into town, to the apartment above the Harmony Agency office. She planned to let him stay there, if he liked, while he was in McGrath, or else he could come out to Malachy's house.

"What does Mom think about Danny?" Scout asked as they walked.

"Oh, you know. She supports Dad. Even if she doesn't agree, they usually present a united front."

"*Does* she agree?"

"She was upset when you left. They argued about it."

Scout prayed that Danny Kilbourne wouldn't settle in McGrath. Or remain at her parents' place, for that matter. Or even stay in Alaska…

They met Jeremy after school and went back to the house together, and that evening Scout drove her brother to Mary's to look at the bitch Mary wanted to sell.

Quiet settled over Holden as they rode together in the car.

Of course, Scout reasoned, he'd be shy when he first met Mary.

But if they could talk about dogs… Surely Holden could talk sled dogs with anyone.

As Scout and Holden climbed out of Malachy's truck, Mary glanced at them with as much interest as she'd given Malachy's arrival when Scout had first showed up with him. Eyes fastened on one of her dogs, going over to check a paw, she seemed almost oblivious to the newcomers who'd set every canine in her yard singing.

"Hey, Mary," Scout said. "This is my brother, Holden."

Holden had flushed already.

Mary held out her hand in a businesslike way, trying to meet eyes that wouldn't meet hers.

Holden made a sound that was supposed to pass for greeting and dropped her hand swiftly.

With an enigmatic glance at Scout, Mary said, "Let's look at this bitch, then."

No attempt to ask Holden about himself. Well, Scout had told Mary that her brother was shy. Maybe Mary was taking her cues from him. In any event, she'd done the only thing that could've put Holden at ease—immediately fixed her attention on something outside him.

This might work.

Scout thought with a certain wistfulness of times and cultures in which *matchmaker* was a viable career. It would be easier than what she did now. After all, in those times and places, divorce was virtually unheard of. Once a match was made, dowry exchanged, troths pledged, all of that—well, the unravelings were probably rare.

She'd taught herself not to worry about her clients, but she also found herself rooting for some of them. Martin the mosquito man, for instance, was immensely likable. And, although Andy Case wasn't a client, when she'd last seen him, he'd told her he was going to Florida in February. Scout doubted he planned to go just for a bit of sun. She didn't necessarily care whether her clients ended up single, dating or married; she wanted them to find happiness, to feel content with themselves.

But in Holden, she had more invested. And Mary's accusations about Scout's ending up with Malachy had made her nearly as interested in finding Mary someone nice.

As far as Scout was concerned, men didn't come nicer than her twin.

What if Mary treats him like she did Malachy?

But oddly enough, Holden would probably *expect* to take a back seat to the sled dogs. He might even treat Mary in kind.

The bitch was smaller than most of Mary's dogs.

"I've run her in lead," Mary said, not even looking at Holden when she spoke but frowning in concentration at the dog. "I used to do a regular eighty-mile run with her as leader. She's just…"

Scout saw Holden actually look at Mary, who stayed focused on the black-and-white bitch.

"Truthfully, she's not that interested in speed. She's not scrappy. My best lead bitch will get your hands, but Newer here is real calm."

"Newer?"

He speaks, Scout thought. *Hallelujah!*

"Yeah. I had one called New, and then I got her, and she was Newer." Mary shrugged, glancing at Holden.

He turned scarlet and stared at Newer.

Mary averted her gaze from him, as though embarrassed by his embarrassment or perhaps mirroring his feelings. "I'm going to have puppies on the ground in a couple of days, but it'll be awhile before I can pick who I want. With a few exceptions, though, I'm generally open to hearing offers on any of my dogs. So if one catches your eye, let me know. How long is your trapline?"

Scout trailed after them, certain that Holden wouldn't be able to answer.

Her prediction came to pass. Her brother muttered something inarticulate while looking toward the road.

Scout was torn between irritation that Holden couldn't hold up his end of the conversation and a renewed anger at the way her parents had raised him, at how they'd fallen short in failing to make sure he developed social skills. Pity took over. "The kennel's also big business," she told Mary, as though Holden's reply had been coherent and she was just adding to it. "Well, not big business, but they do sell a fair number of dogs. They should have a Web site, but my father eschews technology."

"That's my favorite thing about Alaskans, some of them," Mary said. "I mean, sometimes I think of not even having a phone. I'd like to live farther out, farther away from everything."

That must be an arrow straight to Holden's heart, Scout thought, stealing a glance at her brother. He didn't turn his head at Mary's remark, yet Scout was sure she read *something* in his almost immobile expression.

It stirred a feeling that nagged at her from time to time.

Malachy had paid her the highest compliment, asking her to be his wife. She knew, as well, that he considered her his best friend.

But he'd never said he loved her.

It wasn't his way. No more complicated explanation than that. He just wasn't a man who said *I love you.*

He'd certainly never said to Scout that he loved Mary Clarke, only that he'd wanted to marry her. *Now he wants to marry me.*

And we're engaged.

Whenever she needed to remind herself of that, she only had to look down at her ring.

"Do you guys want some lemonade?" Mary asked. "I'm on this kick where I'm making it with my grand-mother's *secret* recipe."

A love potion. Scout smiled with approval. "That sounds delicious."

"Thanks."

Her brother had spoken *again.*

WHEN THEY LEFT Mary's it was with the arrangement that Holden would come back by himself the following morning to see Newer, the bitch Mary wanted to sell, run with the rest of her dogs behind a four-wheeler. Scout had clients. This evening had been so easy, had gone so well, she could hardly believe it.

Holden said their father was planning to fly home that night. Either he'd return for Holden another day or Holden could fly home with someone else.

"I just hope he takes Danny with him," Scout muttered as she turned Malachy's truck into his driveway. Holden was going to stay at the house with them that night.

They found Malachy, Jeremy and John in the kitchen. Jeremy had a textbook open on the table and was doing homework, and Malachy looked as though he'd just gotten off work.

"He rented the apartment behind the general store," he told Scout.

Too much to hope that "he" was someone other than Danny Kilbourne.

She tried to appear unaffected. "Thought he was dying to show his worth in the bush during the winter."

"McGrath is the bush," John said.

It won't be so bad, Scout told herself. *I'll get a restraining order, and I won't have to deal with him. He won't be able to come near me or talk to me.*

"Where did he get money for rent?" Holden, whose shyness around John MacCullagh had evidently been trumped by the news, looked both suspicious and baffled.

Malachy shrugged, then eyed Holden. "Why?"

"Oh, he claimed he had nothing. I think that's part of why Dad took him in. Supposedly he was trying to sell—" Holden snorted, apparently barely able to finish the sentence "—bibles."

Everyone in the room gaped at him.

"That's his story," Holden explained. "He said he came up to Alaska to tell Scout how he's born-again or whatever he claims to be. He's selling Bibles to benefit some Irish missionary group. He says."

Scout blinked once. "And he's indigent?"

Holden nodded. "He says."

"Then, Dad gave him money."

"Looks like it," Holden agreed.

"I'm going to be sick."

"That's okay, Scout," Jeremy said. "You don't need them. John and Malachy will be your family."

Scout cracked a grin. "And you? What about you?"

Jeremy's cheeks grew pink. "Yeah, whatever." He turned the page of his math book.

The first few notes of Ravel's "Bolero" suddenly played in the kitchen.

Malachy picked up his cell phone from the counter, looked at the number and answered it.

Scout opened the refrigerator and consulted John with a glance. "Shall we have some of that venison?"

"I thought I'd sauté it," Malachy's father volunteered. "Look at these zucchini Martin brought by." Martin the mosquito man was a friend of Malachy's father.

Malachy had walked around the corner into the hallway, and Scout saw him leaning against the flimsy fake-wood paneling. His face had a frozen, arrested look, and he kept his eyes averted. He said something, but Scout couldn't hear what.

A moment later, he closed the phone and came back into the kitchen.

Scout wasn't sure why she'd gone cold inside.

Everything had become slow-motion, almost as though she could see every molecule in the still air.

Behind her, John filled a stainless steel pot with water.

Malachy said, "Holden…" But his eyes locked on Scout's. "Let's…go out on the deck. Scout…"

What? What? What?

Holden's chin, so strong, so handsome, seemed to be quivering when it couldn't be because Holden was un-shakable. It was her vision that had become strange.

There were Adirondack chairs on the deck. Scout sank slowly, hesitantly, onto one with stuffing coming from its faded cushion.

"Your father's plane," Malachy said, "went down."

CHAPTER TWELVE

IT WAS IMPOSSIBLE that a Berensen should crash an airplane.

And in summer.

"But he's okay." Scout heard herself.

But she'd seen Malachy's face, and Holden's face was wobbling, everything falling apart.

"He's dead, Scout."

Malachy said this, but she couldn't believe it. Her father had not spoken to her that afternoon, except for his remark that he could pick his own passengers. *That was the last time...* The last time she'd see him alive. The last time she *had* seen him.

"Where? Where is he?" She had to see him, to see *something.* He'd just been alive.

Holden said, "Mom. Does she...?"

"Yes. I'll take you," Malachy said, knowing they'd want to be with their mother. "Let's... Let's pick up what you need and get going."

Scout's cell phone—a jangling bell—rang in the kitchen. "I'll bet that's her." She tripped as she stood up, then hurt her hand opening the screen door to go inside, clumsy in her haste.

In the kitchen, Estelle jumped on her, and Scout

kneed the puppy in the chest as she spilled out her purse and answered the phone.

"Scout, it's Serge—"

"Serge, this isn't a good time. I'm sorry. Is this an emergency?"

"Well, I thought I'd like to do some process with you."

"I'll have one of my partners talk to you. Good-bye." She ended the call and pressed in her parents' number.

The line was busy. Who was her mother talking to? Why wasn't she calling her and Holden?

At least he hasn't had time to change his will in Danny's favor.

This reaction was so irrational, so unlike her. She didn't care about an inheritance. She was just worried for her mother, knowing her mother couldn't manage that place without her father.

I can't manage. He died not loving me.

Strange that until she'd learned he was dead she would've claimed he *had* loved her.

He did. He just thought I was challenging his authority.

"What's happened, Scout?"

She looked at John, and Jeremy was there, too. Did Jeremy care about her father at all? "My father's plane… He's dead."

It wasn't real. Everything looked so strange, too bright and too sharp. Why didn't she feel? She pressed redial.

Her parents' phone rang.

"Hello?"

"Mom, it's Scout. Malachy's bringing us home."

"I can't believe it. It happened on the other side of the river. I saw it go down. I couldn't believe what I was

seeing. I thought Holden… I didn't know… Hal's here."
Their nearest neighbor.

"Hang on. We'll get there soon—"

"Tell Malachy to be careful."

"Yes."

SHE HADN'T EVEN gone inside the kitchen on her last visit to the family home. Danny had come up from the river, and she'd walked back to the plane. This was what she thought of as she made her way across the muddy ground toward the fragile-looking woman at the edge of the family airstrip. Danny Kilbourne was a monster.

Her mother had seen her father's plane fall from the air. It was mostly in one piece, nosed into the bank.

Malachy had sought more details as they drove to the McGrath airfield, but there'd been no warning, no sign that the plane was in trouble.

"I wonder if he had… But he was the last person to have a heart attack!" Scout said to Holden.

Her twin nodded.

But it had to be something like that. Her father was a seasoned pilot. Even in the event of mechanical failure, there was a good chance he could've brought the plane down safely.

Troopers were walking the area across the river, near the plane.

"They won't let me go over there," Dora said.

"I should think not," Malachy murmured.

Holden embraced his mother, and Scout hugged them both. "I'm sorry about the way I left the other day, Mom."

"Let's not talk about that. It doesn't matter. It didn't matter."

But it *did*.

I had no time to talk to him.

Because he'd talked to Danny instead. Because he'd believed, trusted and forgiven Danny, although her father hadn't been the injured party.

Even if she could forgive Danny his bigamy, his abuse, his lies, he had finally come between her and her father. For that, she would never forgive him.

And she'd never forgive herself—for letting it happen, for letting her own relationship with her father deteriorate to the point that it could happen and *had* happened.

Scout picked the first chore she could find indoors. Pulling laundry off the line to fold. The dogs would need to be fed, too, but Holden was here.

Her father never would be again.

The house had changed so little since the last time she'd been inside, years before. The skeins of yarn spun from dog hair hung from pegs along the rafters; they might've been the same yarn she'd produced as a teenager. The house retained its earthy scent. The walls smelled the same, vaguely burnt, vaguely damp. And there was the hidden smell of blood, of skins, of fish, of greens and berries, of gone summer and presaged winter.

Dad never wanted to add anything, never wanted to modernize, never wanted to make life easier.

Now what would her mother do? Stay here alone with Holden?

Dora seemed diminished, shrunken. Yet she also seemed more important, more noticeable, than she ever had before. And she was not falling apart. Scout didn't want to see her cry for Frank Berensen, but knew she would see it, would hear it, and it would be something she couldn't deal with. She, who'd gone away from the place of her birth.

I can't stay here. I can't stay here to take care of her, because I hate it up here. I always have.

Yet the cast-iron excuse she would've given for returning to McGrath immediately was now out of the question. When she'd called the home office to say that her father had died, Victoria herself had said she'd come to McGrath.

Scout, Dana and Victoria were equal partners in the business; that was true. But Scout and Dana had admitted to each other more than once that Victoria was always, in some sense, *in charge.* They had explained this to each other with justifications ranging from *Well, she's married* to *She can be such a bitch.* In any event, it was Victoria, fresh-faced and beautiful, somehow the essence of Eternal Bride with her excruciatingly large diamond and matching wedding ring, who would be coming to McGrath.

Friends were friends. Yes, Scout was going to need some help up here because her father had died; she'd need someone to cover for her at the office. But the reasons for Victoria's visit to McGrath must have more to do with Malachy and Jeremy than wanting to see the place for herself.

There was a relief in Victoria's coming. Yes, it wasn't Dana, Dana with her extreme fashion sense—*Could we tone it down a little?* Victoria would say about certain outfits—Dana who could make Scout laugh and who herself laughed easily and often. Victoria was sober, thoughtful and yet comforting. Sometimes Scout had the feeling that nothing could actually go wrong on Victoria's watch.

Scout was so keen for Victoria to have the unforget-table experience of dealing with Serge that she consi-dered giving him a gift certificate for a free session when her partner came.

Also, there was the fact that in coming to Alaska Victoria was doing something terribly brave. Victoria was a City Girl who'd never been camping and had no desire to go. She lived, with her husband, in a luxuri-ous condo. Her only pet was a declawed Persian cat named Pillbox. No doubt the shower at the apartment, which was framed in wood and whose taps had to be handled in a very particular order, would present her with quite a challenge.

Yet she'd agreed to come.

And Scout missed her and would be glad to see her. The thought of being with a girlfriend filled her with nostal-gia for the days when she could just meet Dana or Victoria for a drink or at the gym. McGrath was so far away from the circle of people who'd been her strength after Danny.

But would there ever be a true *After Danny?* Would he leave her alone now?

Malachy and Holden came into the house, and Holden brought Estelle. It had been his idea to bring the puppy with them, which had surprised Scout. To her knowledge, no sled dog had ever been inside this house.

"She's Scout's lead dog, Ma," he said, deadpan. Estelle wasn't his idea of a sled dog of any variety, but he'd warmed up to her. Scout had twice caught him calling her *Goofy Girl.*

Scout saw her mother's eyes, red-rimmed with unshed tears or perhaps because of tears that had fallen before the arrival of her children, fall upon the white dog.

"She's a little sweetie," Dora exclaimed, reaching almost tentatively for silky ears.

It occurred to Scout for the first time that she wasn't sure, beneath it all, who her mother really was. Hadn't Frank Berensen's personality demanded that everyone around him adhere to certain rules?

Her mother loved him, yes, had been his wife, partner, the mother of his children, but who was she without him? Who could she become? Who had she always been inside?

"Your father would…" Dora's voice trailed off.

Grab Estelle by the scruff of the neck and throw her outside?

Estelle's tail wagged back and forth, smacking chair legs, her rear end bouncing against Malachy's shins.

Scout admitted, "We haven't spent a night apart since I got her."

"Like a baby," Dora said with no derision but only kindness in her voice.

Yet Scout realized the words held more when her mother stole a look at her daughter's fiancé.

A wish for something so normal, so regular, as grand-children? Yes.

Holden went out to feed the dogs, perhaps to run them. Malachy, Scout and Dora sat at the kitchen table. Hal, the nearest neighbor, who was seventy-five, popped in and out with news and lack of news from across the river.

"It'll take time," Malachy said, "until they know what happened." By virtue of his status as a state trooper, he had faster access to information, but he was no more welcome at the search across the river than were Scout and her mother.

"He would've liked to see you married," Dora said sadly.

"He *what?*" Scout's mouth engaged before her brain, something she'd spent most of her adult life training it not to do. When no one else spoke, she made her voice soft, confused rather than incredulous. "He wanted me back with Danny. He liked Danny. My last sight of—"

She had to stop this, stop blurting out things that would hurt her mother.

"Mine, too," Dora said.

They'd both last seen Frank side-by-side with the man who'd pretended to marry Scout.

"He was angry," Malachy said abruptly, "because you'd been away so long and wouldn't come home to visit."

Scout turned to face him. "Did he tell you that?"

"That isn't it," Dora interjected. "He wasn't sure whether Scout's story was the whole story because he couldn't understand her never telling us any of this before Danny showed up."

"I did exactly what he would've done!" Scout realized this only as she spoke. If someone had made a fool of her father, he would've revealed the fact to as few people as possible and never to those whose esteem he most needed—his family's.

Dora nodded. "I told him that, Scout."

Nobody asked if Danny knew Frank Berensen was dead. It was as though this final catastrophe had done what had been impossible while Scout's father was alive. It had completely uncloaked Danny in the way that what was real—in this case, love and death—could brightly illuminate what was false.

In any event, Dora seemed disinclined to waste her breath defending him.

Scout's eyes flooded. She would never speak to her father again, never again experience the rare, soaring feeling when he actually did approve of something she'd done. Moments of praise were infrequent, yet even the stingiest was as valuable as precious gems.

Her mother moved her chair, and they sat together crying.

"I want to see him," Dora said. "They really must let me see him."

"Yes," Scout agreed.

But all knew and none needed to say that there was no telling what remained of Frank Berensen's body.

THEY VIEWED HIM in Anchorage and were allowed to see only a separated circle of restored face, the rest of him draped. The result looked nothing like him in life and yet the features were clearly those that had once belonged to him.

Afterward, Scout, Holden and their mother went to a Starbucks where Scout wondered how much of the shell-shocked expressions of her family came simply from the overwhelming shock of being in a city. No one had asked whether Dora would want to remain in the bush without her husband. She could, if she wanted, sell the property, including the kennels and the trapline.

Only that morning, when Scout had stepped outside to find her brother splitting wood with an ax, she'd been unable to resist blurting out, "Can you say hydraulic log-splitter?"

Some people, Holden had replied good-naturedly, *prefer to do things the hard way.*

The answer had made her smile. He'd admitted to splitting logs the hard way. And said that he preferred it.

Why, she still wondered, had she never been able to accept that her father was like that, too?

Because he wasn't. He was never able to laugh at himself—or at the idea of someone who *enjoyed* doing things the hard way. It was all deadly serious with him, all an expression of being close to the earth and close to an older way of doing things, even if that way had little to do with his own heritage.

Sipping a latte—which she'd accepted at Scout's suggestion—Dora finally said, "I suppose someone's told Danny."

"Well—let's say I'm sure he knows by now," Scout replied, determined not to get angry over this. Her mother didn't deserve her anger.

Holden asked, "Mom, are you going to give him money?"

Dora said, "No. I can't afford to."

Their father's death would make finances tighter for their mother.

"I hate him." The words escaped Scout.

"Well, you shouldn't. It's bad for you, Scout, to feel like that about him. Just let the past go," her mother said.

"I was able to do that when the past was the past, but unfortunately he's been attacking me in the present."

"I don't see how you can think that," Dora exclaimed softly.

Had Frank Berensen's spirit returned to take possession of his wife's body? *Keep your temper, Scout.* "By trying," she said carefully, "to make my family love him more than they love me."

"That's ridiculous," Dora told her. "We could never do that. Never."

Did her words soothe? Scout wasn't sure. But if she clung to the topic and fought with her mother now, then Danny would truly have won. Yet hatred simmered within her, blackening her spirit, dragging at her like disease.

Couldn't she convince even her mother that Danny was a predator and a liar?

Scout forced herself to change the subject. "Mom, are you going to stay up there?"

"Oh, Scout, I couldn't think of moving anywhere else. That place was your father's dream, and we shared it."

The place or the dream? Was there a difference?

"I know you think you lost out on certain advantages growing up in the bush—" Dora said.

"I don't," Scout protested. "I just wasn't cut out for it. I wasn't good at it."

"You've always been too hard on yourself, Scout. I missed you when you left." She sighed. "It was important to both of us to raise our children that way. We wanted you to know where food comes from, to have the satisfaction of catching fish, hunting, dressing out your own game, not being dependent on things people in cities take for granted."

"I have no resentment whatsoever," Scout told her, "over how I was raised." Yet she knew that wasn't true. Didn't she resent that her brother was so shy? And that her father had always wanted her to be different—stronger, more self-reliant, happier without the conveniences the city offered? "I always believed Dad would love me more if I was better at the things he thought were important."

"He wanted you to *like* those things, Scout."

Scout changed the subject again. "Mom, will you be able to manage up there without Dad?"

"I'll have Holden."

Holden nodded. "That's right."

"I don't expect you to give up your life and come live somewhere you never liked, Scout," her mother continued.

There was such freedom in those words, in her mother giving her blessing for Scout to have her own likes and dislikes. Dora did not expect her daughter to sacrifice everything to come home.

"McGrath's not far away. I'll be able to visit more often."

If only Danny would leave. Leave McGrath. Leave her and her family alone. Scout reflected on the lengths she'd gone to, past and present, to avoid her ex-husband. "I have to go home and see Victoria," she said.

"You told us that," her mother answered. "How soon do you need to be there?"

"Well, Malachy promised to meet her plane and show her the office and the apartment. She knows what I'm doing, so there's no real schedule. Do you like your latte?"

"Very good. It seems more bitter than regular coffee, but I like the milk with it." Dora frowned. "I want to see Jeremy. How is he?"

"He enjoys being with Malachy's father."

"You know," Scout's mother said, "I think what he did—the fight with that boy—haunts him more than he

shows. He seems convinced that he's bad and doomed
to remain so."

Scout wasn't sure what Jeremy believed about his
part in that incident. He'd never said he regretted it.
Even during the counseling sessions they'd attended
together, he'd said nothing about it. "Was there a particular thing he did or said that made you think that?"

"Actually…I don't know. We were talking at the
dinner table about a woman across the river whose child
was stillborn. We talked about parents suffering the loss
of children. He got up and went outside and didn't communicate again before bedtime. Did he, Holden?"

"No. But he could've been thinking about himself,
about his mom not being around for him."

The conversation wound back to Frank, to reminis-
cence, to what sort of memorial service they should have.

"People up and down the river will want to come,"
Dora said.

Scout's cell phone rang. "Hello?"

"Scout, it's Danny. I heard about—"

Scout hung up.

"Who was it?" Dora asked.

"Wrong number." And more evidence for a restraining order.

"I'M GOING BACK tomorrow," Scout told Victoria. "She'll
need help getting ready for the service, for visitors. And
I think she needs both Holden and me."

Gazing thoughtfully at Scout, Victoria nodded.
She looked out of place in the setting of the McGrath
office. Pink cashmere sweater, black canvas pants and
blocky high-heeled boots were her concession to the

environment, yet her makeup remained flawless over her unmarked, pink-cheeked complexion, and her light brown hair held its long pageboy.

She and Scout were curled up on the office sofas to visit, and Scout had caught her up on everything in McGrath and listened to her news about the southern California Harmony office and about her husband, whom Scout and Dana sometimes called The Perfect Man.

Aaron, the constable, had notified Scout that an Anchorage judge had approved her restraining order, and Scout had picked up the document.

"If he has even a dime," Scout said, "he'll get an attorney and fight it. That's how he is. He'll behave as though I'm smearing him somehow."

"What's he doing up here?" Victoria squinted around the office, but her look seemed to take in McGrath and all of Alaska. "There's nothing for him here, and he can't seriously hope to renew his relationship with you. He must know how you feel. It's not like you've ever sent him mixed messages."

"He just can't bear to see me happy. I don't want to think about him, but Victoria, I'm not sure I can stay in McGrath if he's here."

"Your fiancé is here, Scout. You're not going to break your engagement because Danny Kilbourne's following you around, are you? That *will* be letting him win."

"Of course I'm not going to break my engagement because of him! But I can't go on living here if he is, too. He's done too much damage. I'm not wallowing in what he did, but I don't want to be reminded of it, either."

"Let the elements take care of him," Victoria suggested.

"What?"

"He's a southern California boy, when all is said and done. He's not going to last more than one winter here."

Scout considered that. "It'll be a long winter," she predicted.

WHILE SCOUT HELPED her mother up at her parents' home, Malachy stayed with his father and Jeremy. He saw how accustomed he'd become to living with Scout, to sleeping with her each night, to telling her what had happened at work. He'd never before lived with a woman day in and day out. Now he missed it.

Victoria had offered to see Jeremy for counseling; like Scout, she was a licensed family/marriage therapist. Jeremy said he didn't need to talk to anyone. In fact, Malachy knew Jeremy talked to his father. John kept his secrets.

To Malachy's shock and alarm, he learned that Danny had been hired as a tutor at the high school. Malachy went to the principal and revealed what he knew of Scout's ex-partner, but the principal shrugged it off, although she said she'd double-check his credentials. All that was required for the position was a bachelor's degree, and Danny's—apparently earned in the last few years from a California state college—was in English.

He told Scout about it over the phone.

She said, "I'm appalled. Didn't she hear you?" The principal.

"I think she found herself in a difficult situation, having already hired him. She'd checked his references. Apparently, he pulled off something similar here to what he was doing when you and I met him."

Silence. He knew Scout's stomach must be falling hard and fast.

"I can't wait to see you," he said.

"Really?" She sounded interested and vaguely disbelieving.

"Really." The memorial service would be the next day. Frank Berensen's body had been cremated, and the family planned to scatter his ashes in the river that bordered his land.

"A bear's been getting at the fish racks," she said. "Mom and Holden are listening for him. When he shows up again, Holden's going to shoot him."

Her voice was strange, resigned and quiet.

"Do you hate it that much?"

"Yes," she said, then hesitated. "How did you and your father live—when you were growing up?"

"He taught school. He didn't hunt, but I did. And we both ate the game. We didn't live like you did, Scout, but it was pretty primitive up there on the coast. It still is."

"I don't suppose you'd ever consider moving away from here. From Alaska."

"What gives you that idea?"

More silence. "You're kidding."

"No, I'm not. I don't want to pack up and go right now. I have a house, and I have other property. McGrath is my home, but that doesn't mean I'd never live Outside."

Far away, in the kitchen of the house where she'd grown up, Scout realized how many assumptions she'd made. Her fear of being imprisoned in her place of birth was a chimera. Malachy had no extreme attachment to Alaska.

"Thanks," she said.

"There's nothing to thank me for."

Malachy, do you love me?

He did, at least as a friend to whom he was sufficiently attracted that they could be lovers. And, in her heart, Scout believed that would make for a very solid marriage. During the time she'd been in McGrath, the two of them had become closer friends than ever before. He had understood immediately about Danny. He understood what she hated about how she'd been raised, the aspects of Alaska she had no desire to relive.

She said, "Do you want to think about setting a date? You know, for our wedding?" They'd discussed it before her father's death. But the plane crash had overshadowed all thoughts of their wedding.

"Yes. Do you have many friends you want to invite from Outside?"

"Well, Dana and Victoria and Victoria's husband. There are a few others, too. Some of the Harmony counselors. Some friends from California. But it's an expensive trip. I don't know if they'll come."

"What season?"

She didn't want to wait another year. "How about Christmas?"

"Works for me. But the travel will be harder—and more expensive—for your friends. And they might not want to leave their homes during the holidays."

"I'll talk to Dana and Victoria. If they can come… That would be plenty," she said. "A big wedding doesn't matter. I just want a dress. I wish your father could marry us."

"He probably does, too, Scout."

THEY STOOD on the banks of the river, bundled in wool and fleece clothing, shivering in the autumn morning.

Jeremy and John MacCullagh had both come, and even Victoria had dared the bush plane to stand beside Scout.

Dora had decided that words would not be meaningful, so the entire service consisted of the scattering of the ashes. Afterward, everyone went inside the house Frank Berensen had built. They ate food gathered, grown, hunted or caught through methods he'd learned when he came to Alaska from a Kentucky coal town decades earlier.

Victoria followed Scout outside to see the working dogs that had so prejudiced Scout against Alaskan dogs for years.

"I knew the way you grew up was rustic," Victoria admitted. "But it's quite different seeing it, different from what I'd pictured. I mean—I can smell blood around here."

"Yes."

"I'm sorry about your father, Scout."

Scout squeezed her friend's arm in acknowledgement of her sympathy. "The hardest part is that he died liking Danny. He died because he'd flown Danny to McGrath. There was no reason for him to come, and he and I—" Scout shook her head. "We didn't even speak. I let Danny come between us."

"You followed precepts that were right for you."

"But I knew my dad wouldn't be pushed around and that he'd perceive my 'precepts' as an attempt to dictate what he did. Danny used to say I don't understand men, that I break them because I don't understand them."

"Consider the source."

Malachy came around the side of the kennels. Scout waved, and he joined them.

"What's Jeremy up to?" Scout asked.

"Your brother's trying to teach him to spin. I think your father tried to teach him, but Jeremy resisted. Personality differences."

"That I can believe."

Scout flew back to McGrath with the others that night, and she and Victoria spent several hours reviewing Victoria's work with their clients.

"What's with this Serge character?" Victoria asked. "He told me you'd arranged a discount for him?"

"That's not true!" She'd never even given him the gift certificate she'd considered in jest.

"Well, bill him for an hour, then. I said I'd let you bill him. What a piece of work."

It was most unlike Victoria to express anything so negative about a Harmony client. Of course, Scout could remember no other Harmony client lying about the rate he was being charged—at least not to his counselor.

"Martin seems very nice. He's decided that rather than settle on the one woman who came up to see him, he's going to try corresponding with some other women, too." She paused. "So, Scout, since I've been here, I've been thinking."

That had the sound of a thought not yet voiced.

"We need to open an Anchorage office. I know you'll want to keep your clients here in McGrath, especially those who have contracts, but could I ask you to start working on something in Anchorage, including recruiting counselors?"

"I can do it, but you and Dana and I have always made personnel decisions together."

"I know. It's just that Alaska's so far away, and I think we're going to have more success keeping our employees if we recruit from people who already live here and know what it's like. I didn't feel that way until I started meeting your male clients in particular and realized how many of their problems with meeting women were truly geographic—Serge excluded."

"They are a nice bunch, aren't they?" Scout said. She'd had nothing to do with the caliber of McGrath men coming to the Harmony Agency, yet she felt proud of her clients. Those who'd signed up for relationship counseling had seemed surprisingly comfortable with receiving guidance.

"Now, some new people came in yesterday," Victoria said, "and they came for counseling in an existing relationship. They wanted an emergency session, so I agreed to do what I could, but I said you'd have to decide if you were willing to see them for ongoing therapy. *He* is apparently paying and seems to have ulterior reasons for going to counseling. I didn't get the whole picture. I got the feeling that she couldn't afford it and was willing to go along with it only because he insisted."

"Who are they?"

"Jackie Crestone and Mark Hopkins?"

Scout's heart thudded. "I don't think I *can* see them, Victoria. Jackie Crestone is Jeremy's mother. But I have to admit I'm curious." She knew that, as she wasn't planning to see the couple, Victoria would reveal no more about their meeting. "I hadn't heard she was in town," she added. "That's bound to make a difference in Jeremy's life, though for better or worse, I can't say. She didn't know that Malachy and I are engaged?"

"If she did, she didn't mention it." Victoria's expression had grown a bit grim.

Scout longed to grill her partner, to ask a million

questions. *What was she like? What did she look like?*
Was she drunk? On drugs? Who's the guy?

Then there were the questions to which Victoria
could not possibly know the answer: What impact
would the return of Jeremy's mother have on Jeremy?
Would he be glad to see her? Why was she back in
town? Was she still working as a prostitute?

Even if the changes in her were good, it would still
be stressful for Jeremy.

And Scout's experience with people, both clinically
and personally, told her that it was highly unlikely
they'd find Jackie Crestone clean and out of "the life."
I'm afraid for Jeremy. Surely, someone must have told
Malachy by now that Jackie was back.

I'll call him anyway.

"Victoria, you're not thinking we should close the
McGrath office?"

"Of course not. I'm happy with the response. I wish
I could have you in Anchorage, but you can't be two
places at once, and I'm not sure you'll be able to recruit
someone else to come to McGrath. In any case, new
counselors need initial training and supervision."

"Are you saying you really want to leave the hiring
up here to me?"

"Don't you *want* to do it?"

"No," Scout admitted. "Not alone. We've never done
things that way. Anyhow, who'll train and supervise
new counselors in Anchorage? As you said, I can't be
in two places—"

Victoria nodded. "I suppose you're right. Well,
then either Dana or I will fly up to help with the hiring
and training."

"I'm so glad you're here now." Scout hugged her friend impulsively.

"It's been traumatic, hasn't it? Even without what happened to your dad. I'd like to meet Mary Clarke, by the way. Any chance of that?"

"Sure. Why? Want an autograph?" Scout teased.

"No, I'm just professionally interested in the kind of woman a man can be so sure he wants to marry, then change his mind about. Unless you two don't get along."

"No. Listen to this." Scout told Victoria about introducing Holden to Mary. "And they actually managed to *talk* to each other. Usually the other person talks and Holden says nothing."

"I noticed," Victoria agreed. "I think in the two times I've met Holden, he's said a total of two things. Maybe."

Scout picked up the phone and dialed Mary Clarke's number. She answered on the third ring, and Scout told her, fairly candidly, that Victoria wanted to meet her.

"Sure," Mary said. "I'm game. Hey, I'm sorry about your dad. I wanted to call and talk to Holden, too, but I didn't know how to reach you up there."

"Thanks. Let me give you the number. I'm back in McGrath, but I'm sure my brother would love to hear from you."

They drove over to Mary's house. As Scout turned the truck into the driveway, Victoria said, "I don't get the dog thing. Living with this many. The number you have seems sufficiently crazy for one person. And I must've passed ten houses with a million dogs staked outside."

"I used to hate it," Scout said. "You saw how many dogs my dad and Holden have—Holden has. And not the world's friendliest, either. I have to admit, they've grown on me since I have my own. But when my dad was there, they weren't allowed to be *pets*. They were working dogs, and he wanted everyone to know it." She shrugged. "I shouldn't be saying this about him. He's dead. I'm sorry he's gone."

"Well, it doesn't sound as though he was an easy man. And I know his allegiance to Danny really upset you."

"I still feel enraged." And a little sick.

They climbed out, and walked over to join Mary in the yard.

Mary said, "Did you see that Jackie's back?"

"Really," Scout said, knowing that Mary would show none of the discretion Victoria had to.

"She's with Mark Hopkins." Mary made a truly disgusted face.

"Who's he?"

"Oh, he's really awful. He's a drunk, and he used to deal cocaine."

"Lovely," murmured Scout, terrified for Jeremy. But Malachy was Jeremy's legal guardian.

"Jackie's sweet and really tough. I mean, she's had some hard times. Jeremy's dad wasn't that bad, but Mark Hopkins is a creep."

Scout and Victoria nodded, Victoria's face betraying nothing.

But Mark Hopkins had wanted them to go to counseling. Why was that?

"You'll probably be seeing Mark," Mary said. "He needs court-ordered counseling."

"For what?" Scout's voice had become oddly lifeless. There was time to explain later that she wouldn't be seeing Mark for counseling because he was too closely connected to Jeremy.

"An inappropriate relationship with an underage girl."

Victoria tucked her hands in the pockets of her pink snow jacket. "How many dogs do you take when you run the Iditarod?"

Change of subject.

LEAVING VICTORIA at the apartment, Scout drove to Malachy's house, stopping on the way to pick up her mail. When she arrived at the cabin, she found Jeremy in his new room, fooling around on the Internet.

"Hey," he said when she looked in the half-open door.

Did he know that his mother was back in town? She thought not. It was Saturday, and he'd been at the memorial service the day before.

"Where is everyone?"

"They're outside, fixing kennels."

Scout went out and saw Malachy and his father affixing a new metal roof to one kennel structure.

"It looks good," she observed as she reached them.

"Thanks," Malachy murmured. He turned on a screw gun.

Scout watched them work, then stand back to admire what they'd done.

At last, she said, "Did you know Jackie's back?"

Malachy did not even move his head to look at her. "I do know."

"Does Jeremy?"

"No." He rubbed his jaw thoughtfully. "I figured I'd tell him tonight."

"Would you rather I did it?" Scout asked.

He gazed at her, clearly mulling over the suggestion. "I wonder," he said, "if Jeremy would."

JEREMY WAS LEARNING to use Adobe Photoshop by altering a digital photo he'd taken of the school principal. He was giving her facial hair and a mohawk when someone knocked on his door. He was also learning Adobe GoLive so he could make a Web site. Maybe he'd sell bumper stickers or something.

He got up, went to the door and opened it.

Scout stood there. She looked depressed, probably because her father was dead. Jeremy supposed she must've loved him even though he was a jerk to her.

Jeremy missed his father. He would always miss his father. He hoped it wouldn't be that way for Scout.

"Can I come in?"

He stepped back.

She walked into his room and said, "Your mom's back."

Was *this* why Scout looked depressed?

"Back where?"

"In McGrath. I don't know where she's living, but she's with a man called Mark Hopkins."

Jeremy detested Mark Hopkins. Jeremy wanted to be with his mom, but he couldn't be if she was drunk all the time. And he hated being around Mark Hopkins, who was sleazy. People thought prostitution was sleazy, but as far as Jeremy was concerned, Mark Hopkins defined sleazy. "Okay," he said. "Am I still going to live here?"

Scout's expression changed. She seemed surprised. "Of course."

He nodded and sat down at his desk.

She noticed *The Adobe GoLive Bible* on his desk. "Thinking of launching a Web site?"

"Sure."

"Do you have the program?"

"John gave it to me."

"Ah." Scout said. "I've had this idea the last couple of days. I'm not a Web site person myself, but I thought *someone* could create a good site about living in the bush. There are tons of people Outside who find it fascinating."

"And you think someone should do this?" he asked. "You hate the bush. Everyone knows that."

"Everyone?"

"Well, me and Malachy do."

"Malachy and I. Do you understand why?"

"Because it sucks."

"No, do you understand why you should say 'Malachy and I'?"

"So we won't have to talk about it anymore."

"Because 'Malachy and I' was the subject of the sentence."

"I think I could've gone my whole life not knowing that."

"I pick on you," she said, "because it supports the notion, for me, that I'm important in your life."

Jeremy said, "If I'm going to put together a Web site, I want to make money at it."

"You could sell advertising," Scout said. "Heck, the Harmony Agency might even buy advertising."

"There's an idea. Crazy women who think they want to live in the bush can meet other crazy people."

Scout laughed. *Actually, that's kind of what my job's about.*

THREE DAYS LATER Victoria returned to California, leaving just before the first big snowfall. Scout and Malachy set their wedding date for December twenty-first, in McGrath. Victoria and her husband and Dana would be able to come then, combining the trip with work in the newly planned Anchorage Harmony office.

In early October, Scout got a call from Serge, who'd finally paid his bill for the time he'd spent with Victoria.

"I need to talk," he said. "I need a *friend*, Scout."

"But you and I have entered a therapeutic relationship of sorts. Which makes it ethically incorrect for me to be a friend to you."

"I need to talk. Is it going to cost money?"

Patience, she told herself.

"Look, it's Mary. I'm in love with her. I've never stopped being in love with her. We've been seeing each other again these past few weeks."

Scout put a lid on her instantaneous reaction. Mary Clarke and her brother were just friends. If Holden thought of Mary as a girlfriend, he'd never said so. They seemed to talk on the phone a lot, and Mary had gone up to the Berensen property twice, but it still didn't seem precisely *romantic*. And the idea had been for Holden to become more comfortable making friends.

"Anyhow, we—well, we start talking—and then all of a sudden she starts flying into these rages and screaming at me never to come near her again. And I know it's because of things that happened between us in past lives—"

"Are you sure it's not because of something that happened in *this* life?" *Scout, you need a vacation.*

"Ha ha," said Serge. "She says I don't respect her boundaries."

"Well, if you want to talk about this, you should make an appointment."

"Anyhow, now *I'm* angry," he said, "because she's seeing someone else, and she didn't tell me."

Holden, Scout thought.

"She's seeing your ex-husband."

"He's not my—" She stopped. "Who?"

"That guy Danny from Ireland."

"Danny Kilbourne is not from Ireland." *I have to be careful what I say.* Danny would love a reason to come after her with a defamation suit.

"Well, his family is or something. She says."

Scout bit her lip. Should she call Mary and warn her or leave her to fate? If she were Mary, would she believe Scout? Or would she be too smitten with Danny?

"If you want to talk about this," Scout repeated, "let's set up a time when you can come into the office."

"I was hoping we could talk about this as friends. I know you're *her* friend, and Aaron told me you've said this Danny character isn't the world's greatest guy."

Scout did not acknowledge this.

"I wanted you to know, because I thought you were the one person who might be able to protect Mary from this guy."

"Do you want to come in for counseling?" Scout asked.

"I want a *friend,*" Serge said. And hung up.

A bad feeling crept over Scout. *This town is too small for the business I run.* It wasn't primarily the fact that Mary was seeing Danny that troubled her—or what

Holden would think about it. No, it was the distress in Serge's voice when he'd hung up.

She knew better than to call him back. She didn't want to be his friend and couldn't be. But she worried, and she called Malachy and asked him to drive past Serge's place, just keep an eye out. Scout suspected that Serge might be bipolar, and autumn could be a difficult time for mood disorders.

Two days later, Holden flew down to McGrath to visit—and to warn Mary about Danny. Although Scout was unwilling to get involved—and had mentioned Serge's phone call to no one—Malachy had learned about Mary and Danny and told Holden. Scout met him at the airfield and drove him back to the house. He and Jeremy were looking at Jeremy's start on his new Web site when Malachy came home. He walked into the kitchen, where Scout was making dinner, and when she saw his face she thought of Serge, wondering if something had happened.

But Malachy said, "Danny's disappeared."

CHAPTER THIRTEEN

HOLDEN EMERGED from Jeremy's room, and he and Scout listened to everything Malachy had to say about Danny's disappearance.

Mary had made the discovery. She'd been out running dogs for two days, on the new snowpack. She'd just returned, and had called Malachy's cell phone because she'd gone by Danny's cabin and discovered food left standing out.

The thought that immediately crossed Scout's mind was, *Somebody finally killed him.* It horrified her that it was the first thought she had.

Did she hate him? Did she *wish* him dead?

How many times had she been over these issues, everything relating to Danny, to his relationship with her father, to his relationship with her? How many times had she reminded herself that if she didn't forgive him, it would damage her?

He still had the power to get to her.

And now he was missing.

People did disappear in Alaska—and sometimes other people made them disappear. There were too many people in Scout's life who had reason to make Danny Kilbourne disappear.

Holden wouldn't have done anything to him.
Nor Malachy.

"No one suspects that a crime's been committed," Malachy told her, as though reading her mind. Aaron had gone to Danny's house to investigate; Malachy wasn't on duty. "We'll probably call out Search and Rescue if he doesn't show up."

Scout remembered Danny singing for her in Irish and even teaching her some Irish. She recalled times he'd made her laugh—and that she'd made him laugh. But those recollections were overshadowed by his cruelty. Telling her she was fat. Lying, lying about everything. And finally...

Yes, finally worming his way into her father's affection. Winning her father's love and taking love that should have been hers.

I'm not going to think it, she told herself. And she didn't think it, *I hope he's dead.* The things Danny had done would never go away, but his being dead wouldn't *make* them go away.

So she tried to dismiss him from her mind altogether.

WHEN MALACHY WENT on duty, Scout and Jeremy took the snowmobile into town, to the general store. The rows of goods still made Scout wish for other stores in other places, where particular brands of dressing she liked sat in rich variety, where no shortage of orange juice not-from-concentrate ever occurred, where the vegetables were fresh and diverse. As they turned down the baking aisle, a woman beside the shelf glanced up. She was small, and she and the man with her were scooping bottles of vanilla extract off the shelves. Their basket was already filled with cough syrup.

Beside Scout, Jeremy froze.

The woman's eyes grew round. "Jeremy."

"Hi, Mom." He didn't acknowledge the presence of her companion.

"I wanted to see you," she said.

Neither Scout nor Jeremy spoke. She *could* have seen him. It would've meant coming to Malachy's house or approaching him at the station or in the street.

But seeing Jackie stocking up on vanilla extract and cough syrup, last resort of alcoholics in dry communities, Scout suspected that Jackie would never change, never free herself from the prison of alcoholism.

After Jeremy had hugged Jackie, Scout introduced herself as Malachy's fiancé. She also gave Jackie his home number and encouraged her to call so she and Jeremy could get together. Jeremy seemed pleased by this, as pleased as he ever was by anything.

When they returned home, Malachy was there waiting for them. "We found Danny's body," he said.

Dead, then.

Dead.

He'd been her lover once. Once, she'd loved *him,* loved who she thought he was, had even tried, in some way, to love the Danny who was underneath it all—until she'd realized that allowing him to remain near her was incompatible with developing a healthy life of her own.

"What happened?"

"A moose. It seems he went out for a walk. The moose charged, it looks like."

Iditarod mushers carried rifles because of moose.

Moose would not yield to dog teams—or, apparently, to Danny.

At one time, she'd wished him dead. Just so she'd never have to deal with him. Then years had passed when she *hadn't* seen him, and that had suited her. But he'd come to McGrath, threatening her and her family. Had she wished him dead then?

All she'd wanted was for the pain to stop, the pain of her father's rejection. Was Danny evil? she wondered now as she had many times. Or was he pitiable? Could he be both?

"You know, I'm not sure he even has any family," Scout murmured, almost to herself. "I never met them. And he never said what the *real* story was. Not to me, anyhow."

"Well, a look around his place turned up something interesting. He's married."

"Again?" His real wife divorced him when she discovered the bigamy.

"Yes. Her name is Georgia. She's a graphic artist in San Francisco. They were estranged because she discovered he was involved with someone else, but she's very upset that he died."

"I'm glad someone is."

Malachy glanced at Scout curiously.

"I mean it. It would be so awful to die and have no one be sorry." She paused for a moment. "I used to wonder whether he was a sociopath or a true psychopath."

"What did you decide?"

Scout shook her head. "I didn't. My vision of him was too clouded by my experiences with him to know. Did you tell Mary?" she asked.

"Aaron did."

"And she's all right?"

"She didn't fall apart, and I don't think she will. She's very…hard. She looked angry."

Jeremy sat on a bench beside the woodstove, watching the two of them, and Malachy lifted his eyebrows, silently inviting him to speak.

But Jeremy said nothing.

Scout left the room, pensive and sad-looking, and Malachy said, "Have you seen your mom?"

"Just now. At the store. Buying vanilla extract."

"You can't control what she does, Jeremy."

"I figured that out a long time ago. I just wish *she* would. Stop. You know."

Malachy nodded, wondering if Jeremy really had figured out that he couldn't stop his mother from drinking. He said, "This is your home. You know that."

"What's your mom like?" Jeremy asked.

The question hit Malachy's chest like a rock, because as he spoke with Jeremy, his own mother's abandonment had surrounded him. "She left us when I was a baby. I haven't seen her since."

"Where did she go?"

"Home. She was from the Aleutians."

Jeremy contemplated this—or something else—for several minutes. Malachy wished the boy hadn't asked, wished he hadn't been forced to say this shameful thing out loud. It did seem shameful, and for the first time he noticed his own feeling.

"Have you ever tried to go and see her?" Jeremy asked.

Malachy shook his head.

"I can see why," Jeremy said.

Malachy knew instinctively that Jeremy *could* see why. Yet he said, "Which is?"

"You must think she doesn't want to know you. It's kind of like my mom."

"Your mom spent a lot of time with you, Jeremy."

"But if she wanted me around, she'd stop drinking. She wants to drink more than she wants anything else."

Malachy said, "*We* want you around."

Jeremy glanced at him once, maybe assessing the truth of this, then slowly rose. "Well…" he said. "I wonder where old Danny is now. I wonder what happens to people like him."

"So do I," Malachy said, but what lay in his mind was that he was a grown man still deciding to honor a choice made by his mother when he was too young to remember her.

JEREMY HEADED down the hall to his room, still wondering what happened to people like Danny Kilbourne when they died.

What would happen to him.

John's office door was open, and Jeremy walked in to see what Malachy's father was doing.

The older man glanced up. "Hello, there. I'm packing some carvings to send to buyers. Lend me a hand?"

"Sure."

"Something on your mind?"

Nothing it would help to say, Jeremy thought.

Studying his face, John shut the door. "Something about Danny?" he asked.

"In a way. He was…a creep— But he never tried to kill anyone. I mean, I *wanted* to kill Rayburn."

The not-a-real-priest just sat there looking at Jeremy. Finally, he said, "God forgives everything and everyone, but it can be very hard to forgive yourself."

"*If* there's a God."

A small smile on Malachy's father's face. Jeremy knew that this man believed there was a God and no calamity would shake his faith. But John said, "Well, I think we agree that *you* exist."

Which left the thought that it was hard to forgive oneself.

He couldn't stand what Rayburn had said. Even if he *had* killed him, the thought would still be there, and the thought was like a sick question, the kind of question you couldn't ask of anyone, couldn't even say out loud. The kind a thing you could only try to kill someone for saying.

But if he'd succeeded in killing Rayburn...

I'm lucky he's not dead.

He wasn't sure he'd actually thought that before, because he was still mad about the image he'd been given—his mother with someone *his* age.

She wouldn't do that.

"He said something about my mom." And he told Malachy's father exactly what Rayburn had said.

"You don't think it's true, do you?" he asked John, who'd lived in McGrath long enough to have an opinion, but who wasn't Malachy, who might have a different opinion.

"What do you think?" John asked. "You'd know better than I."

For the first time, Jeremy thought through the things he'd *known* his mother to do for alcohol and many things she hadn't. He'd been afraid to ask the question, and now that John had asked, he was no longer afraid. Because he knew the answer.

"She never would."

And he no longer wished that he could wipe Rayburn from the face of the earth—or his words. They didn't matter.

Because it was a lie, a story Rayburn had made up.

NONE OF THEM WENT to the service for Danny.

Scout took the dogs out in the snow, letting Estelle run along beside them. She seemed to have a gift for bossing the other dogs by nipping and growling at the ones who showed signs of scrappiness and urging forward any who lagged.

On the run, Scout contemplated the hardness in her that kept her from the memorial service. She just couldn't bear to hear people who didn't really know him—Mary, for instance, whom Holden had escorted to the ceremony at the community center—singing the praises of Danny Kilbourne. He had caused Scout too much grief. Not only that, she still didn't *know* him. He remained a mystery to her, but she resented the respect in which he was held by other people. She could not honor him in death.

And yet she knew with certainty that she *must* let go of her grievances against him. In some way, that was the lesson of death and of life. The letting go that was forgiving *and* forgetting. Oh, if she could manage the last, somehow... As she ran the dogs, she prayed that Danny's spirit be guided to a place where no one would believe his lies. To his spirit, she tried to find something nice to say. A farewell, nothing else.

She'd never been certain of his goodness in life and was unsure if anyone was purified by death.

So she closed her mind against any sense of him and headed for home.

THOUGH SNOW LAY on the ground, Scout now had to make weekly flights to Anchorage, where she usually spent two nights before coming home. Occasionally, Malachy flew her. Other times, she went on mail flights or with local pilots.

In Anchorage she stayed in hotels and remembered how much she preferred civilization to the bush and how much more civilized Anchorage was than McGrath. She could have dogs in Anchorage. Why couldn't they all live there? But Malachy's father liked McGrath, and John was obviously good for Jeremy.

One weekend in October, both Dana and Victoria flew up. Scout's mother had agreed to come, too, and together in Anchorage they found a wedding dress for Scout and bridesmaids' dresses for her two business partners. Dana would wear a dark pearly-gray, Victoria a light blue. Scout's dress was a sheer Grecian-style gown over a fitted satin sheath. The veil was a wreath. The three younger women talked Dora into a special dress for the mother of the bride. Dora, who said that she couldn't remember the last time she'd worn a dress, agreed to a flowing rayon gown in silvery-gray.

The wedding was to take place at the community center in McGrath, with Holden as Malachy's best man.

As the winter solstice approached, Scout made sure family and friends had suitable accommodations and finalized plans with the caterer—owner of McGrath's smallest restaurant and the only restaurant besides The Tug. The dinner would include fresh game—and, of course, champagne.

Malachy and Holden reserved tuxedos in Anchorage, and John agreed to retrieve them the day before.

The night before the wedding, the party—family, plus Dana, Victoria and Victoria's husband, Skip, aka The Perfect Man—enjoyed a casual rehearsal dinner at Malachy's house. Then Scout rode back to the apartment with her friends to spend the night.

The three friends settled down together on the collection of folding futons. Victoria planned to join her husband downstairs in Jeremy's old bedroom—*We especially like the black walls,* Skip had teased with a smile. Now Dana asked, "Is Malachy's mother dead?"

"I don't think so." Scout told her friends what Malachy had said about his mother and father.

"Does John ever mention her?"

"Never. I'm not sure how he feels about her. He gave up his vocation for her and Malachy, and then she took off. But I've never heard him talk about it."

"Isn't Malachy curious about his mother?" Victoria asked.

Scout shrugged. "I don't know if he's curious, but I do know—because he's said so—that he feels *she* doesn't want a relationship with him."

"Does he have pictures?"

"He must. I've never asked."

An hour later, Victoria went downstairs to be with her husband, and Scout and Dana turned out the light in the upstairs apartment.

Tomorrow, Scout thought, *Malachy and I are going*

to be married. She wasn't sure she'd be able to sleep. Not right away. After the wedding...a baby? Tomorrow would be a wonderful day.

MALACHY LONGED to call off the wedding. Over the last few days, the feeling had crept over him like clouds gradually obscuring the sun. He said it to no one. Calling off the wedding would mean losing Holden's friendship and probably any allegiance of Jeremy's. His own father would be disillusioned and disappointed. The desire for escape was so overpowering he wasn't sure he wanted Scout anymore. How had he ended up engaged to her, anyhow?

He'd been on the rebound from Mary....

No, you left Mary because you wanted Scout.

As he'd left the woman before her, because he'd decided he preferred Mary.

Part of him wanted to escape that pattern. Another part suspected that his current course of action was the only way to do so.

So, I'm getting married. We can always get divorced.

He hated himself for the thought, even more for what his desertion would do to Scout. Lying alone in his bed, he missed her and also wished that she could simply remain his friend and lover and nothing more complicated.

But what else, he asked himself, was a wife?

Till death do us part.

Neither of us will leave.

Then he slept.

IN THE MORNING his terror returned. He didn't want to marry anyone, that he was only going through with it because it was Scout, Scout who'd been so badly hurt by Danny Kilbourne. Scout who was his best friend, the easiest person he knew to be with and talk to.

Can't we go on as we have been?

He dressed, and his father came in with flowers that had been refrigerated the night before, to pin a boutonniere on his lapel. He glanced into Malachy's eyes. "Holding up?" he asked.

Malachy smiled. "It's a bit too late to change my mind."

"Oh, no it's not. After the wedding is when it's too late to change your mind."

Malachy looked out the part of the window that wasn't iced with fresh snow from the night before. "Is that when you did?"

John lifted his head sharply, eyes like a raptor's. "What do you mean?"

Malachy shook his head. This wasn't the time for confrontation. Why had he spoken?

"I never changed my mind," John said.

"You never changed your mind about the first vows you took," his son countered. "I think you wavered, and during the wavering I happened into the picture."

His father paled.

But didn't speak.

Didn't refute it.

Only looked at the floor.

Malachy reached out with his hand, to touch his father's arm in its tuxedo, but his hand seemed unable to make contact. He lowered it and walked to the door. "What time is it?"

"I'm glad—" John stopped.

Malachy glanced at him.

"That after I knew you," his father said, "I never had to choose. The choice was already made, and it was right—because of you."

"I don't believe you feel that way."

John fixed him with his blue eyes again, then abruptly strode from the room ahead of his son.

No, Malachy realized. It would never be right for his father. His father loved him. But he'd never forgiven himself the transgressions that had led to Malachy's conception and birth—and had deprived him of the life he'd loved more than he ever came to love his son.

Strangely, Malachy decided, it didn't bother him. There was integrity in his father's allegiance to his first vow.

And my mother, Malachy thought, *was just a casualty of the situation.*

For the first time he could remember in his life, he discovered that he wanted her to be safe and happy and loved. She was not some distant and vaguely resented person but someone who'd been hurt. Now he felt concern for her and for the young woman she'd been, torn from her family and her people, left with a man steeped in regret, a man in some quiet way ruined.

He followed his father, thinking of Scout and deciding again that he could be her partner and she his.

THE SCHOOL PRINCIPAL played the wedding march on the piano, and Dana entered the main room of the community center, walking slowly. Scout saw Victoria go next. Then it was her turn.

She saw Harmony clients in the audience, people invited by Malachy because they were his friends or his father's. Martin the mosquito man. Serge.

Who invited him? Scout wondered and immediately realized he must have invited himself. She bit back a smile. Mary sat with Andy Case and another musher. And Malachy stood at the front with the pastor of McGrath's non-denominational church, who was to marry them. John was with him and Holden and Skip.

Malachy met her eyes, his jaw unmoving for a moment. Then he smiled.

As Scout reached him, she looked up at him and saw something in his eyes she'd never seen there before. He clung to her hands tightly. His eyes seemed both darker and filled with fire.

She was as beautiful as Malachy had ever seen her, her skin a dark golden against the white of her gown. And that dress had been made for a goddess—not a celebrity goddess of the earth, but one of other realms. And yet, she seemed infinitely fragile to him, as all humans are— as Danny Kilbourne, killed by a moose, had so recently proven—and Malachy wanted to protect her from everything, especially from his own worst impulses, the impulse to abandon before he could be abandoned.

No longer was there the slightest possibility that he would not marry her. Caring for her, *not* leaving her, was his destiny, and a warm contentment spread over him as the mayor began to speak.

CHAPTER FOURTEEN

THEIR HONEYMOON WOULD be brief. Malachy had planned a four-day excursion, keeping the details secret from her, only telling her to pack a swimsuit and some clothes for warm weather. He wasn't sure how she'd feel or if the gift he'd planned was even what she wanted.

At the Anchorage airport, she finally learned their final destination. "San Diego?"

He nodded.

Scout sighed with a blissful smile.

He watched the relaxation ease through her. She liked sun, liked the ocean.

Whatever he'd done to try to make her like Alaska hadn't worked. She didn't like it. Not really. She tolerated it, but this was what she truly wanted, to live Outside.

As they sank back against their seats, he saw Scout's mouth twitch in a way that meant she was troubled about something.

"What?" he said.

"Now that we're married," she said rather tightly, "don't you think it would be good form to verbally express affection for me?"

He knew exactly what she was asking for. He put his arm around her shoulders and pressed his mouth to her ear. "I love you. You're my best friend. It's why I married you."

Scout heard him with a warm shiver. Of course, he hadn't said he was *in love* with her, but maybe he wasn't. Still, when he'd looked into her eyes, when he'd seen her in her wedding dress, she'd thought he seemed overwhelmed—exactly like a man very suddenly in love.

Well, it didn't matter. He loved her and he treated her well.

They flew to Seattle, San Francisco and then to San Diego. There, a rental car awaited them, and Malachy drove them, with Scout navigating, to a hotel on Mission Bay.

It was different than it would have been to visit during the summer, but Scout still inhaled the salt air as though it were a medicine she needed for health, even for life.

"We can rent wet suits," Malachy told her, reaching for her waist, pulling her close. "Later."

THAT NIGHT, digging through Malachy's pack looking for one of his T-shirts, her preferred garment even for a honeymoon night, she felt the canvas portfolio inside and pulled it out. It had been stowed hastily, wasn't zipped, and papers fell out, fanning out on the hotel room's carpet.

As Malachy sprang up from the bed, Scout saw what was printed on the pages.

His résumé.

She studied him.

He shrugged. "I have…an interview."

"Here?" Her heart hardly dared to believe—even to understand.

Malachy gave a small nod. "Monday."

"I can't leave McGrath very soon," Scout said. "I really can't. I mean, if you got the job, I could talk to Dana and Victoria, and we could try..." She blinked. "Do you *want* to live down here?"

"I wouldn't mind more challenges on the job."

The thought of that terrified her. For a state trooper in California, challenges might include motorists trying to kill him if he pulled them over on the highway, a greater chance of a car accident—all hazards increased. At least, that was how it looked to Scout.

But you're the one who'd like to live Outside.

"Are you unhappy with being an Alaska state trooper?"

"Not necessarily."

But on Monday he went to the interview and said the prospects were good.

Soon they were back in Alaska and Scout was back to her schedule of flying from McGrath to Anchorage and home again every week.

Jeremy had finally launched the Frank Berensen Memorial Alaskan Bush Web site. This involved a distance trip by dogsled with Holden from McGrath to the place where Scout had been born and raised. On the trip and at her family's property, Jeremy took many photos, which he included on the site.

A Portland, Oregon, woman, whom Martin the mosquito man had met via the Harmony Agency, moved in with him.

IN JANUARY, Scout participated in her first sprint race— five miles, running six dogs. She ran Malachy's Ices in front with Pigpen, whom Ices tried to kill while never slacking on the tug.

Scout came in fourth out of four competitors in her group, but it didn't bother her. She'd never raced before, so just to finish without ending up in a heap with her dogs was a success.

At the end of January, she missed her menstrual period. Two weeks later, she started throwing up. Other people in town had a stomach flu, but Scout refused to believe that she did. When she wasn't profoundly nauseated, she felt fine.

After the third day of morning sickness, she told Malachy, "I think I'm pregnant."

"I think you are, too," he said. It was a Saturday, and she had climbed out of bed only to be sick.

She curled up with him again, looking wretched and peering at him anxiously. "Is it okay?"

"Of course it's okay," he said. "We've talked about it. I've told you it would be okay. Want some crackers?"

"Okay. But I think protein's the solution. That's what I've read."

Malachy got up, pulled on some sweatpants and went to bring her some crackers and a glass of milk. He couldn't help wondering if his mother had awakened alone with morning sickness. Of course, she must have. Her father had told him once that they'd never even spent a whole night together before they were married.

Malachy tried to imagine her realizing what she had to tell the parish priest. She must have been terrified of his reaction.

When had she found out that he loved his vocation more than he'd ever loved her?

Returning to the bedroom, he said, "Some time I think I'd like to visit the Aleutians."

Scout blinked up at him with her eyes like a wolf's. She didn't ask what had caused this change. Maybe she felt too sick. "Thank you," was all she said as she sat up to take the food.

Malachy thought, *We're going to have a baby. Am I ready for this?*

Strangely, he was. He was glad Scout was pregnant. She wouldn't leave him or this baby, and it seemed a way to cement something that was the antithesis of his parents' situation. This was an affirmation that his unusual birth did not mean that everything in his life must be sundered, be a mess, be strange or unsatisfactory. "Are you excited?" he asked.

"Yes. And nauseated."

He smiled and watched her eat some crackers. "You still look like my Scout."

Comfort spread through her. *My Scout.*

"Does that make you my Malachy?"

"Well, that's definitely who I am."

Scout bought a pregnancy test at the general store, which was as good as announcing to the entire town of McGrath that she was pregnant. When it showed positive, she called her mother and Holden to tell them.

"Take care of yourself," Dora said, "and eat plenty of protein."

"I will."

"I'm glad, Scout," she said. "So glad."

Scout's heart soared at this approval and happiness from her mother. There was actually something she could do right; even her father would have probably approved.

ON THE SECOND Monday in February, Scout flew to Anchorage, where the new office was now open and accepting clients. She, Dana and Victoria had hired a likable Athabascan woman named Caroline to run the office, with Scout supervising her. Andy Case, on his way to Florida to see his ex-wife, was on the plane flown by a local bush pilot named Merv, who had become Scout's most frequent carrier. This wasn't because she liked the way Merv flew, but because he made himself readily available, both for Monday flights to Anchorage and Wednesday flights home.

When she returned from Anchorage that Wednesday, Malachy flew her in the plane he and John owned. It was dark, and she sat in the co-pilot's seat, completely happy and relaxed.

There was a moment, an instance that had its own stillness, right before the engine stalled, when she knew it was stalling.

Immediately alert, thinking of the baby, thinking of the baby instead of her own peril or Malachy's, she watched him take the plane through steps her father would have recommended to try to get the engine going again.

Time slowed down.

The engine was gone and did not restart.

Why is this happening? God, don't let this happen. Maybe we'll all die together.

No, we're not going to die.

Malachy gave their coordinates to the McGrath tower, now closer than Anchorage, and said that he'd have to attempt an emergency landing.

Scout had no idea where they were. She had greater

confidence in Malachy's ability to land the plane than in her own—which wouldn't have been the case had Merv been flying.

"I'm going to try for Rico," Malachy said in the eerie quiet of the gliding plane.

Rico was a ghost town south of McGrath. The area around it had been cleared of trees, which had never returned. But that meant they'd be coming down in deep snow miles and miles from McGrath.

Reaching the tower, he told them his intention.

Scout shifted in her seat, torn between surrender to the physical sensation of being in an airplane without power, an airplane that seemed to be falling too fast, and bracing herself, wanting to take the controls from Malachy when there was no control.

It was impossible that she'd die this way, so soon after her father's death.

The falling time wasn't long, and she absolutely did not fear death, so certain was she that she wouldn't die.

Her flesh was bruised in one bullet-fast moment, when she was thrown against her shoulder and seat belt with the impact. The belt was cutting her at her hips, squashing the baby. Help help help.

Baby!

The cockpit lights went out as the plane plowed on, driving through something thick and dark, burying them, swallowing them.

A cramp tore at her lower abdomen.

No.

"Malachy?"

He said nothing. She could see nothing.

She reached out with her left hand, and it touched his warm body.

He made a sound.

Light. She had to find light. She knew where Malachy kept flashlights and a headlamp, but could she get to them?

Her abdomen cramped again.

Am I going to miscarry because of this?

I have to keep us all alive.

She unfastened her seat belt and moved gingerly, reaching behind Malachy. A bag containing a head lamp and other equipment had been stowed in a cupboard behind his seat.

She found the head lamp and switched it on.

The plane was crumpled and broken and, as far as she could tell, buried in snow, which meant she had to do something about air first thing. Still, she played the light over her husband, over his short dark hair, over his face.

"Scout?"

"Don't move." What if he'd broken his neck? Well, if he had, she was going to take care of him. "Can you feel your toes?"

"Yes." He didn't move. "It's the left leg."

In other words, *There's something wrong with my left leg.* "Are you in pain?"

"A bit."

Which meant, *Yes, definitely, lots.* That seemed good. An absence of pain would mean something more complicated, more difficult.

I can't remember any wilderness first aid. Or not enough. She'd have to make sure he'd refrain from moving.

Scout didn't notice the change that came over her,

because there was no change. Simply a complete ability to cope. Whatever this emergency required, she would do.

Coping became automatic.

The windows hadn't broken, and though the windshield had cracked, some of it falling in, digging out by that route would involve tangling with glass.

So be it. She decided it was the best way. Wrapping her hand in her Gore-Tex shell, she removed more broken glass, then hit the windshield with a heavy Maglite. "I'm just going to dig for air," she told Malachy.

"There's a shovel. In the back."

Yes, but getting to the back would be tricky. Snow had come in from somewhere. Assessing damage to the plane was disorienting. She crawled over snow and dug through it with her bare hands, looking for the place where she remembered he kept a shovel.

Finally, her hand touched the handle.

Her abdomen still cramping, she spent another few minutes getting the shovel loose, then awkwardly made her way back to the cockpit and began to dig upward, knocking snow down into the plane, carefully avoiding the windshield's broken glass.

Flares. We'll need flares so they can find us. We should stay here. Then, more people will come and take care of Malachy.

But she'd have to keep him warm in the meantime.

How far to the surface? She had to stand on the instrument panel to dig. Then the shovel broke through. She dug her way up, poking her head out. Falling snow whipped her face and hair. Now she was cold and frightened and knew that the latter would only make the former more intense.

More pain in her abdomen.

She disregarded it. She couldn't afford to lie down and do nothing so as to prevent a miscarriage. She had to keep herself and Malachy alive. Night, storming, the middle of nowhere. Those were her concerns. As far as she could tell, they hadn't set down in Rico—or anywhere.

The radio.

She went below.

No signal. Nothing.

"Malachy, where's the beacon?"

The device that would direct help to them more surely than flares.

"Over here. I tripped it as we went down."

"Excellent. Is there anything I can do for you?"

"No. Don't talk to me."

That way, he thought, he could float. He was outside his body and outside the pain, seeing clearly that part of the cockpit was embedded in his thigh. The secret was not to move, not to pull anything out. Eventually, the nerves would stop sending pain signals. He felt nothing now. Scout moved beside him, working to widen and strengthen the sides of the hole she'd made through which cold chilled her. He saw the cold touch her but didn't feel it himself.

He had experienced something similar once before, when he'd dislocated his shoulder as a child. Then, too, he'd made some sort of decision to leave the pain behind, and in doing so he could watch everything happening without being part of it.

"Does anything else hurt, besides your leg?" Scout asked. "Your neck?"

"Just my leg. Don't worry about my neck."

If she could believe him, Scout reasoned, that was a load off her mind.

Her stomach cramped painfully again.

A miscarriage could come with associated hemorrhage, but she wouldn't worry about this now. She had to keep herself and Malachy warm until help arrived.

There had been—earlier—sleeping bags in the bag where she'd found the shovel. Wearing the head lamp, she went back again, her stomach cramping as though with the most painful menstrual period she'd ever had, and used the small avalanche shovel to toss snow aside and reveal everything buried beneath. One sleeping bag in a stuff sack. Yes. Another? She couldn't find it—not right away—and when her abdomen gave another painful throb, she grabbed the one bundle and headed back for the cockpit.

Warm moisture gathered between her legs. Blood.

It was her Alaskan upbringing that came to her in that moment, not with the tools that could save her life and Malachy's, but with an acceptance of certain natural processes. Her body had just known trauma, and the baby within her wasn't strong enough to withstand what had happened. It was nature, and she didn't fight it, either with mind or with action.

Sitting down and doing nothing was not an option. She returned to Malachy and pulled the sleeping bag from its sack and placed it around the side of his body that wasn't pressed against the crushed part of the cockpit and instrument panel. She felt for blood on him and found relatively little, just stickiness near his thigh where she thought metal was stuck inside. She examined his face, trying to remember how his pupils

should look if they were all right. Her father hadn't
been one for formal first aid classes. What she'd learned,
she'd learned in high school and college, both a long
time ago. A slight smile formed on Malachy's lips.

His eyes seemed all right to her, fairly normal, but
he was pale, and sweat beaded his upper lip, his cheeks
and forehead. They both wore hats, parkas—she'd put
her Gore-Tex back on—Sorel-style boots, insulated
pants. It was cold in the plane this time of year, even
without a crash, and the outside temperature must be
twenty below. Malachy had been flying because it was
an unusually warm day.

*I should've said no to these winter trips. It was silly
to keep doing it.*

Her family had usually kept their plane grounded in
winter.

The cold had been one thing about Alaska that she'd
hated. In the past weeks she'd spent time cursing
engines and motors that wouldn't start without intensive
heating and coddling and had embraced travel by dog
sled. The dogs always wanted to go.

But there were no dogs with them now.

Even besieged by painful cramps, with the blood on
the legs of her insulated pants freezing, she knew she
could keep herself alive and sufficiently warm for quite
a while. But Malachy couldn't move. To try to pull him
off the piece of metal that had pierced his leg would be
to risk worse injury—rapid blood loss, for instance.
Scout weighed that against the necessity of keeping him
warm. The human body could endure massive environ-
mental stress. As a child, she had witnessed it in herself
and others.

I'm going to have to trust that his neck and spine are all right.

"Malachy, I want to try to move you."

His eyes shifted—his eyes but not his head. He said nothing.

"I need to get you warm."

"We should stay here. The beacon's working."

How he knew that, Scout didn't ask, but she was sure he *did* know it.

Malachy brought himself firmly into the present, into the pain of his leg, pain that would become agony if he or Scout managed to pull from his thigh whatever was impaling him and keeping him immobile.

He felt her unfasten his seat belt.

"I don't think you can get me out of here," he whispered hoarsely.

"But you can."

She was right.

"I think my ankle's crushed on that side. Or broken."

She didn't respond. He couldn't remain where he was, or he'd suffer even more from the cold.

He tried shifting, and the effect on his leg was what he'd expected. Agony that made any sensation in his ankle dull to nothing. *Keep going,* he thought. And he moved through the pain, using his good leg to force himself up and sideways, away from the thing that was impaling him.

As he freed his leg, he saw, in the light cast by Scout's headlamp, that it had been impaled on part of a sled runner he and his father had used to build a cache in the cockpit. Now the metal, two inches wide, gleamed dark with blood.

He grabbed what Scout passed him—her long under-shirt, it looked like, and pressed it through the gaps in canvas and insulation to his skin. Scout handed him her water bottle, which hadn't frozen because she kept it tucked inside her clothes during flights. She hated being without water.

They chose to do nothing more with his wound than keep her shirt pressed to it, for now. Stop the bleeding.

Scout did not mention her own.

Her cramps eased with less activity. She and Malachy huddled together in the one sleeping bag, and she got up periodically to clear away snow and to listen for sounds of aircraft. The storm had stopped, but the temperature had dropped again, making air rescue less likely.

There were no snowshoes in the plane, but she even-tually climbed out and dug a path to a nearby stand of scrubby trees. She knew how to fashion snowshoes—not good ones but sufficient for a brief period of time—out of branches like these trees provided. It was now cold enough that she'd covered her entire face, as well as her hands. When she paused to pee, she carefully examined her underwear and pants in the light of the head lamp.

Only blood.

No sign of a lost pregnancy, even one as early as hers.

She cut branches and dragged them back to the plane with her. At least, making snowshoes would occupy her for the time being.

They had no rifle with them, just Malachy's service weapon. She could make snares, too, for animals, but she hoped they wouldn't be there long enough to catch anything.

We need a dog team.

Not possible.

Make do with what you have, Scout.

It was her father's voice but not stern—encouraging. She felt his presence with her so strongly that she could almost smell him. And for once, that presence didn't seem to be looking down on her in despair for what she couldn't accomplish but praising her for what she'd done—and reminding her of other things she could do.

Scout didn't think she'd ever felt so close to Frank Berensen in life—or so loved by him.

While Malachy lay beside her, she checked out his handgun, a .38 automatic that annoyed her because it wasn't a rifle. A rifle would be so useful now, if they should be lucky enough to stumble on something edible.

Her father seemed to be suggesting that she go up again and look at the lie of the land. She considered this option—and the cold that made it so unappealing.

More warm clothes. Where do I find them? And why didn't I take warmer clothes with me on the flight?

It occurred to her that she'd grown a bit careless in McGrath.

Though McGrath was, after all, the bush, it was less remote than where she'd grown up. *I've been stupid.*

No point talking to yourself that way. That thought seemed to come from her father, as so many other unexpected things had in the past hour.

She consulted her watch to determine how long until brief daylight. More time had passed than she'd realized since the plane had gone down—yet not enough, either. It was after midnight, but only just.

As the next hours passed, she talked to Malachy and examined his ankle, which appeared to have been at least partially crushed. How long could he go without medical attention before infection set in?

There was some food in the plane, the kind of canned stuff that made decent survival fare but no more. A stove, as well, for emergencies, but no fuel.

By morning, rescue still hadn't come, and Malachy had developed a fever. They agreed that Scout should clean his wound. She did this, sensing by his sudden intake of breath when she was causing pain, which was most of the time.

Then she took his gun and went outside. He had plenty of ammunition in the plane. A handgun was much better than no gun. At 5:00 a.m., she dug a snow blind for herself and began to wait.

IT WAS TOO COLD for anyone to fly. She realized that much, just as she realized that the longest she could tolerate outside the plane was ten minutes. She had built a protective frame, of sorts, to cage Malachy's injured foot, and he dragged himself out of the plane, too.

The fever, however, took its toll on his strength.

That afternoon, in circumstances nothing short of miraculous, she shot a rabbit. She liked rabbits and hated killing them. *I'm sorry,* she thought as she butchered it outside, not far from her snow blind, and took the meat in to Malachy.

They ate some raw and froze the rest, and she returned immediately to the snowblind to see if the rabbit's intestines and blood had attracted anything else. It had. Ravens. And a wolf.

She could not shoot a wolf. They were too much like dogs. Instead, she watched this one, a female who looked young. Lacking Holden's particular gift with animals, she made no effort to approach her but instead remained in the blind until she became too cold and went back to Malachy.

Her cramping had ceased completely, and she was surprised by how strong she felt. She'd made another ventilation hole after breaking one of the plane's rear windows, and she built a small fire inside. Even after their landing, the plane hadn't given off a noticeable scent of fuel, and she decided that the risks of fire were outweighed by its necessity.

She melted snow and ice for water, and she used the heated water to create compresses to wrap around Malachy's wound, trying to draw out the infection.

As she did this, twenty-four hours after their wreck, he said, "You're enjoying this, aren't you?"

Scout gave a shrug.

True, something had begun to happen to her, something she could recall from no other time in her life. Extreme self-reliance. She was strong, capable of survival in the situation Alaska had dished out to them. They had an ax, a knife, a gun, strike-anywhere matches… far more, in short, than her father had allowed when teaching Holden and her survival skills.

But she couldn't stop Malachy's fever—or rather, the infection that seemed to be growing in his leg. To stay warm during the long day, she had dug out from the plane everything she'd thought could possibly be useful.

Now, she considered a fifth of vodka.

She showed it to Malachy.

He frowned, undoubtedly reading her mind.

"Okay," he said.

"More warm compresses first."

They'd cut the fabric away from his insulated pants to expose the wound, which was jagged, four inches wide at its widest point. Malachy drew around the red area that surrounded the wound with a ballpoint pen.

"What's that for?"

"We can see if the infection continues to spread."

"All right."

Twenty minutes later, Scout poured vodka into the open wound as Malachy shuddered, soundless.

She went outside and threw up, then recognized something familiar about her nausea. *I'm still pregnant.*

BY THE NEXT DAY, the red patch surrounding the wound on Malachy's thigh had grown smaller. Now his foot was the bigger problem. Though circulation seemed unimpaired by the injury, parts of the foot seemed to be dying. Scout spent hours holding his bare foot against her stomach, keeping it warm.

She began dismantling the plane, taking cables and wire from the interior—and the exterior when she could get to them. With these, she constructed two types of snares, which she set nearby.

On the third morning, she caught another rabbit. After they ate, it and some canned refried beans, Malachy produced a black jewelry box from his pocket.

Scout, warmed by the fire they were enjoying, her body pressed against his right leg, gaped at him.

"Happy Valentine's Day."

"I don't even have a card for you."

"You're a resourceful woman. You have hours yet to make one."

She grinned and shoved the box back at him. "Then wait till I'm ready."

Taking advantage of the remaining daylight, she worked outside part of the time, inside at other times, on a rabbit's pelt. Inside it, with her knife, she etched the words, *Thank you for making me love Alaska. Your wife.*

They exchanged gifts, each with a mouthful of the life-and-limb-saving vodka, to celebrate.

Nestled close to Malachy, where she'd spent so much of the past few days, growing more intimate with him than sex or pregnancy could make her, Scout opened the box.

Silver earrings, each set with a ruby and other, smaller stones.

Matching her engagement ring.

She lifted her eyes.

He said, "I love you."

Scout rested her forehead against his throat, breathing slowly and deeply.

Watching her, Malachy rubbed the rabbit's fur against his face.

That afternoon, the weather warmed slightly, and finally they heard a plane.

Scout went out with a flare gun and laid a bright orange rain slicker on the snow above the plane.

She watched the bush plane approach, and she fired the flare gun.

The plane flew over and tipped its wings.

CHAPTER FIFTEEN

SCOUT NEEDED to clear a landing strip for the rescue plane, but with only an avalanche shovel, the task was Herculean.

Still, she set out on the snowshoes, which were too flimsy and required frequent repairs, to find a place for a plane to land safely. She tried dragging a panel of metal, from the side of the plane, behind her, to clear larger sections.

She'd cleared an area of about twelve feet by twenty-five, not nearly big enough, when she heard barking dogs.

She turned, and even at a distance she recognized the distinctive look of Mary Clarke's dogs—then of Holden's. Two sleds.

It was Mary's arms she fell into first.

"Malachy's in the plane," she told Holden. "His ankle's messed up."

Two hours later, the two dog sleds headed for the ghost town of Rico.

Scout rode in her brother's sled. Mary's was the faster team, and they'd decreed that, with Malachy as passenger, she should race for the area where Holden and Mary had landed with the dogs and sleds that morning.

"Dad would be proud of you," Holden called through

the wind as they stood side by side, each on a runner, behind his team.

"He was with me," Scout said and tried to tell him about her sense of her father's presence over the recent days. "I felt like I was doing things right for once."

"You look great," Holden said. "Like a Berensen."

She grinned, but her smile soon faltered. "I'm worried about Malachy's foot."

"Nothing to be gained by worrying," her brother answered, his face wearing a similar expression.

THE FOOT COULD BE repaired, to a certain extent, with surgery. Malachy was flown back to Anchorage, had already been taken away by the time Holden and Scout reached Rico, where Mary awaited them. She told them that Jeremy and John had already been told she and Malachy were alive and in relatively good physical shape.

Scout said, "Did this screw up your team—for the race? I know these are your best dogs."

The Iditarod was in March, a few weeks from now.

Mary shook her head. "I wouldn't have been resting them today in any case. And I've picked up a good handler."

Holden?

She scrutinized Scout. "Could I have the pair?" she asked. "Both twins?"

Holden and her.

Scout had just come out of a wilderness ordeal that had turned into far less of an ordeal than it might've been for someone else. Somehow, in the last few days, Alaska had become more than the place where she was born, where her parents had forced her to grow up. It had become her home.

And Mary's asking her to be part of her Iditarod crew, to clean up campsites when she was gone, to pick up dropped dogs, was more than a compliment. From Mary, it was a peace offering, a way of acknowledging all they could put behind them—Malachy's past with Mary...and Danny.

Being a couple of months pregnant shouldn't affect Scout's ability to be a competent crew member. And helping Mary on the Iditarod Trail should not endanger the baby.

"You're on," she said and added, "if—Malachy— you know..."

Because none of them knew what kind of shape Malachy would be in the next month.

Mary stepped toward her, away from her dogs and up to Scout, and wrapped both arms around her. "He looked good, Scout. And surgeons these days can perform miracles."

Alaska had given her one more thing to make it her home: a friend.

THE LAST THING Scout wanted to do was get in another plane, but the next Cessna that landed, piloted by Merv, took her back to Anchorage and to Malachy.

A surgeon was working on his foot when she arrived. When the staff learned she was pregnant, an obstetrician was summoned, and he ordered an ultrasound. She was still carrying the baby, and it had implanted in a good and safe spot.

Jeremy and John showed up three hours later.

Jeremy seemed very young, his not-yet-grown face extremely white. Scout spent a long time hugging him. "The doctors say he probably won't be running the Boston Marathon, but he'll definitely be walking—and, in general, getting along pretty well."

"Will it disqualify him from law enforcement?" John asked.

"It might." Scout didn't want to think ahead to the impact that would have on Malachy.

John surveyed her. "How did you do? And the baby?"

"All's well, as far as I know. I bled some. I thought I was going to miscarry. But we're still together." She touched her abdomen. This, at least, would help Malachy's spirits.

She was the first person allowed to see him when he came out of recovery.

"Painkillers are amazing, aren't they?" she said, as she remembered pouring vodka onto the wound in his thigh.

The surgeons had examined that wound with laparoscopic and done their best to repair his crushed ankle.

"There's metal in there now," he murmured. "Holding it together."

She sat with him and told him that she and Holden would be part of Mary's crew. "If it's all right with you," she finished.

"Of course it is. I'll still be immobilized."

The surgeons had opted for a splint rather than a cast, assuring a faster recovery.

"I can't go back to my job," he finally said.

"Are you sure?"

"Completely. One of the other guys went through something like this two years ago. I remember it vividly."

Jeremy and John were in the cafeteria, and Scout noticed that Malachy had chosen to make this announcement while they were gone. "Any ideas about what you'd like to do instead?"

"I'll check regulations for the public land agencies. I might be able to get on as a ranger somewhere."

And if not? She couldn't bring herself to say it.

"Otherwise, I suppose I'll build things."

Scout looked at him in surprise. He *could* build things—and well. Bookcases, tables.

"I'd like to learn to make dog sleds. Or we could become mushing outfitters. Expand the kennels." He shrugged. "I'll do something. Don't worry. Unemployment's unattractive."

At least they'd have his health insurance for a while. Malachy's was better than the plan Dana, Victoria and Scout had arranged for the Harmony Agency.

"What about Fish and Fur?" Scout asked, using the nickname for the U.S. Department of Fish and Wildlife. She wondered what role the U.S. Fish and Wildlife played on the Aleutians.

MCGRATH PREPARED for the Iditarod, the town's event of the year, swelling its year-round population of five hundred to five thousand. Rooms were readied to board the journalists and others who'd come to see the race. McGrath wasn't just any place on the Iditarod Trail. It was the halfway point, and there was a trophy for the driver and team that reached the checkpoint first.

Two McGrath residents besides Mary Clarke would be racing this year. Both were women, a twenty-two-year-old, new to McGrath that fall who went by the name of Denali—*I had a dog named that,* Mary had said blandly when telling Scout about her fellow McGrath competitors—and a forty-two-year-old wife and mother from the bush outside McGrath. Her name was Bridget Corson.

Learning that Scout was pregnant, and recognizing that she'd want to remain close to Malachy, Mary asked her and Jeremy to crew at the McGrath checkpoints. That would involve being ready with dog food, fresh booties for any dogs who needed them, a replacement sled and much more.

Scout spent hours studying the rules with Jeremy to make sure neither of them unwittingly did something to jeopardize Mary's chances.

Scout visited the house that served as McGrath's Iditarod checkpoint often and helped prepare it for the mushers who'd flood the area during the race. She and Jeremy and Holden also spent hours at Mary's kennel, helping her train dogs, feeding, cleaning. Scout had a new appreciation for how hard Mary worked and how independent she was.

Scout also began to understand why Mary had won the Iditarod. One: She did not give up. Two: She infected her dogs with the same attitude. Three: She kept herself and the dogs completely upbeat, an outlook that suffused her even more strongly as the Iditarod approached.

By the week of the race, Malachy could walk, carefully, on his splint, and had devised a warm bootie that allowed him to go outside. He'd begun to apply for jobs with the Bureau of Land Management, the forest service and the Department of Fish and

Wildlife, hoping he'd be walking without the splint by the time he was asked to interview—*if* he was asked to interview.

Jeremy spent the week before the race photographing outhouses for a page on the Frank Berensen Web site and was brainstorming ideas for T-shirts to sell from the site.

They watched the beginning of the race on Malachy and John's television.

"What if she doesn't win?" Jeremy asked.

They'd just spotted Mary among the mushers at the start, along with her passenger who'd bid at auction for the opportunity to ride on her sled for the first eight miles. The race had two official starts—the ceremonial in Anchorage was the first, and the time from there to Eagle River didn't count toward overall time. The next morning, the real race would begin at an old airstrip in Wasilla.

Scout shrugged. "If she doesn't win, she doesn't win."

"I think she'll tear someone's throat out if she doesn't win," Jeremy opined.

"She *looks* so great," Scout said.

"Aye," John agreed.

The race would take at least nine days. Over the next few days, members of the family checked the television periodically, watching to see where CLARKE was. She seemed to be running about eighth.

"Last year," Malachy said, "she picked up a few spots on the way to Finger Lake and then held her own till Rainy Pass. She's told me her tactic is to pace the dogs the entire way."

"She wouldn't tell you her *real* tactics," said Jeremy.

The local race volunteers had set up a big-screen television in the community center. The media reporters and photographers spent part of their time there, and almost as much at the actual McGrath checkpoint.

"Did she get the halfway trophy last year?" asked John.

"No. She says she doesn't care about it."

"Another lie," remarked Jeremy.

Holden was flying between checkpoints with another handler, picking up dropped dogs and cleaning campsites.

"Where's Lakota?" asked Jeremy as they got a shot of Mary at the Finger Lake checkpoint. She had changed lead dogs, switching from the bitch who'd led her to past victories, and was now running a dog called Geordie alongside Thorlo.

"On her sled," Malachy said. "She must be hurt."

Scout squinted at the television screen, where a commentator soon revealed that Lakota had begun limping and was being dropped.

"This is not good," Scout said.

"Geordie's faster," Jeremy told her.

"That doesn't necessarily make him a great leader. He's young."

"Well, she's giving him a chance," John said.

By the time Mary reached McGrath, she was in twelfth place. Also, the weather had worsened, the temperature falling as winds blasted dry snow through the streets and around the checkpoint.

"Geordie's doing really well," were the first words out of Mary's mouth to Scout, and Scout had never liked her better than for her confidence in the young dog. "And he enjoys running with Thorlo. You're a good boy, aren't you?" Already she was preparing the dog's food, and Scout went ahead, picking up after dogs as they relieved themselves.

Mary had chosen to take her mandatory twenty-four-hour rest stop farther along the trail but was taking eight hours in McGrath.

Scout watched her check the dog's feet, one by one, all four paws.

Geordie was smaller than Mary's other dogs and more streamlined, a lot like the dogs Malachy had gotten in Unalakleet.

"Have you seen Holden?" Scout asked her.

"Yes. Don't worry. Your family's definitely gone beyond the odds on plane wrecks this year. He should be here soon. I want to know how Lakota's doing."

Mary tucked her unruly curls back into her caribou-fur hood. She was clearly tired but also looked healthy—and like she could go on for another week.

"We all want you to win," Scout said.

"Denali passed me. Did you see that?"

The twenty-two-year-old.

"She's a rookie, isn't she?"

Mary nodded. "She should get Rookie of the Year, at least. I have great dogs," she said. "Geordie hasn't slacked on the tug once."

Just before she pulled out of McGrath, Mary asked Scout to look after Lakota.

This took some compromise on the part of Estelle, who objected to the dominant bitch's certainty that she could rule the world, but Malachy and Scout went to bed that night with both dogs sharing the floor, together with Pigpen and Trooper.

Days later, all four dogs sat in front of the television as Geordie's nose crossed the finish line garnering Mary fifth place.

THE BABY WAS due at the beginning of October. By May, Malachy was working again, doing fish counts with the U.S. Department of Fish and Game. His foot had mended enough that he could now hike four miles at a stretch.

Scout welcomed the return of light. She'd stopped supervising the Anchorage office after Malachy's plane crashed, telling Victoria and Dana she couldn't make the weekly flights anymore. Victoria had sent another supervisor from California to run the office full-time.

Even as the Harmony Agency thrived, Scout was in demand as a counselor for local teenagers. Having grown up in the bush, she felt particularly suited to this job.

She spent several days every month at her family's property, with Holden and her mother. During Scout's visit late in August, her mother broached the subject of where the baby would be born.

"On September fifteenth—depending on whether the baby has dropped—Malachy and I will fly to Anchorage."

Her mother was not one to blurt out either criticism or her own feelings of disappointment. Nonetheless, Scout was too familiar with Dora to miss the meaning behind the silence that greeted this announcement.

"I never had any trouble, and you were twins," her mother finally said.

Why didn't I anticipate this? Scout asked herself.

But she'd planned what to say in any event. "We're renting a house there for a month. John can't come because of the dogs, or Jeremy because of school, but we'd love it if you could be with us, Mom."

Her mother considered this. They'd spent the afternoon canning berries, and now Dora retied her long gray ponytail. "Well, I don't know how I'd do living in the city that long. A whole month... Perhaps I could come when your labor starts. Or when the doctor says you're close. You know, your dad and I loved doing it out here by ourselves." She gazed out the window at the fish rack. "When you and Holden were born."

"Twins," said Scout. "That's high risk."

"It's all in how you look at things. Anyhow, it was December, and the weather was bad. We just had faith. It's how we did everything. We knew we had to depend on ourselves, so we were careful. Not that you can control the process of birth."

"No," Scout agreed. *Which is why I'm going to a hospital.* She ventured, "I really want you there, Mom."

Dora glanced at her. Unexpectedly, she smiled. "Then of course I'll plan to be there."

As Scout embraced her mother, a question occurred to her. "If Dad were here...would you still have come?"

Dora's smile faded. "I know you had a hard time with him, Scout."

"Would you?" she repeated. "If he hadn't wanted you to?"

"That's a question we don't have to worry about," her mother replied.

And Scout knew the answer—that Frank Berensen would've made the decision. He would not have approved of his daughter giving birth in a hospital, so he wouldn't have gone to see her there or let his wife go, either.

Would he?

She remembered the sense of her father she'd felt after the plane crash, the feeling of being aided and protected by him.

"Dad would've come to the hospital," she said at last. "Sometimes I make him into an ogre in my mind, but he loved us. He would've come."

"I think so, too."

THE ANCHORAGE house was an old shotgun-style Victorian. One story, two bedrooms. Scout kept Estelle, Pigpen and Trooper with her during the days.

Malachy flew often for work, and he divided his weeks between Anchorage and McGrath, staying in nearly constant phone contact with Scout.

When she went into labor, he'd just returned to Anchorage, bringing her mother with him. It felt to Scout as though the baby had simply been waiting for them to arrive.

In Anchorage, she'd been seeing a certified nurse-midwife named Alice, and when Scout got to the hospital, she found Alice accompanied by an older Talkeetna midwife, Francesca, who would be assisting.

The room in the hospital's birthing suite was bathed in a comfortable golden light. As Scout experienced the cramping of early labor, the two midwives chatted in low voices with Dora.

Malachy, beside her and more restless than Scout had ever seen him, kept looking at his watch, timing her contractions himself. "Have some more water," he urged.

The midwife named Francesca, whose long graying hair fell in curls like Mary Clarke's, came over to listen to the baby's heart. Then she handed the earpieces of the fetoscope to Malachy and said, "You listen. It'll give you something to do."

Alice said to Dora, "Scout says she and her brother were born at home."

Dora nodded. "We did everything ourselves. We were committed to that ethic—their father and I. But I think now…" Watching Scout, she blinked. "We thought we were prepared to deal with whatever might happen— and by that I mean prepared to accept nature. But, thank God, there was no tragedy. They were healthy, and they came at eight months. We really managed, but as I sit here…" She smiled at Scout, and her lips trembled. "When it comes down to it, I'm glad Scout's here."

"Thanks, Mom. Oh, here's another—" She focused on her breathing as the contraction waved through her, a force beyond anything that could be contained, as uncontrollable as—well—Alaska itself.

A knock sounded on the door.

As the contraction drifted through and past her, Scout saw John, Jeremy and Holden in the doorway. "Come in. Jeremy," she said, "I'm so glad you're here."

She reached for his hand, and he came to stand beside her, holding her hand comfortably. He seemed small to Scout, and she thought of the way his life had been disrupted by first his mother's death, then his father's and his stepmother's alcoholism and prostitution. He was still very much a boy, not yet grown, not yet free of childhood.

He said, "You look wild. Your eyes look like you're on drugs."

"Women in labor can look that way," Alice said.

Malachy made introductions, and he held one of Scout's hands, Jeremy the other, as the labor intensified.

Then John said, "Holden and Jeremy and I will be in the cafeteria. We're going to have a bite to eat."

Scout wanted something to lift her away from the pain. "Mom, tell me about our birth. About Holden's and mine."

Her mother sat in the nearby chair, offering a washcloth for Scout's forehead, then a cool, gentle hand, which Scout preferred, remembering it from childhood illnesses.

"It was the seventeenth. The date doesn't mean anything," Dora said, "except that your father was gone on the trapline."

Scout moaned with the contraction and with the thought of a husband out on a trapline when his wife went into labor.

"I started getting cramps, rather like menstrual cramps…."

"Weren't you afraid?" Scout murmured.

"I had faith. I suppose it was a kind of…grace. I didn't think of myself as being in peril. And I didn't think either of you were in danger."

"You knew there were twins?" asked Francesca.

"Yes."

Scout felt Malachy go still beside her. Was he thinking of his own birth?

But abruptly, he turned to her and began stroking back her hair.

Her body folded in on itself, contracting, and she heard nothing else in the room.

Then her mother's voice continued. "I was in hard

labor—transition, I suppose—when I heard the dog team. As soon as your father came in, he could see your head."

The midwives were quiet, but one of them wanted to know the life of each twin. Both expressed amazement at the ease with which Holden, breech, had been born.

Scout felt caught in some surf of sensation, and the sensation had definitely become pain. What had felt good, now felt difficult. The next time Alice checked her, she said, "Shoulder."

This seemed to mean something to Francesca, who immediately joined her.

Scout wanted to scream as Alice asked her to take a deep breath and hold it. *I want painkillers.*

She remembered Malachy's silence as she poured vodka into the hole in his thigh.

Why can't I be that tough?

You are that tough.

Her father.

Frank Berensen was with her again, close by, holding her hand, and Scout was far away, on the banks of the river, trying to start a fire in the rain as her father emptied out the canoe.

Crying.

Why was he crying?

There had been a dog in the canoe. The dog had drowned.

Hookah. The dog was named Hookah, and he was black, and he'd followed her father around the yard. He'd been the lead dog of the trapline team.

Her father had cried when Hookah drowned.

She had to start a fire, because they were soaked, and her hands were already freezing.

You are tough.

She couldn't do it. She couldn't do it.

You got that fire going, Scout?

Where was Holden? Not with them.

Pain. Holding her breath because a woman's voice told her to.

"Now push. Gently. Good girl."

A cry escaped her, the scream of birth.

"Another push. You're doing great, Scout. You can see your baby."

But what she saw was Malachy beside her, reaching out to touch their child.

"HE SHOULD BE named for someone in a book," said Jeremy. "Like Scout and Holden are."

An adult, perhaps, would not have ventured an opinion in this highly personal manner.

Malachy, with one glance at Scout's face, peaceful as she gazed down at their son, said, "Let's see what Scout has to say."

"I want to hear Jeremy's suggestions," she said.

"Lestat," Jeremy put forth without hesitation.

Scout burst out laughing, and the baby made a tiny face.

"Harry," said Holden, "for Harry Potter."

Scout closed her eyes.

"No, Severus," Jeremy said.

"Jay," Holden suggested. "For Jay Gatsby."

Scout shook her head mutely at this duel.

"Jean Valjean." John had spoken, and Scout turned to him.

Holden said, "Colter."

"The *dog?*" asked Jeremy.

"Richard Sharpe. Or Aubrey."

"Or Call. For the dude in *Lonesome Dove*. Woodrow Call, and we can call him Call. But Lestat's better," Jeremy insisted. "I mean, Lestat's *alive*. You know what I mean?"

"I think Lestat pretty much defines 'not alive'," Holden answered. "He's a vampire."

"Lestat MacCullagh," Malachy said, laughing as he tried the sound of it.

Scout tried another one. "Valjean MacCullagh."

Jeremy said, "Cthulhu."

"When he's older," Scout told Jeremy, "I'm going to tell him you suggested that."

"It's got a great ring to it. Cthulhu MacCullagh."

Too many choices. Scout hadn't thought of this child in terms of a name. And she'd thought it would be a girl.

She said, "I have to pee."

"Ah." Francesca came to the edge of the bed. As Scout held out the tiny boy, who still smelled so different from anything she'd ever known, Francesca took the child. "Malachy?"

Malachy had already held his son. He said, "Jeremy. Start being a big brother."

Jeremy blinked, then put out his arms.

"You want to support his head," Francesca told him. "There you go."

Jeremy sat in the chair, feeling the innocent vulnerability of the baby. He thought the baby should have a powerful, all-reaching kind of name, like a god's. Maybe not a star-spawn from H.P. Lovecraft—Cthulhu, which would be his, Jeremy's, first choice. He tried to remember all the gods of mythology. Zeus. Neptune.

Something Alaskan? He said, "I want him to have a strong name."

"John," Malachy said.

Scout, hobbling to the bathroom on Francesca's arm, paused.

"Yeah," said Jeremy, who thought John MacCullagh was pretty damned strong, as human beings went. And then the baby would have the same name. He glanced from Malachy's father, who looked startled, to the infant, to Scout. "How does that sound?"

"Perfect," she told him, gazing at the baby in his arms. "John Francis Berensen MacCullagh."

Beside the bed, Dora put her hand to her face, suddenly streaming with tears. Through them, she said, "That's a very strong name."

CHAPTER SIXTEEN

"THEY'VE ASKED ME," Malachy said early that December, "to fly to the Aleutians."

Scout, sitting in the Harmony office in McGrath, nursing Johnny—as people seemed unable to stop calling him—eyed her husband. He'd just brought Johnny down to her from the apartment above so the baby could nurse between clients.

Unsure whether she should mention the obvious thought suggested by mention of the Aleutians—*Will you search for your mother?*—Scout said, "Why?"

"To count birds."

"Ah." She looked into Johnny's eyes, which seemed to be turning the topaz, wolf's-eye color of her own. "When are you going?"

"I want you to come."

Will you search for your mother?

Now she didn't have to ask.

"Of course I'll come." A chill touched her. Malachy's mother had left him more than thirty years before, and she'd never come to look for him. She had never, to Scout's knowledge, contacted John MacCullagh to learn what had become of her child.

Malachy's seeking her, whether to ask questions or

just to see her face or for some other reason, was terrifying and therefore also courageous.

"Do you have a plan?" she asked.

"Her maiden name was Eleanor Gordieff. She never sought an annulment from my father, so if she decided to marry again it wasn't in the Catholic Church. But people will know who she is. It's not that big a place."

Scout didn't want to utter the next thought. "Are you prepared for—"

"That she might not want to see me?"

"Or she's dead."

He shrugged, his jaw as steady as ever as he finished dressing for work in regulation gray.

"When are you going?" she asked, deciding not to mention her hatred of winter flights in Alaska.

"Next week—for the first time. I'll have to go back."

Scout nodded philosophically.

A BUSH PLANE transported them to Anchorage, but from there a commercial carrier flew them to Atukan. Although the plane was still small, Scout felt more comfortable in a commercial aircraft—comfortable enough, in fact, to peer out the windows at the islands as they appeared below, at the immensity of the ocean and at the white lines where water and land met in surf.

"Malachy, do you like working for Fish and Wildlife as well as you liked being a cop?"

"No. But I have to be able to run, and I'm not there yet."

"We're lucky you got this job."

"Very." Absently, he held Johnny's small foot. "I talked to Jeremy before we left. I told him I was going to try to find my mom, to meet her. He said I must feel the way he feels with his mom—Jackie, that is. He said my mother left me to go home, and his mother left him to be a drunk."

"I wish Jackie would make an effort to see him."

"Maybe it's better if she doesn't," Malachy said.

"Because you think she did turn tricks for a boy Jeremy's age?"

He shook his head. "I can't imagine her doing that. I just know she's not ready to walk the straight and narrow—and I'm not sure he wants to spend time with her until she's sober in some kind of lasting fashion."

The plane circled over the coastal village where Malachy had been born. Soon they could see the buildings of the fishery, which was the village's chief industry, and then they were down, into clean, brisk cold sea air.

As they stepped off the plane, Scout made sure Johnny's hat covered his ears completely. Though the sky was blue, her cheeks immediately felt the sting of wind. A woman in a Fish and Wildlife uniform and jacket waited for them inside the small terminal. Her long dark hair was Malachy's dark color, but her face was Aleut. The woman's name was Daphne, and she told them they'd be staying in vacant government quarters for the next two days. She'd come in a truck to take them there.

The government houses were less than a half-mile from town, and Scout and Malachy settled in quickly, Scout giving Johnny another chance to nurse, then gratefully passing him to Malachy for a diaper change.

Malachy had no work obligations until the following day, and when Scout came out of the bath she found him looking through the slender local telephone directory.

"Eleanor MacCullagh," he said. "She kept her married name. She must not have remarried."

"Did she ever divorce him?"

"Oh, yes."

How sad for your father, was Scout's thought, but she kept it to herself. "Are you going to phone her?"

"I guess that's the thing to do." He grabbed his cell phone and painstakingly punched in the number. Johnny lay asleep beside him on the bed.

Scout half-wished she hadn't come, that Malachy hadn't come. What could his mother say to make him feel better?

"Hi, this is Malachy MacCullagh, calling for Eleanor MacCullagh."

Scout could hear nothing, and Malachy's face had become pale, paper-like.

"Yes. Right," he said. "I'm here in Atukan, visiting. I work for the U.S. Department of Fish and Wildlife, and my wife and son are with me."

He was so brave, Scout reflected.

"If it's all right," he said. Then, "Thank you. Yes, I've got a pen...."

THEY WALKED INTO the village, Scout carrying Johnny against her chest in a sling, monitoring him constantly in the cold and wrapping her coat around them both, binding them together.

Malachy's mother lived in a tiny government-built house on the edge of the village with her mother. When Scout and Malachy came up the walk of hard dirt and stone, the door opened, and a dark-haired woman stood there. She had an Aleut face, and the lines around her mouth and eyes were fine, delicate.

She did not look like an unhappy person.

"Hello. I'm Eleanor," she said, holding the door open for them.

A tiny silver-haired woman emerged from the shadows. The place was modest, the interior cheaply furnished, yet it showed care. Handmade rugs and afghans brightened floor and couch.

"I'm Malachy." He held out his hand. "And my wife, Scout, and our son, Johnny."

"Ah," said Eleanor, reacting, Scout thought, to the baby's name.

They sat on the couch, and Eleanor brought them herbal tea, and her mother sat in a rocking chair, crocheting as they talked.

Eleanor admired Johnny and finally said, "May I hold him?"

Scout nodded and carefully handed the infant to Malachy's mother. Her hair was probably dyed to stay dark—yet she couldn't have been very old when she'd become pregnant with Malachy. Scout didn't want to think of the sadness she must have suffered when she'd realized her husband would never love her as much as the work he'd left for her.

Eleanor said, "Is your father still alive?"

"Thriving," Malachy said, with no apparent emotion.

Eleanor smiled gently into Johnny's face and seemed to be seeing something out of the past instead of the infant in her arms. Yet she was seeing him, too. "He has eyes like his mother," she said, glancing at Scout.

Scout stood up and feigned interest in a carving on

a shelf. Eleanor's mother rose, too, and said, "My uncle gave me that when I was a little girl. I'll show you a picture of him."

Johnny mewed, and Scout took him from Eleanor and settled herself on a stool as her son's great-grand-mother brought down a framed photograph of an Aleut man. Eleanor invited Malachy to come and see photos of her father, but Scout suspected they were going to talk in private.

"I LOVED HIM," Eleanor said without pretense in the room with the quilt-covered bed where she showed Malachy a photo of a man in Aleut ceremonial regalia. But she wasn't speaking of her father; she meant John MacCullagh. "He loved me, too. You mustn't think he didn't. But we had to live far from my family. And he wasn't happy. He felt guilt and regret. So I left."

Malachy wondered if he really wanted to know the answer to his next question. But he had to ask. "Why didn't you take me?"

She gaped up at him. "I just said. Because I loved him. If I'd taken you, he'd have had nothing. He loved you. He thought you were wonderful."

Malachy didn't ask whether *she'd* loved him, her son. It seemed clear that whatever she felt about her role in John MacCullagh's life, her regret had taken prece-dence over maternal feeling.

"I have a picture of you."

And there it was, on the bedside table. Her holding a child, perhaps a year old, on her lap, hugging him tightly.

"You have this here all the time?" he said, not quite believing.

"Do you think not having it would've made it easier to bear?"

He shook his head. And said what he'd come to say. "I felt bad for you. I knew it must've been—" He stopped.

"Yes, well, he regretted what we'd done, although he tried to hide it. But that kind of thing is hard to hide."

"He's like that," Malachy agreed.

HE SPENT SEVERAL hours with his mother and grandmother over the next few days, sometimes with Scout and Johnny, sometimes without, and he promised to return when he came back to work on the bird project.

As the plane lifted off, taking him and Scout and Johnny home to McGrath, Scout glanced at Malachy. "Has it made a difference?"

"Meeting her?"

"Yes."

He shook his head. "I didn't expect it to. She left for the reason I thought, the reason he'd told me."

They didn't mention the subject again until they were back in McGrath, back at the house.

John and Jeremy stood in front of the cabin running the hydraulic log-splitter, which they usually kept under wraps all winter. But a tree had fallen in the yard, so they were cutting up the trunk.

"It did change something," Malachy said.

Scout knew immediately what he meant, as though no time had passed since they'd last spoken of his mother and father. "What?"

"Jeremy. You and Johnny. Our whole family. But also, he's changed. There's something more for him."

Scout knew without being told. Because it had

become valuable to her, too. She said the word softly, like a benediction. "Alaska."

He smiled, looking from her to Johnny and back as he parked the truck outside the cabin. "Where we were born."

* * * * *

*Experience entertaining women's fiction about
rediscovery and reconnection—warm,
compelling stories that are relevant
for every woman who has wondered
"What's next?" in their lives.
After all, there's the life you planned.
And there's what comes next.*

*Turn the page for a sneak preview
of a new book from Harlequin NEXT.*

*CONFESSIONS OF A NOT-SO-DEAD LIBIDO
by Peggy Webb*

*On sale November 2006,
wherever books are sold.*

My husband could see beauty in a mud puddle. Literally. "Look at that, Louise," he'd say after a heavy spring rain. "Have you ever seen so many amazing colors in mud?"

I'd look and see nothing except brown, but he'd pick up a stick and swirl the mud till the colors of the earth emerged, and all of a sudden I'd see the world through his eyes—extraordinary instead of mundane.

Roy was my mirror to life. Four years ago when he died, it cracked wide open, and I've been living a smashed-up, sleepwalking life ever since.

If he were here on this balmy August night I'd be sailing with him instead of baking cheese straws in preparation for Tuesday-night quilting club with Patsy. I'd be striving for sex appeal in Bermuda shorts and bare-toed sandals instead of opting for comfort in walking shoes and a twill skirt with enough elastic around the waist to make allowances for two helpings of lemon-cream pie.

Not that I mind Patsy. Just the opposite. I love her. She's the only person besides Roy who creates wonder wherever she goes. (She creates mayhem, too, but we won't get into that.) She's my mirror now, as well as my compass.

Of course, I have my daughter, Diana, but I refuse to be the kind of mother who defines herself through her children. Besides, she has her own life now, a husband and a baby on the way.

I slide the last cheese straws into the oven and then go into my office and open e-mail.

From: "Miss Sass" <patsyleslie@hotmail.com>
To: "The Lady" <louisejernigan@yahoo.com>
Sent: Tuesday, August 15, 6:00 PM
Subject: Dangerous Tonight
Hey Lady,

I'm feeling dangerous tonight. Hot to trot, if you know what I mean. Or can you even remember? ☺ Look out, bridge club, here I come. I'm liable to end up dancing on the tables instead of bidding three spades. Whose turn is it to drive, anyhow? Mine or thine?
XOXOX
Patsy
P.S. Lord, how did we end up in a club with no men?

This e-mail is typical "Patsy." She's the only person I know who makes me laugh all the time. I guess that's why I e-mail her about ten times a day. She lives right next door, but e-mail satisfies my urge to be instantly and constantly in touch with her without having to interrupt the flow of my life. Sometimes we even save the good stuff for e-mail.

From: "The Lady" <louisejernigan@yahoo.com>
To: "Miss Sass" <patsyleslie@hotmail.com>
Sent: Tuesday, August 15, 6:10 PM
Subject: Re: Dangerous Tonight

So, what else is new, Miss Sass? You're always dangerous. If you had a weapon, you'd be lethal. ☺
Hugs,
Louise
P.S. What's this about men? I thought you said your libido was dead?

I press Send then wait. Her reply is almost instantaneous.

From: "Miss Sass" <patsyleslie@hotmail.com>
To: "The Lady" <louisejernigan@yahoo.com>
Sent: Tuesday, August 15, 6:12 PM
Subject: Re: Dangerous Tonight
Ha! If I had a *brain* I'd be lethal.
And I said my libido was in hibernation, not DEAD!
Jeez, Louise!!!!!
P

Patsy loves to have the last word, so I shut off my computer.

Want to find out what happens to their friendship
when Patsy and Louise both find the perfect man?

Don't miss
CONFESSIONS OF A NOT-SO-DEAD LIBIDO
by Peggy Webb,
coming to Harlequin NEXT
in November 2006.

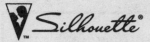

HARLEQUIN®

NeXt™

**Entertaining women's fiction
for every woman who has
wondered "what's next?"
in her life.**

Receive $1.⁰⁰ off

any Harlequin NEXT™ novel.

Coupon expires March 31, 2007.
Redeemable at participating retail outlets
in Canada only. Limit one coupon per customer.

52607178

REQUEST YOUR FREE BOOKS!

2 FREE NOVELS PLUS 2 FREE GIFTS!

HARLEQUIN®

Super Romance®

Exciting, emotional, unexpected!

YES! Please send me 2 FREE Harlequin Superromance® novels and my 2 FREE gifts. After receiving them, if I don't wish to receive any more books, I can return the shipping statement marked "cancel." If I don't cancel, I will receive 6 brand-new novels every month and be billed just $4.69 per book in the U.S., or $5.24 per book in Canada, plus 25¢ shipping and handling per book and applicable taxes, if any*. That's a savings of close to 15% off the cover price! I understand that accepting the 2 free books and gifts places me under no obligation to buy anything. I can always return a shipment and cancel at any time. Even if I never buy another book from Harlequin, the two free books and gifts are mine to keep forever.

135 HDN EEX7   336 HDN EEYK

Name	(PLEASE PRINT)	
Address		Apt.
City	State/Prov.	Zip/Postal Code

Signature (if under 18, a parent or guardian must sign)

Mail to Harlequin Reader Service®:

IN U.S.A.
P.O. Box 1867
Buffalo, NY
14240-1867

IN CANADA
P.O. Box 609
Fort Erie, Ontario
L2A 5X3

Not valid to current Harlequin Superromance subscribers.

Want to try two free books from another line?
Call 1-800-873-8635 or visit www.morefreebooks.com.

* Terms and prices subject to change without notice. NY residents add applicable sales tax. Canadian residents will be charged applicable provincial taxes and GST. This offer is limited to one order per household. All orders subject to approval. Credit or debit balances in a customer's account(s) may be offset by any other outstanding balance owed by or to the customer. Please allow 4 to 6 weeks for delivery.

Silhouette®

nocturne™

USA TODAY bestselling author

MAUREEN CHILD

ETERNALLY

He was a guardian. An immortal fighter of evil,
out to destroy a demon, and she was his next
target. He knew joining with her would make
him strong enough to defeat any demon.
But the cost might be losing the woman
who was his true salvation.

On sale November, wherever books are sold.

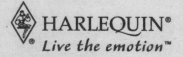